"Sounds to me like you need a coach," Keane said.

"A coach? For fun? Is there such a thing?"

"If there isn't, there should be." Given people's lives these days, he couldn't imagine Marella was the only one who needed help. "I'd think it would be a challenge, teaching someone how to loosen up and not take things so seriously." He glanced at her. "Learn how to just go with the flow."

"You volunteering?"

He knew she meant it as a joke, but it wasn't a horrible idea. He liked her. He'd liked her the second she'd stormed past him on the beach, before she'd even noticed he was there. He'd been excited at the prospect of her being on the cruise tonight and thoroughly entertained watching her interact with her family; a family he could tell was filled with love and concern for one another. Marella's current predicament acted as prime evidence in that case.

"Maybe I am."

Dear Reader,

Every once in a while, I need to pinch myself as a reminder that I truly have the best job in the world. I don't know that anything can top writing happily-ever-afters one after another. Unless it's writing stories that take place in one of my favorite places on earth, Hawai'i.

I fell in love with the islands when I was eight. It just felt like home from the second I stepped off the plane. I think in a way, this Hawaiian Reunions series is my attempt to recapture that feeling.

In this second story, we meet overworked, stressed-out Marella Benoit who, after a rather disastrous first few hours post-arrival for her sister's destination wedding, finds herself in the arms of a handsome stranger. What could be wrong with that? Nothing that Keane Harper can find and hey, he's always happy to help a lady out, especially one as entertaining and intriguing as Marella. But love at first sight? That just doesn't seem possible for either of them. And yet...

Despite such blatant differences, these two are so meant for each other and I hope you enjoy all the fun and games that come along with Marella and Keane falling head over heels for one another.

Anna

HEARTWARMING

Their Surprise Island Wedding

—

Anna J. Stewart

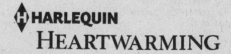

HARLEQUIN®
HEARTWARMING™

ISBN-13: 978-1-335-47546-6

Their Surprise Island Wedding

For questions and comments about the quality of this book, please contact us at CustomerService@Harlequin.com.

Harlequin Enterprises ULC
22 Adelaide St. West, 41st Floor
Toronto, Ontario M5H 4E3, Canada
www.Harlequin.com

Recycling programs for this product may not exist in your area.

Printed in U.S.A.

USA TODAY and national bestselling romance author **Anna J. Stewart** is living the dream writing for Harlequin. She gets to fall in love with each and every book she writes and thrives on falling into new adventures. These days when she's not writing, you can find her in Northern California binge rewatching her favorite television shows and attempting (in vain) to wrangle her two monster cats, Rosie and Sherlock.

Books by Anna J. Stewart

Harlequin Heartwarming

Hawaiian Reunions
Her Island Homecoming

Butterfly Harbor Stories
Bride on the Run
Building a Surprise Family
Worth the Risk
The Mayor's Baby Surprise

The Blackwell Sisters
Montana Dreams

Visit the Author Profile page
at Harlequin.com for more titles.

For Patti & Matt and your happily-ever-after.

CHAPTER ONE

EVEN ON A regular day, Hawai'i displayed an indescribable majesty that took one's breath away.

On its best day? Well, on its best, the islands—the small town of Nalani in particular—put on a show that left everyone in its vicinity, including Keane Harper, speechless and more than a little humbled.

With its pristine glittery beaches and thick, swaying trees arching protectively over its guests, Nalani's air carried the slightest hint of hibiscus and the promise of cooling breezes. In the distance, verdant, rocky mountains rounded into the sky, sloping and dipping as if entertaining those in its vicinity. Errant clouds pushed by as a reminder of the afternoon shower that would soon cleanse the day and send steam rising off the pavement.

There was, Keane told himself as he had every day since he'd come back to the town he'd called home one summer long ago, no other place like it. It was also exactly what he'd needed.

Straddling the bright orange surfboard that until recently belonged to his best friend, Remy Calvert, Keane bobbed far out from shore, bouncing on the familiar waves he'd been riding off and on ever since he was a boy. The same waves that welcomed him home six weeks ago when he'd finally come back to say goodbye to Remy.

While others possessed serious trepidation where the wild unpredictability of the ocean was concerned, Keane welcomed every moment he could spend either in or on the water. Its power, the almost seductive peace it promised in combination with the absolute respect it evoked, acted as a spiritual aphrodisiac for Keane. A reset of the spirit. A recharge for his soul.

He hadn't realized just how hollowed out he'd been these past few years until he'd dipped his toes back into that frothy surf. The ocean was healing him. Slowly. But he was healing.

The midafternoon sun had just about hit its zenith and bathed the residents and visitors of Nalani in presummer warmth. The humidity had yet to reach full strength but would in the next hour or so. The morning breezes had long burned off. Around him, the lapping, slapping, comforting sounds of the water gently nudged him back to shore.

Or maybe it wasn't only the water doing the nudging. Guilt he had yet to shake continued to knock on the back side of his heart. For months Keane had resisted Remy's pleas to return to Nalani, the small town on the eastern shore of the Big Island. To leave the mainland and the troubles Keane found there far behind and start over.

Nalani needs you, K. I need you. Please. I've got a place for you.

Even now Remy's voice was as clear in Keane's mind as the blue water that surrounded him. Regret tainted the memories of the arguments he'd offered, the excuses he'd made in an effort to refuse Remy's request. There would be time enough for Nalani later, he'd told his friend. There will always be time to come back.

Except there hadn't been any time. Not for Remy at least.

Remy was gone and he wasn't coming

back. His ashes had been sprinkled into the ocean around the exact spot Keane currently occupied. Even if Keane hadn't watched the video his friend Daphne had taken from the beach on the day of Remy's memorial paddle-out, Keane would have known where to go.

He could feel Remy's presence all over town, in every store, with every resident. But on the water?

The water magnified Remy's energy to the point Keane could all but feel his friend breathing around him. It was that energy that drew Keane out, part in apology, part in reminder to live every single day to its absolute fullest.

The heat of the sun pounded against his back as he took a deep breath. How he wished it hadn't taken his friend's death to embrace that idea. Would that he'd have listened sooner and understood what Remy was really telling him: that Nalani was his home.

But he had a life back on the mainland. A job to get back to, if he still wanted it. The only problem was, Keane didn't know what he wanted. Remy's death had thrown his entire being into flux and until he saw a sign pointing him in a direction, he wasn't going to make any decisions about anything. He was just going to hang loose as the locals said. And go with whatever the morning sun offered.

His internal clock dinged in the familiar way that told him it was time to head in. The day had begun as usual, early, just after sunrise with him greeting three of his ongoing surfing students at the beach. That was followed by a quick catamaran jaunt up to Honu Bay, located about twenty miles north of nearby Hilo. While he was free and clear this afternoon from his job with Ohana Odysseys, the local tour company Remy had started almost a decade before, it didn't mean Keane could skive off checking in. He was here to help Remy's sister with whatever she needed—tours, excursions, activities, and to his credit, he'd already doubled their surf lesson business. He expected, or rather hoped, his go-along attitude would at some point result in that sign he was waiting for.

But right now, he needed to get his head out of the ocean and back to work. With guests arriving in town at a steady flow, schedules could change as quickly as the overhead clouds.

Paddling in, his energy resurged. June was the beginning of the tourist season. The waves tended to be calmer, the water warmer, which made Ohana Odysseys's sea turtle experience all the more popular. Recent arrivals staying at the Hibiscus Bay Resort had assumed the morning trip would be a hands-on excursion. Keane made it clear, as he did for every voyage, before anyone stepped on the boat, that the turtles were a protected species and this was an observation cruise only. No touching allowed. Visiting the wildlife was all well and good, but only if appropriate respect was paid. Humans were visitors on the water. End. Of. Story.

Grumpy comments aside, the trip had gone off without a hitch thanks to help from his fellow crewman and Ohana Odysseys's jack-of-all-trades, Wyatt Jenkins.

They'd concluded their morning with a stop at Hut-Hut for *loco moco*, the island breakfast of champions that included steamed rice, a hamburger patty—in Keane's case two—and topped off with a rich, thick gravy and runny fried eggs. Wyatt preferred his with fried Spam, another island delicacy, but to each their own. Considering the number of years Keane had spent bulking up calorie-wise to sustain his championship swimmer's physique and stamina, *loco moco* was practically diet food.

He snorted. No, it wasn't. But some delusions were okay to embrace.

Unable to resist temptation, as Keane neared shore and identified what could be the day's perfect wave, he leaned over and coasted forward, dipping up and over the edge of the wave as it headed toward the beach.

He remained mindful of the other surfers, mentally calculating their movements and distances reached as well as his own. Etiquette on the waves was instinctive for most and especially him. They all knew to stay away from each other so as not to cause a wipeout.

Keane could feel the thrumming of the ocean beneath him, a vibration that soon matched the beating of his heart as he gripped the edge of his board and pulled his feet in and under him.

The second he was up, he felt like he was flying.

There was not a better sensation in the world than that perfect wave run. Feet planted, knees bent, he worked in rhythm with the wave, riding it as it crested over itself. Water splashed over his shoulders and head as he ducked down and into the center spiral before he shot out the other end and pushed the board up and to the left as a somewhat elegant dismount. He went under soon after, and came up sputtering and laughing as he shoved his wet hair out of his face and dragged his board close by the leash.

Slogging out of the tide, he made his way up the shore, catching sight of a trio of friends—two women and a man—in what appeared to be a heated discussion on the other side of a secluded cove. Keane's attention, however, was quickly captured by the sight of the familiar shorts-and-tank-top-clad woman standing ankle deep in the surf. Remy's sister. The woman who had taken up Remy's torch of bringing his closest college friends back to Nalani. Back home.

Dozens of other beachgoers moved in and around, heading to and from the water. A squealing toddler in a sagging-butt bikini wobbled her way to the waves before getting scooped up by her big brother and tossed over his shoulder.

"You haven't lost your touch," Sydney Calvert called as he made his way over. "You still find the perfect wave, don't you?"

"Not sure that was perfect." His riding of it certainly hadn't been. "But it came pretty close." He shoved his hair back, plowed the bottom end of his board into the sand. "Everything okay? You need me for something?"

"No." She shrugged. "I'm meeting Theo at the Hut-Hut for lunch, thought I'd take the scenic route." With her thick blond-streaked hair tied back from her face, Keane could almost see hints of Remy grinning back at him. "You still good to help crew tonight's sunset dinner cruise?"

"Sure." Like he was going to say no to any opportunity to get back out on the water. "I'll do my best to represent Ohana Odysseys with class and dignity." He crossed two fingers over his bare chest.

Sydney grinned. "That I'd pay to see," she teased. "Tehani and I just finished up the final itinerary for the Benoit-Harrington wedding party and I have to admit, after spending the last couple of days organizing schedules and time sheets, I was ready for a break."

"Can't believe you're closing Ohana Odysseys down for this group," Keane said.

"We aren't closing per se," Sydney said. "They want our undivided attention and are willing to pay for it. Plus, the wedding has a social media following that'll end up being great advertising for no cost on our part. Provided everything goes right." She nodded. "Potential win-win for us. Tehani and Daphne are assembling the gift baskets we're delivering to their rooms at the Hibiscus Bay before dinner. They kicked me out because I apparently have no creative bent in that area."

"You have other talents." Like the wherewithal to cater to a party of fifteen for the next six and a half days. "I hope it's worth the time you're putting in. What activities do they want to do?"

"You name it," Sydney said, and waved his question away. "Oh, that reminds me. Six of them signed up for surfing lessons tomorrow morning, but not until eight. So you can sleep in."

Keane shook his head. Surfing at sunrise was one of the best things about island life, but like Sydney said, they were paying top price to set the rules.

"Fair warning," Sydney said and he pulled his board up as they walked along the shore. "None of the wedding party has ever been to the islands before, so they might be a little—"

"Unaware?" he suggested.

"Oh, you do have a way with words. Perfectly put. And in case I forgot to say it, thanks for helping crew the dinner cruise tonight on the *Nani Nalu*."

"Not a problem. Is there a reason we aren't hosting it on the *Kalei*?"

"A couple," Sydney said. "First, we're not set up for, well, for want of a better term, a more upscale experience. We're more island casual."

"And second?"

"Ah." Sydney planted her hands on her hips and seemed to look anywhere but at him. "Polunu and Akahi need the business. I've tried to shuffle some other clients their way, but they're being selective about what they take on. This was one they couldn't say no to. Of course, that was back when I figured they'd have a full crew. Even having Kiri around as backup was great and I know he was supposed to be here—"

"Kid got the chance to work on an actual science vessel studying the local coral reefs," Keane said, not liking the idea of one of Nalani's most popular businesses—Midnight Seas—might be going under. Still none of them were about to let the high schooler miss out on such a great opportunity. Even if it meant adding to Keane's and the rest of the Ohana team's responsibilities. "It's practical experience that'll look great on his college application. I'm happy to take on extra jobs to help him achieve his dreams."

"Always the teacher," Sydney teased.

"Coach," he corrected a bit more sharply than intended. "I'm a swim *coach* not a teacher." He certainly didn't want any of his "students" taking life lessons from him.

She shot him a look that told him she clearly didn't see a difference. "Honestly, I'm happy the wedding party agreed to ease in with a relaxing evening event. It'll give us a chance to get a feel for them moving forward."

Translation, Keane thought. It would give them the opportunity to see if any of the guests had the tendency to be big pains in the...

"Feels like things are starting to fall into place around here for Ohana, yeah?" Sydney's smile was almost relaxed. Far more relaxed than it had been when Keane first arrived weeks ago. She'd struggled considerably with her brother's death, but even more so with the idea of taking over the tour business he'd built from scratch.

As a helicopter pilot who specialized in search-and-rescue operations, Sydney had plans for opening her own flight school out in South Carolina when Remy had passed without telling anyone he was sick. The last thing she'd ever expected was to move back to the small island town where she'd grown up and pick up the torch Remy had lit so brilliantly.

"Any more word from Golden Vistas about buying you out?" Keane asked as she ducked down and scooped handfuls of ocean up to wet her legs.

"Not a peep. I think that worries Theo more than it does me."

Her reference to boyfriend Theo Fairfax, an accountant who until recently worked for the California-based corporation that had attempted to, without his knowledge, swindle Sydney out of ownership of Ohana Odysseys, brought a smile to Keane's face.

Theo had done a complete one-eighty where his life was concerned within the space of a month. Not only had Theo fallen head over heels for Sydney, he'd done so in spectacular fashion by quitting his job and putting his apartment in San Francisco up for sale before making the permanent move to Nalani. The two had become inseparable and odds were, at least according to island gossip and Maru, Nalani's *malasada* queen and island wise woman, it was only a matter of time before wedding bells started chiming.

Better them than him, Keane reminded himself. As thrilled as he was for his friends, and he and Theo had become rather good ones, the idea of being tied down for any length of time to any one person was simply unfathomable.

He blamed his parents' tumultuous relationship for that emotional wound. He'd learned firsthand that love rarely lasted longer than the first anniversary or, in his parents' case, the first kid. They'd always said that divorce simply wasn't an option, but it was one his mother and father should have both exercised. By the time Keane was ten, the unhappy times far outweighed the good ones. Thus he'd come to the conclusion love was a flash-in-the-pan illusion where mutual respect wiped out faster than a novice swimmer in a national surfing competition.

It also explained Keane's proclivity toward short, intense relationships that didn't have any strings attached from the jump. He was not the happily-ever-after kind and he never hesitated to announce it pretty much to anyone within hearing range.

"So I heard Theo's moved out of the rental cottage," Keane said when Sydney stood back up.

"Word travels fast," Sydney chuckled. "Yes, he's moved in with me. Why? Staying at a fancy resort getting to you?"

"Getting to my wallet more like," Keane joked. "And that's with Mano giving me the family discount." Mano Iokepa, part owner and on-site operations manager of the Hibiscus Bay Resort, was also a good friend, but Keane wasn't about to take advantage. They could easily be charging double for the room Keane currently occupied.

"Well," Sydney said. "The place is yours if you want it. For as long as you do." She tossed out a more than generous amount for rent that had him breathing easier.

He wasn't stretched for cash, and he had a modest income from Ohana, but it was nice to know he could leave his savings alone for a while. That should give him more time to make some big life decisions he'd been putting off.

"I don't have any plans to rent it out anytime soon," Sydney said. "I've got enough to juggle right now. You'll be doing me a favor by not letting it sit empty."

"I'll even throw in handyman work if it's needed," Keane offered. "I'll keep it in good order, don't worry." He loved the resort. It was one of the nicest hotels he'd ever stayed in across the islands, but there were a lot of people coming in and out, and while Mano had cut him a significant deal for an extended stay, the room didn't include an ocean view.

Keane Harper needed an ocean view like everyone else needed oxygen. He simply wasn't alive without it.

The one-bedroom cottage would be absolute perfection, from its semi-isolation to its large wraparound porch to its step out the front door onto the beach location.

"Don't forget," Sydney said. "The cottage comes with a couple of roommates of the four-legged variety."

"Noodles and his girlfriend?" Keane chuckled at the thought of the golden gecko that had taken up residence in the main cottage. The little guy was partial to, well, noodles and had become quite possessive of Theo's refrigerator contents. The second female gecko, which Sydney had named Zilla, had yet to show off her individual personality. She was still pretty leery of humans from what he understood. "I can cope with them just fine. And any Menehunes that might be lurking around."

"Shh!" Sydney smacked at his arm and frowned. "You say that too loudly, those little tricksters are going to land on you like a ten-ton wave."

"I'll just have to call Haki and have her catch them for me." The local Menehune hunter was known for her eccentric outings and encounters with the locals. "She's like our own Nalani ghost buster, yeah?"

"Don't let her hear you say that. The last thing we need is for her to start advertising her services. I've got the keys at the office. Tehani knows where they are."

"I'll do that first thing in the morning." He'd spent a good year after high school and before college living in a van chasing waves at beaches up and down the Hawaiian coast. Having his own place right on the beach? He couldn't think of a better turn of events. "Mahalo, Syd. For everything."

"You're *ohana*, Keane, you know that. No thanks necessary," she told him. "You showing up when you did saved me. I was so stuck, trying to decide what to do about running Ohana Odysseys. Besides, we both know I'm not in a position to offer surfing lessons and they are one of our most popular offerings."

He had yet to be able to convince her that the opportunity Remy—and she—had presented had actually saved him. In so many ways. Instead of attempting to explain again, he found himself turning at the sound of angry, raised voices coming toward them. It was the same trio of friends he'd seen around the other side of the cove.

One of the women, a curvy brunette with doll-wide eyes and perfectly bowed lips, stomped past, her head ducked, but not so far as Keane didn't see the tears in her eyes. Her heavy sneakers kicked up sand as she swept by, slapping up against her snug jeans and oversized yellow T-shirt.

"Marella, wait. You're overreacting!" The man running to catch up knocked Keane's shoulder as he passed. Not quite as tall as Keane, and a good twenty pounds heavier, he turned and held up both hands. "Sorry, dude. Marella!"

"Dude?" Keane balked and looked at a disbelieving Sydney as the man ran off. "Did that guy just call me dude?"

"I believe he did. Whoops. Hang on." Sydney grabbed Keane's arm and pulled him out of the way. "We've got a third one."

The tall, busty redhead slinked past them with what Keane could only describe as a self-satisfied smirk on her face. Another time or place, he might have warned her that her sunblock had worn off. Her shoulders and back—bared by what some might generously call a swimsuit—was already boiled-lobster red.

"Marella!" The man's voice carried back to them as other beachgoers started to pay attention. "I'm sorry! I didn't think—"

Marella, long, wavy hair flying around her shoulders, spun around so fast her pursuer all but plowed into her.

Keane's interest piqued and his lips curved. Maybe it was the temper flashing in her deep brown eyes, or maybe it was the energy he felt coursing off of her in waves. Whatever the reason, it could very well be the complete package she presented in full, show-stopping splendor. As a result, he could only think of one word to describe her: glorious.

"Stay away from me, Craig," Marella snapped. "I don't abide cheaters. Or liars."

"It wasn't what you think." Craig stepped back, the desperation in his voice telling Keane whatever Marella saw was precisely what she thought. The guy's blond hair and blue-eyed good looks were almost stereotypical in their display of *my charm can get me out of anything* attitude.

"No?" She advanced and Craig scrambled back, lost his footing and landed flat on his back. She stood over him and glared as he flailed around like an upside-down crab. "Are you really trying to tell me you weren't playing hide the seaweed with one of my sister's bridesmaids?"

Intrigued, Keane stuck his board back into the sand.

"I...uh." From his prone position, Craig held up his hands again. The man just seemed to know his way around an excuse. No doubt it added to his slipperiness. "It was an accident?"

"An accident?" Marella stood up straight. "The two of you looked like a hyper octopus with the way you were groping each other."

"Okay, *accident* may have been... I didn't think you and I were that serious," Craig tried again.

"We've been dating for three months. I brought you to my sister's wedding! I paid for your airfare and hotel! How could you...?" She shook her head and in an instant seemed to pull herself together. "You know what? I don't care." She let out a laugh. "I actually don't care." She gestured at the air, spun around, then faced him again as Craig scrambled to his feet, kicking up a mouthful of sand. "You're the one who pursued me. You're the one who... You want him, Alexis?" she offered as the redhead slipped past. "You got him. I'm done with him."

"I've had enough, thanks," Alexis said over her shoulder as she continued down the beach toward the Hibiscus Bay.

"Marella, you're making a scene." Craig looked around as if only noticing now that they had an audience. "We can talk about this when you've calmed down."

"Tell me again to calm down," Marella said in a deliberate tone that had Keane grinning. She took another step forward and had Craig nearly tumbling into the surf. "I. Dare. You."

"She's fun," Sydney murmured from beside Keane. "Spunky. I like her."

"Yeah." Keane did too. Something unfamiliar and wholly unexpected flipped inside of Keane.

"Marella, you're making more of this than is necessary." Craig obviously wasn't going to take the high road and admit defeat. "We can work this out. I know I made a mistake. I didn't understand where we stood. At the very least don't let this get in the way of you recommending me—"

Marella froze, the icy glare in her eyes making Keane shiver. "You can't seriously think I'm still going to recommend you for a job at my father's company."

"So you're going back on your promise because I made a mistake?" Craig demanded. "What about for the Phoenix Coffee account? I'm the one who helped you come up with that entire advertising pitch. I'm the reason you got them signed as a new client for Benoit & Associates."

"You know darn well they were on my radar before I even met you," Marella said. "And the final pitch was all mine. You had nothing to do with it."

"I'm the one who convinced you to go after them. You owe me."

"You got a trip to Hawai'i out of me," she spit. "A trip designed for you to make a good impression on my father." She stepped closer and frowned at him. "Look at my face, Craig.

How do you think that'll go after I tell him about all…this?"

Keane could hear Craig swallow.

"Go home, Craig. Before I cancel your ticket." Marella's gaze drifted and seemed to land immediately on Keane, who, had his feet not been planted in the sand, might have stepped back. "And just to make it clear, you're not the only one who can find some-one else." She sidestepped Craig and walked straight over to Keane. There wasn't a force on this earth that could have made him look away. She stopped directly in front of him, hands planted on her hips. She inched her chin up and looked straight into his eyes. "Hi."

"Hello." Keane's mouth twitched as the world moved into slow motion.

"Help a girl out?"

"Sure." There wasn't a force on this earth that could make him refuse. "What do you have in mind?"

"This." Marella's hands came up to his shoulders. He could feel her fingers tremble against his bare skin. Rising up on her toes, she kissed him.

Keane knew, intellectually, at least, that

her purpose was to make a point. But that point was entirely lost on him the second her lips touched his.

He could feel, he could taste, her anger, but only for an instant before it melted into what he perhaps arrogantly interpreted as shock when she gasped. He lifted his hands from the curve of her hips. It took every ounce of control he possessed not to pull her closer.

There was a wildness about her that drifted through his senses and locked down his brain. Every thought he'd previously possessed evaporated like steam out of a volcano. It was part need that he felt, part need and part desire that surged through his entire system as if he'd been lit like a torch.

He expected her to back away, to break all contact, but instead she took a small step toward him, held on and deepened the kiss.

Keane heard muted laughter in the distance, laughter and cheering and applause, but none broke through loud enough to counter the sensation of this woman in his arms. A woman he'd only just seen for the first time moments ago when he'd paddled in to shore.

A woman he didn't want to let go.

When she did break the kiss, when she lifted her mouth and continued to gaze at him, lowering her heels into the sand, he could see the surprise he'd felt in her body. And then, gradually, the shock rose in her eyes as her cheeks went firepit red.

"Oh." She pulled her arms down, eyes widening as she stepped back. "Oh, I am so—" She looked over at Sydney. "That was— incredibly inappropriate. I'm sorry."

"Don't be," Keane assured her and earned a snort-laugh from Sydney, who shoved her hands in her pockets and rocked back on her heels.

"What was that meant to prove?" Craig's voice cracked like a whip and broke the spell before he reached for Marella's wrist and turned her toward him.

"That I've already moved on. Now let. Me. Go." She wrenched her arm free so hard she nearly slugged Keane in the chest. She instantly winced.

Keane's smile vanished. Without thinking, he moved in front of her and stood between them, glaring at Craig, who looked torn between sputtering and protesting.

"I suggest you do as the lady asked. Walk away."

Craig's eyes fired with irritation. "This isn't any of your—"

"I'm bigger than she is." Keane took one step forward and felt a surge of satisfaction when the man paled. "And meaner. Go. Now."

Craig turned and half walked, half jogged away, leaving heavy-sneakered footprints in the wet sand. Keane felt himself shrink back a bit. He wasn't one to use his physicality, but there were times...

"Are you all right?" Sydney asked Marella before Keane had a chance to. Keane turned and noted Marella seemed to finally be taking in her surroundings.

"I'm fine, thanks. I'm just...mortified." She lifted her hands to her cheeks, shook her head. "I'm so embarrassed. We made such a scene. I'm just..." She looked around as if searching for an escape route.

"Why don't you come back to my office," Sydney suggested. "Marella, is it?"

Marella nodded. "Yes. Hi. Marella Benoit."

"Well, Marella, I'll fix you some tea and you can relax a little. Keane, why don't you—"

"No, please." Marella shook her head, sending her hair cascading around her shoulders. "I appreciate the offer, thank you. But I have to get back. I've got… I'll be okay, really," she said as she moved away. "Um, thanks. For…the assist."

She quickly glanced at Keane, but the second she met his gaze, her cheeks flooded with color once more. Unlike Craig, she didn't scamper away, but slogged through the sand until she disappeared down the path through the coconut trees leading to the main street of Nalani.

"Keane Harper, Nalani's own knight in shining armor," Sydney said when she faced him. "You attract them without even trying, don't you? Marella." She seemed to be testing the name on her lips. "Pretty name. Beautiful lady."

"You're all beautiful." Keane attempted to keep his tone light. Sydney was right. Marella was stunning. Stunning enough that she may have just singed herself into his memory. "But you know me, always happy to help someone in need." He felt something odd under his foot, stepped back, bent down and picked up a beaded-bracelet smart-watch. "Must have come off when he grabbed her wrist." He brushed it off, blew on it, exposing the sea-colored beads and stones. "I'll drop it off at the front desk for her when I get back to the resort."

"Or you could hold on to it," Sydney suggested in a not-so-innocent way. "You never know when you might run into her again. Seems like one heck of a meet-cute opportunity if you ask me."

"Don't go playing matchmaker, Sydney," he warned. "And stop watching those goofy romantic movies you always have on."

"Hey, I'm living one of those goofy romantic movies," she huffed and smacked him gently on the arm. "Go grab your board and get cleaned up. We need to be at the dock by four so we're there when the guests begin to arrive. I'll check in with you later."

"Yes, ma'am." He gave her a silly bow before he yanked his board free. He stood there, ankle deep in sand, watching as his friend and boss walked off.

"Marella," he murmured as he clasped her watch in his palm. She certainly knew how to make an impression. Maybe it was worth holding on to the watch for a few days, just in case he ran into her again. Or…

A slow smile curved his lips. Or he could attempt to make as big an impression on her as she had on him.

"One quick stop, first." Rather than making his way back to the resort, he took Sydney's lead, and headed into town.

CHAPTER TWO

"MARELLA!"

Hotel room key card poised to slip into the slot of her door, Marella dropped her chin to her chest and sighed as the whirlwind that was Crystal Benoit raced down the hall at top speed.

"So close," she whispered. She'd been so close to the solitude her hotel room offered. All she wanted to do was lock herself inside, burrow under the comforter of the king-size bed, pity-gorge on the bag-load of snacks she'd bought at the market and forget today ever happened.

Instead, Marella straightened, and dragged out an overly bright smile that she turned on her ever-ebullient, bikini-clad stepsister. She shifted the reusable fabric grocery bag into her other hand and wished she'd indulged in the ice-cream-and-mochi section of Luanda's. Yeah. She really should have given that a try.

"Hey, Crystal." Marella didn't want to open her door. She didn't want the overcaffeinated, overexcitable bride-to-be intruding on the only place of calm Marella would have for the next week. The room that doubled as her work space and a safe haven from the frenetic, overscheduled, whirlwind of a wedding week their father was paying more than an arm and a leg for.

Crystal was in full prewedding mode as she geared up to become Mrs. Chad Harrington. Her custom-made yellow-accented tiara announcing she was indeed the Bride To Be had been perched on her head from the second they'd boarded the plane.

The rhinestone lettering specifically matched Crystal's self-branded #ButtercupDoll yellow. She'd used the color as inspiration to build her brand as a social media influencer, which, in the past eighteen months, had taken her to more than five million followers and counting.

The blinding, can't-miss-the-crown color and matching bikini only reminded Marella she was crownless and had been trying to take off the same twenty pounds for the better part of two years.

Crystal had picked up a beautiful sarong from one of the cute little stores down the street. The splashes of blue broke up the blinding walking rainbow that doubled as her twenty-four-year-old step-sibling.

"I thought your goal for the day was to remain at the pool until it closes and finalize all the wedding details with Brita." The pool and surrounding area of the resort had been the main reason Crystal had insisted on holding her wedding here in Nalani. The private garden that would host the ceremony was supposedly overblooming with the yellow hibiscus that coincidentally matched Crystal's wedding color scheme.

Marella thought it amusing her sister had chosen the location based primarily on the color of the flowers in the garden. Still, she was pretty sure other brides had made important decisions based on even stranger requirements.

"Brita's got everything in hand." Crystal waved off the comment. "I have nothing to worry about."

"Did your dress arrive yet?" Marella asked.

Last she'd heard, the bride's gown, along with two of the three bridesmaids' dresses, were being express shipped from the mainland. Plus, the custom crystal cake topper Crystal had designed herself. "What about the çake? Has she spoken with the bake—"

"The dresses will arrive Thursday afternoon." Crystal sighed. "If I'm not worried about things, I don't know why you are. Brita—"

"Has it all under control, right. Got it."

"Don't look at me that way," her sister warned. "Brita's one of my best friends. This is literally her dream job. Are you forgetting she planned Alcina Palmer's wedding shower last fall?"

Marella blinked, having absolutely no idea who this Alcina person was. But the idea that Brita and Crystal equated a wedding shower with an actual wedding? Marella bit the inside of her cheek. It wasn't her problem Crystal had insisted on giving Brita full rein with the wedding, and by full rein that meant the flowers, the catering, the music… you name it, and Crystal was thriving on the idea of being surprised come Saturday afternoon.

What Marella needed to do was channel her sister's calm, silence her inner control freak and just do what she was told. Why she couldn't embrace that idea was beyond her. Most maids of honor would probably be thrilled not to be weighed down by the millions of details and arrangements that needed to be treated as a priority. Still, she thought it a big mistake not to at least bring the resort event organizer into the loop.

"I'm sorry," Marella said in an effort to erase the frown from her sister's face. "You're right. I have no doubt your day is going to go perfectly. And you were right about this resort and the grounds. It really is stunning here." As if any place in Hawai'i was unattractive. "You certainly are keeping us busy with activities while Brita brings everything together."

She wasn't lying about that.

The resort's attention to detail with its varying open-air spaces filled with the local flora gave a truly tropical feel, right down to the hibiscus tree situated near the balcony door where it was bathed in sunlight for a good portion of the day. Its bright yellow flowers complemented the decor of the room perfectly. Cool ocean tones mixed with splashes of sunshine yellow and orange across the walls and unintentionally fell in line with everything Crystal's heart could desire.

"So why aren't you at the pool?" Marella asked.

"Well, I *was* there," Crystal said. "We were. Most of us, anyway. The bartender gave me a free drink! Okay, maybe three, but they were soooo good! It was served in a pineapple! I had to ask for an umbrella though." She pouted. "Funny they didn't think of that."

Or the bartender wasn't interested in fulfilling island stereotypes that would place the Hibiscus Bay Resort on equal footing with more touristy and kitschy accommodations. Marella had only been here less than a day and already she felt as if the resort was something different than the typical crash-and-dash hotel. They'd certainly been accommodating with her taking Craig's room off the bridal party account.

"I couldn't very well stay there when you need me."

Marella's stomach clenched. "And why do I need you?"

"Marella." Crystal gave her one of her

perfectly practiced expressions of sympathy. "I heard what happened down at the beach. Between you and Craig." Crystal plucked the key card out of Marella's hand and slid it into the slot. She whipped her head around so quick, her long, recently highlighted gold-blond hair nearly swept across Marella's face. "I couldn't wait another second to come find you and hear all the details." Never were Crystal's eyes more alive than when potential scandal lay in the offing.

"Of course you couldn't." Marella tried to hide her sarcasm. She loved all three of her step-siblings to bits: Lance, only a few years younger than Marella; Tag, the baby who was still attempting to figure his life out; and Crystal, who from day one had arrived with her own special instruction manual. The young woman simply did not have an off switch. And in wedding mode? It was like someone had left the fast forward feature running on their remote control.

"Come on in and tell me everything!" Crystal ordered.

Grateful she hadn't succumbed to that bottle of island rum she'd seen at the grocery, Marella slow-walked herself inside and closed the door behind her. She set the bag on the floor, drew her cross-body purse over her head and placed it on the coffee stand directly across from the spacious bathroom.

Making herself at home, Crystal flung open the glass balcony door and filled the third-story room with the calm ukulele-led Hawaiian music played by those welcoming guests to the resort. She'd thought the added cost of ocean view rooms had been an unnecessary splurge. They weren't going to be spending a whole lot of time inside for the next few days, but as Marella felt that luscious breeze drifting through and she caught sight of those magnificent waves tumbling up onto the sand, she welcomed the offering. There was something meditative and calming about the ocean. From a distance, that is.

Being around water had never been a problem for her. Being in or on it? She shivered even as anxiety circled in her chest. She'd spent the better part of the past few days trying to come up with an excuse to get out of going on tonight's dinner cruise, but she knew nothing short of falling off a

cliff would allow for her to skive off this—
or any other—prewedding event.

"So?" Crystal stretched her arms out across
the railing and hit a pose that would have
made a top fashion photographer proud.
"Craig. Spill."

Marella sank onto the edge of the bed. "I'd
rather my social life not be a feature spotlight on your TikTok channel."

"YouTube is channel. TikTok is page."
Crystal rolled her very bright blue eyes, but
her smile didn't dim. "Honestly, how are you
in advertising when you can't get the social
media platforms straight? And FYI, I left
my phone at the pool."

Marella arched a brow before she dropped
her gaze to the rectangular bulge beneath the
knot of her hip-slung sarong.

"Oh, right. Oops. I meant to leave it at the
pool." She yanked out the phone and waved
the screen at Marella. "You sure you don't
want to—"

"Yes, I'm sure and no, I don't want to,"
Marella said with patience that actually
hurt. "Nor do I want to have this conversation again. I promised to participate in your
online…thing—"

Crystal scowled.

"I promised you could record me the day of your wedding. That's it." Marella pointed to the phone. "You want to talk, great. But turn that off first." She blinked down at her bare wrist. "Oh." She jumped up, spun in a circle as she patted her pockets and her chest. "Oh, no."

"What's wrong?"

"My watch." Marella raced over to her purse, but the thing was barely big enough to carry her cell and ID let along her smartwatch. She'd thought she'd gotten lucky and she hadn't had any alerts to deal with. But nope. The thing was just…gone. "Darn it, I knew that bracelet thing you gave me wasn't going to be strong enough. Geez! I just got that watch. It has all my alarms set up and I didn't see a tech store in town. Maybe I missed it."

"My bracelet works just fine." Crystal joined her in the hotel room, waved her arm in the air to display her yellow—of course—stone and beaded watch band. "Maybe you lost it when you were kissing the sexy surfer guy on the beach?"

All concerns about her watch faded. Marella's skin instantly became clammy as she looked at her sister. "What sexy surfer guy?"

"The one you kissed." Crystal enunciated every word for obvious effect. "On the beach. From what I heard—"

"What did you hear?" She advanced, which caused Crystal to back away, and a fleeting expression of panic flashed across her step-sister's cherubic, youthful face. Marella didn't have any issue being known for dumping Craig in front of most of Nalani. Kissing a perfect stranger in public on the other hand… "And from whom did you hear it?"

"Well, I don't think—" She plopped straight down into the oversized padded wicker chair situated by the hibiscus tree. "Who I heard it from isn't exactly important."

"Oh, but it is." Anger flamed from her toes all the way to her head. Marella's face felt so hot she wouldn't have been surprised to learn steam was coming out of her ears. "Let me guess. Craig." She shoved her hands in her hair and resisted the urge to yank. "The creep must have booked it back here so he could start tattling on me and play the victim card."

"He did stop by the pool on his way up to his room."

"I should have known he'd pull something like this. Suddenly I don't feel so bad after all. For the record, he was the one frolicking in the sand with your—"

"So you did kiss him?" Crystal's eyes went wide. "This surfer guy?" She lifted herself up only long enough to tuck her legs under her. "How was it? Was it hot? Was he hot? Craig was steaming so the guy must have—"

"You always have had selective hearing." Marella let out a loud breath, crossed her arms over her chest. "You missed the actual important part, Crystal. I caught Craig making out with Alexis."

Crystal blinked. "Alexis who?"

"Your bridesmaid Alexis. Your BFF, remember?"

"Oh." Crystal pursed her lips. "Eesh. Awkward. Sorry about that. Typical though. She has a thing for attached men." Crystal waved away Marella's shock. "I don't want to talk about Craig or Alexis. I want to hear about the—"

"Sexy surfer guy, yeah. I got it." It seemed easier calling him that instead of using his name. *Keane.* His name was Keane. Not that she was going to share that tidbit of information with Crystal.

Frustration getting the better of her, Marella stalked over to the grocery bag and dug deep inside until she pulled out a heaving handful of locally made chocolate-coconut candy. The second the rich, not-too-sweet chocolate hit her tongue, the rest of her settled. The coconut tasted luscious and tempting and had her bringing the rest with her when she returned to the edge of the bed. She sat and held out the bag to her sister, who looked as if she'd just been offered a package of salmonella.

"Are you kidding? I've already been overindulging enough as it is."

"Okay." Marella sighed and shrugged before shaking the bag closer. "If you don't want to hear—"

"Fine," Crystal snapped, then sighed in near ecstasy when she bit into the treat. "Oh." She sagged back into the chair. "Keep the bag away or I'll scarf down the whole thing."

Marella grinned.

"Okay, I caved. Now spill," Crystal ordered before she licked her fingers.

"There isn't much to spill. I was mad at Craig and he was…"

"Craig," Crystal supplied and earned an acknowledging nod from Marella.

"I said something to the effect of he wasn't the only one who could find someone else and I turned around and…kissed the first man I saw." She blew out a breath. "It wasn't anything special, Crystal. He was there and convenient and I wanted to make a point."

For the life of her she couldn't recall exactly what that point was, but…

Marella pressed a hand against her suddenly racing heart. She was not the kind of woman who grabbed perfect strangers off the beach and kissed them. She wasn't the kind of woman who did anything on impulse. Heck, she was sitting across from the very embodiment of impulse at this very moment. She'd witnessed the trouble not thinking things through caused, the ripple effects that could eke out at unexpected moments far down the line.

"I'm not buying the 'he's nothing special' routine." Crystal circled her index finger in the air in front of Marella's face. "You're blushing."

"I always blush," Marella muttered. It was the Benoit family curse.

"Not about men, you don't," Crystal argued.

"Because I never talk about them. Men." When oh when was this day going to end?

"My point exactly." Crystal smirked. "You liked it. Ooh, I wish I'd been there! You kissed him and you liked it!"

"I honestly don't recall." Good thing they were inside—otherwise Marella would have had to run for cover from the multitude of lightning strikes headed her way. "It was different. From Craig. I'll give you that." Now that she tried to, she couldn't recall a single time Craig's kisses had made her feel anything other than justified in her belief that love—at least the kind of love that supposedly made people's toes curl and their hearts stutter—simply didn't exist. Relationships were about companionship. Camaraderie. Supporting each other as they went through life together. Passion?

Simply put, in Marella's estimation and experience, passion was overrated and frequently overstated.

She nibbled on another coconut bomb and thought about nibbling on her sexy surfer's lips.

"If you ask me," Crystal said.

"I didn't," Marella said.

"It sounds to me as if you've finally got a little excitement going on in your life." Crystal untucked her legs and leaned forward, rested her hands on Marella's knees as she turned on that life-gives-me-nothing-but-jelly-beans-and-confetti expression full blast. "This trip is just what you needed, Marella. It's been a rough few months since Dad's heart attack and you taking the reins at Benoit & Associates while he recovered. But he's better now. You can exhale. No one has earned this vacation more than you, and a bonus vacation, no, an island romance? Oh! What a great sidepiece for the wedding! I need my phone."

"No." Marella grabbed her sister's arm and tugged her back in front of her. "Absolutely not. My life or lack of one is not for public consumption. Today's beach thing was a freak occurrence that will never happen again."

Crystal sagged and looked a bit defeated. "You're about to turn thirty, Marella. You work, you go home, you go to bed and you do it all again. You won't even get a cat because you don't want to alter your routine."

"I won't get a cat because I don't want them horking up their breakfast on my hardwood floors."

Crystal looked at her and for the first time in a while, the facade of internet party girl collapsed. "I worry about you, Marella. Pippy's got a more active social life than you and our grandmother is eighty-three! I'm beginning to think you schedule time to smile. When are you going to actually start living?"

"You live more than enough for the both of us." Marella reached out, touched her sister's cheek, much in the way she had all those years ago when Crystal and her brothers had become part of the Benoit family. Gloria, Marella's stepmother, had lost her husband around the same time as Marella and her father had lost Marella's mother—one of those odd similarities that created a surprising and ultimately much-needed bond. Sometimes she could still see anxious, adorable five-year-old Crystal clinging to her fashion doll as if it were a pair of floaties in the big people's pool. "And lest you forget, me working the hours I do is part of the reason you can afford to have this big splashy wedding of yours. In Hawai'i. With all your friends. If I hadn't signed that big client—"

"I know, I know." Crystal heaved a sigh of dramatic proportions. "Dad's reminded me I have you to thank for arranging to get everyone here, thank you very much. I've said thank you. Not to mention I'm giving the company a featured sponsorship spot on my vlog."

"Because what twentysomething isn't looking for an advertising agency?"

Marella released her hold. She hoped Crystal understood just how much money this entire week was costing. Personally, she couldn't fathom what warranted countless thousands of dollars for what was essentially a big party. To this day she nearly went into shock when she thought about the price tag that came attached to Crystal's custom-designed gown. But that was Crystal, not Marella. At some point she was going to have to get better at not judging people by the standards and expectations she set for herself.

"I understand what you're saying, Crystal, and I appreciate the thought for what it is. But I feel safe in saying that what I did today on the beach is the one and only time I will ever do anything like that."

Crystal giggled.

"What?" Marella asked.

Her sister shrugged as she got to her feet and grabbed her phone. "Just thinking how funny life can be sometimes." She headed to the door. "If you're going to mope around here, you only get until five. That's when the dinner cruise leaves. Don't forget, docking slip four."

Marella stared at the door closing behind Crystal. Her mind spun. Not because of the scent of hibiscus filling the room. And not because of what she now suspected was a life-saving dalliance between her now ex-boyfriend and Crystal's man-eating bridesmaid. Nor was it her missing watch or the idea of having to step foot on a boat that as far as she was concerned might very well go the way of the *Titanic* and deposit the entire bridal party into the ocean.

No. She turned, sat back down and tried to breathe. It wasn't any of those things that had her thoughts spinning like a summer cyclone.

How could one kiss—with a stranger no less—shift her long-held beliefs that passion was a myth? Maybe it had been the surprise of the moment. She'd been upset, off-kilter and not thinking clearly. Obviously. Or, it was an utter and complete fluke. Yeah, that was probably it. But still, he…

She blew out a breath and had the sudden urge to fan herself.

The man had definitely known how to kiss.

The way his mouth had moved on hers, gentle, curious, maybe a bit amused as she'd felt the distinct curving of his lips. His hands had slipped down her back and rested at the swell of her hips, fingers clenching just enough to make her breath catch in her throat.

It had been the kind of kiss she remembered reading about in the romance novels she'd sneaked beneath the covers with a flashlight while growing up. All those stomach-pitchy, toe-clenching, breath-halting feelings she'd long given up hope of ever feeling. The kind of kiss she'd convinced herself simply didn't exist.

From the kind of man she'd never once, in her entire life, entertained the notion of attracting.

"Okay, what was in these chocolates?" She grabbed the bag and tossed them to the dresser that sat beneath the wall-mounted flat-screen television. She'd been in Hawai'i for less than a day, certainly long enough to get her bearings, but not remotely close to the time needed for an entire shift of her belief system. "Fluke. It was a fluke, that's all it was."

Marella had her head in her hands as the breeze kicked up and the turquoise curtains billowed around her. She gazed out the open patio door and shoved the self-pity away.

"I'm in Hawai'i for goodness' sake. I need to soak it in and enjoy it." But Crystal was right. Fun had never been at the top of her list of things to do; nor was letting loose. For most of her life she'd had her eyes focused on the preset horizon of running Benoit & Associates. Since before she'd left for college, she'd been determined to make a name for herself and hopefully bring fresh eyes and ideas to her father's company, take it to the next level. She'd made inroads with both those things in the past few months. "And look what that's gotten you."

Sulking, feeling embarrassed and sorry for herself in a hotel room situated in the middle of an absolute paradise.

It had also gotten her kissed by one very handsome, very, well, for want of a better term, understanding stranger she'd probably never see again. "Thank goodness for that." She breathed a sigh of relief as she headed to the closet for the dress she planned to wear tonight. "Imagine how awkward running into him again would be."

CHAPTER THREE

"ALOHA, POLUNU!" KEANE stood at the edge of the slip where the *Nani Nalu*, a sixty-five-foot catamaran dedicated to sunset dinner cruises, awaited its evening passengers. He was a bit early to report for duty, but he was anxious to see his friends. Already he could smell the familiar aroma of long-roasted pork wafting out from the forward kitchen area. Other than the lapping waves against the hull, the distinctive and all-too-welcoming sounds of banging utensils and muted culinary conversation filled his ears.

A longtime staple of Nalani, the *Beautiful Wave* ran nightly four-hour cruises down south to the Cape Kumukahi Light, circling back to Hilo, before returning to Nalani. The event was a chance to feature local food, history, and provide sightseeing that best showed off the islands. As if there was a bad way to do so.

He'd lost count of the number of parties and dinners he'd attended on board, let alone how many he'd worked over the years. He knew this boat almost as well as he did the water surrounding it. He could still remember the pride he'd felt when Polunu had given him the wheel for the first time and allowed him to steer straight into the sunset. Unlike other moments in his life, that one felt particularly defining.

"Keane!" The hulk of a man poked his dark head up from behind the bench seat on the upper deck and waved, the smile on his face brighter than the setting sun. "Howzit? No need to wait for an invitation, brah. Come on board. Akahi, we're saved! Keane's here!"

After stepping onto the deck, Keane deposited his flip-flops in one of the large buckets provided for that purpose. Polunu and Akahi's catamaran wasn't anything fancy or elegant. They offered a straightforward, practical yet immersive experience for their customers. They liked to think of their boat as their home that they opened up to tourists and locals alike. Few frills, but an authentic experience and lots of attention to detail had kept them in business for as long as Keane had been coming to Nalani.

"Keane." The statuesque woman emerged from the main cabin on the lower deck, a relieved smile on her round, sun-kissed face. The muumuu she wore was sky blue with a white flower print. He recognized it as one of the more popular patterns from The Hawaiian Snuggler, the town's quilt and fabric shop. Akahi hobbled forward, a walking stick clenched in one fist. "Aloha."

"What's this?" Keane frowned as he brushed his cheek against hers. "Sydney didn't say you were having difficulties. What's happened?"

"Ah, this? It's nothing." She waved away his concern, her close-cropped cap of black hair glistening in the sun.

"Don't believe her!" Polunu shouted down from above. "Doctor keeps telling her she needs to stay off that leg."

"Don't listen to him. He frets, which only makes things worse." Akahi hitched up her chin and her eyes glistened with defiance as she glared at her husband. "And I know better how I feel than that Doc."

Keane couldn't decipher what he heard

Polunu mutter, but he'd bet big money it wasn't anything positive.

Akahi held out her free hand and squeezed hard when Keane grabbed hold. It shocked him how old and frail she looked, and his regret over having stayed away for as long as he had surged once more.

"I'm happy to see you, Keane. Thank you for helping this evening. Since our Jay and his family moved to the mainland, we've had problems keeping a steady crew." She sighed as he led her over to one of the cushioned benches along the perimeter of the dining area.

There was a lovely dressed, long dining table positioned across the width of the catamaran, with each setting meticulously arranged and decorated with a lei of hibiscus and ginger blossoms, or the more masculine *kukui* nuts. The dark brown nuts had, at one time, been worn only by royalty. Providing them for sale was a service to Nalani that lei makers took seriously. Everything found on the *Nani Nalu* was locally sourced.

"We've had to stop our morning fishing trips and only stuck with taking on select private cruises," Akahi continued. "Otherwise, it's too much for the two of us. Kiri's been a huge help, but his schooling takes precedence. And then there's Wyatt too, when he hasn't been committed to another job. We still have Edena, of course, who's been a blessing in the kitchen." She leaned forward, her lips curving in a bittersweet smile. "Don't tell her, but she cooks almost better than I do."

"Now that isn't possible," Keane teased. Akahi was well-known for her traditional Hawaiian cooking as well as her take on familiar mainland comfort food. "Do you know, I make a batch of your luau stew every few months? Keeps me fed for days and my house smells like slow-roasted pork and the islands." He didn't mention how hard it had been to find taro leaves in the Midwest, but he'd managed. Eventually.

"I've missed you, Keane." She nodded. "I've missed that smile." But her own smile didn't quite reach her eyes. "Never a gray cloud with you around."

"You and Polunu were two of my biggest supporters back in the day," Keane reminded her. "Those few years my grandparents lived here, and I'd come out for the summer, they were the best of my life. If it wasn't for you rallying folks and holding those fundraisers, I wouldn't have been able to afford to go to San Diego for that surfing competition my senior year of high school." It was that competition that had led to his swimming scholarship to Stanford, which took him almost as far as the Olympics. From there many—maybe too many—doors had opened for him. "I'm sorry to hear you're struggling."

"We all have our challenges to deal with," Akahi said. "I have to tell you, that Sydney really can work a deal. I'm so glad she decided to move back and keep Ohana Odysseys going. The money we're making from this cruise and others from the business will give us some breathing room to decide what we're going to do."

"Do about what?" Keane crouched in front of her, keeping hold of her hand.

"Decide whether or not it's time to retire and shut it all down." Polunu came slowly down the curving staircase from the pilothouse on the upper deck. His girth made the narrow space a bit difficult to navigate, but he was, as always, one hundred percent positive energy as he arrived on deck. Keane stood, shook his friend's hand and found himself instantly pulled into a suffocating bear hug. "Missed you, *keiki*." He slapped Keane hard on the back.

Keane laughed. "I think maybe you're the only person in Nalani who still calls me kid." Never mind the fact that Keane was a good two inches taller than the older man.

"I always will. Still remember that time you and Remy sneaked on board so you could go surfing off Honomu. Never mind that winter had the tallest waves in two decades. You two were determined to get there. Didn't even wait for the boat to stop before you dived in."

"Then we wiped out in about ten minutes flat." Keane rubbed his fingers across the scar he'd gotten on his wrist when he'd gotten caught up in the rocks. "If it wasn't for you and this boat, we might not have made it back."

"You two were the worst sneaks ever," Polunu reminded him. "Never could get away with anything. Not anything bad, anyway. Remy." He shook his head, touched a hand to his heart. *"Hui hou."* Until we meet again.

Resisting the pull of grief, Keane waited before he rested a hand on Polunu's shoulder. "What needs doing around here? Serving? Bartending? I know you aren't going to put me on kitchen duty."

"We learned that lesson the hard way," Akahi laughed. "Sydney and Daphne offered to come and handle the table service. Tehani was planning on it, but she's having a terrible time with morning sickness."

"More like all-day sickness. Boats only make it worse," Polunu confirmed. "Tonight's group isn't very large, so we should be okay."

"What about supplies?" Keane asked. "You have everything on board already?"

"Food, yes." Polunu looked at his wife.

"What?" Keane asked.

"The bar isn't as well stocked as we'd like," Akahi said. "We've been operating on a minimum the past few months to keep expenses down and we didn't want to get ahead of ourselves before—"

"Say no more." Keane forced himself not to cringe. The idea of them closing was bad enough, but that they were afraid they weren't giving their customers the promised experience was another story altogether.

"Let me take a look at what you've got and I'll make some calls, yeah?" He patted Polunu on the shoulder before he headed into the main cabin.

The *Nani Nalu*, despite showing its age with a few dings in the hull and a few chips in the fiberglass, was still a sight to behold. The main cabin displayed a bevy of windows on both sides, giving the space an even bigger feel. The interior amenities boasted a narrow, four-seater bar on one side of the cabin, and a line of plush, slightly worn benches that provided a great vantage point for those spectacular views.

A quick assessment of the liquor supplies confirmed Polunu's concerns. They were low on just about everything, but a quick call to Mano up at the Hibiscus Bay took care of that.

Polunu and Akahi underestimated their standing in Nalani. They'd been operating the *Nani Nalu* for more than twenty-five years and were responsible for providing the perfect setting for a number of celebrations and special events. Weddings, graduations, christenings and their sunrise fishing trips were legendary in the area. Not only had they raised their three kids and welcomed twice as many grandchildren, but they'd also been unofficial parents to dozens of children over the years, always providing jobs, a kind ear or even a room to sleep in when times got rough. Keane had found himself on the receiving end of their generosity on more than one occasion when he'd come back after graduating college.

They'd taken care of Nalani's residents for ages.

It was time for Nalani to take care of them.

When Keane stepped out of the cabin, the couple immediately stopped talking, looking at him with overly wide eyes. "You still have a 5:00 p.m. boarding time for guests?" he asked them.

"Yes."

Keane looked up at the sky. "I need a half hour. Forty-five minutes top."

"For what?" Akahi eyed him.

"To work some of my island-famous magic." Keane retrieved his flip-flops and jumped off the boat. "Just don't leave without me. I'll be back as soon as I can." He jogged down the dock, turning right and headed straight for the ramp toward the harbor entrance just as Sydney and Daphne Mercer, Ohana Odysseys's nature expert, appeared.

"You making a break for it?" Sydney teased.

"Have to pick up supplies from Mano. Make sure they wait for me. Party of seventeen for the *Nani* tonight, right?"

"Ah, sixteen," Sydney said. "Brita, Crystal's wedding planner, called a little while ago."

"Right. So…" He waggled his hand back and forth. "Party of fourteen, so I'll figure twenty-five as a safe number, at two drinks per… Got it." Some math was easy. "Hey, Daph."

"Nice shirt," Daphne joked, pushing her glasses higher up her nose. She had tied her long red hair back and donned a matching shirt to Akahi's muumuu. Even when they'd all been younger, his and Remy's college classmate gave off that studious vibe and more often than not had her head stuck in a book. Or a flower. She'd all but turned her dorm room into a greenhouse by filling it with countless plants. It had been the perfect retreat when exhausted students needed a natural oxygen hit. Fortunately, Daphne liked people almost as much as she loved her flowers, which made her a perfect tour guide of the nearby rain forests, state parks and botanical gardens. He knew some of the story that had brought her back to the islands to work for Remy as his lead tour guide, but he had never wanted to push. If she was ever interested in telling him, she knew he was always a willing listener. Until then, Daphne's and Sydney's khaki shorts were a practical, cool choice for the warm evening.

"I didn't get the memo about the blue." Could anyone really be surprised he had a collection of surf-themed Hawaiian shirts in every color? But no time to joke—he was already on the move again. "Be back in a bit."

He darted past familiar faces, waved at friends who called out. He was tempted to stop long enough to give Kahlua, Nalani's unofficial porcine mascot, a quick pet as the pig lumbered beside his elderly owner, Benji. As usual, the two wore matching shirts, this one with comical bug-eyed lizards on the fabric. Making a mental note to have a coffee and catch-up with the island wanderer— Benji, not the pig—Keane skidded to a halt in front of the Hibiscus Bay Resort as a large group emerged from the wide, automatic glass doors.

Keane easily identified the crowd as the *Nani Nalu*'s passengers. One young woman's Bride To Be tiara was a dead giveaway. The fun energy they radiated was contagious and Keane bit back a grin, finding added entertainment in the memory of Marella's spectacular dumping performance.

Marella. Maybe Sydney was right. Maybe holding on to Marella's lost watch was in his best interest.

One of the young men bringing up the rear wore a sash across his chest that said Game Over, clearly indicating he was the soon-to-be-married groom. If Keane had to guess, he'd suppose the older woman walking beside him was his mother. She had an air of semiconfusion about her that, along with nervous hands clutching the purse at her side, made her appear a bit out of touch with her surroundings.

They were all polite enough, most of them offering a quick smile as they passed him, but for Keane they may as well have been wearing I'm From The Big City signs.

It was obvious some had not read, or more

likely their event organizer had neglected to share, the conditions regarding the catamaran's journey. All those fancy tasseled loafers and high, strappy heels were going to end up in one of those corner buckets of the boat in the not-too-distant future. Plus, he didn't see very many sweaters, lightweight jackets or shawls being carried. Hawai'i might be known for its tropical heat and humidity during the day, but out on the water? The temperatures dipped considerably along with the sun.

Their chattering teeth might keep the sea turtles up all night.

Speaking of chattering teeth. Keane saw over his shoulder a man in disheveled shorts and T-shirt, struggling to exit the hotel via another door. He jerked one suitcase behind him while juggling a large garment bag over his arm.

"Craig." Keane spun easily, caught the door and allowed him to pass. "Allow me. Leaving already?"

Craig glared at him. "She canceled my reservation."

"Did she?" Marella was just leaping up in Keane's estimation. "That's a shame."

"And she changed my return flight. If I don't take it, I'll—"

"Have to pay to get home yourself rather than on your ex-girlfriend's dime?" Keane kept his tone light. "Never easy to play the long con, is it, Craig?"

Craig looked as if he wanted to say something, but shook his head, shoved past him and jumped into the first cab that drove up.

"Aloha!" Keane waved as the cab pulled away. He wasn't sure he was going to stop smiling before dawn. "And good riddance."

"Keane!"

He turned at the sound of his name. "Oliwa." He slapped his hand into the younger man's open palm. "Howzit, *keiki*? Good to see you. Last I talked to your folks they told me you were working at a resort over in Honolulu."

"Was." Oliwa's chest puffed out. "Mano called me a few weeks back, said he needed a new head of bell services at the Hibiscus and he thought of me. I started yesterday. Welcome back to Nalani, brah. You staying long?"

"Remains to be seen," Keane admitted. It was the one question he hadn't let himself dwell on too much over the past few weeks.

Staying here was good for his soul, but it also felt as if he were running away from his life. Running away and hiding. "But it's good to be back. It's really good to see you." Keane motioned inside. "I've got some business with your boss. Hey, you have a good, stable cart I could borrow? One I can wheel down to the *Nani Nalu*?"

"How about one of our new solar-powered golf carts? Most of them have been returned already."

"Oh, yeah?" He'd seen the guests buzzing around the property in the open six-seat vehicles. "That would be great, thanks."

"I'll go find one and get you the keys."

"Mahalo. I'll talk to you soon, yeah?"

As usual, when Keane finally ducked into the lobby, a familiar sense of peace washed over him. That custom scent of hibiscus mingling with jasmine filled the air. It was just enough to keep the senses serene and the promise of what lay beyond in sight. The wide walkway to the front desk that was manned 24/7 by at least two reservation and courtesy clerks provided ample space for those coming and going without luggage crashing.

It had taken a lot of work and dedication on the part of operations manager, Mano Iokepa, to take away the generic hotel vibe and replace it with an extension of the land surrounding the resort. The dark wood structure had been enhanced by the close proximity of trees planted all around the property. Where windows might have been expected, there were none, providing an open-air environment that felt almost otherworldly. One could hear the numerous waterfalls echoing in the distance, blocking out the noise of the bustling town that lay on the hotel's doorstep.

One of Mano's pet projects had been to improve the outdoor landscaping, which had been somewhat overhauled a few years before Mano began running the place. It had been something Mano's then-wife, Emilia, had pushed for when she was still living in Nalani. But it wasn't until Emilia was gone that Mano seemed to realize she was right.

The timing for the project worked out perfectly as it coincided with Daphne's moving to Nalani. It had been one of her first consulting jobs and earned her an excellent reputation as someone who was easy to work with but who also knew her stuff. If she didn't have an answer, she found one. The new landscaping gave her the hands-on experience she'd needed to become an expert in the local plant life. Step outside any one of the many doors in and out of the Hibiscus Bay and you found yourself in the middle of a rain forest.

Word was the world-class spa at the back of the property was just as majestic. But he'd yet to take a walk over in that direction.

Keane waved to the pair of clerks at the desk and scanned the spacious, breeze-filled lobby. It didn't take long to locate Mano Iokepa. In addition to being a man who was impossible to ignore—well over six feet, shiny jet-black hair kept neatly trimmed, Samoan dark skin with hints of tattoos peeking out from beneath the tailored collar of his shirt—there was a presence about the guy that stopped some people in their tracks.

Mano lived and breathed not only the Hibiscus Bay, which he'd helped make the must-visit, in-demand tourist destination it had become, but Nalani as well. The Iokepas' connections went way back on the islands, but in recent generations, Nalani had become their epicenter.

Their heartbeat. Their home.

For as long as Keane had known Mano, and his sister, Tehani, Mano's sole focus had been to lift up Nalani to a place that benefited everyone who lived here, by welcoming all to the small town. He'd worked his way up from a busboy in the resort restaurant to buying in as a partner with the caveat he be the on-site manager. To this day, there wasn't a detail that escaped his notice.

Keane caught Mano's dark gaze and received a nod before he was waved over.

"Of course, Mr. Benoit. I don't think it should be any issue to accommodate that request. Keane." Mano smiled in greeting. "Excellent timing. Keane Harper, this is Armand Benoit. His daughter's getting married this coming weekend in the main gardens here at the resort."

"Mr. Benoit." Keane accepted the older gentleman's hand. "Aloha. Welcome to Nalani. And the Hibiscus Bay."

"Keane Harper." Armand's eyes turned questioning. "You coach swimming up at Cleaver University."

"Ah, yes." Keane plastered on a well-practiced smile. "I do. Or did." Even he wasn't sure where things stood at the moment. "You keep up with the sport?"

"My younger son, Tag, you may have seen him leaving a moment ago." Armand gestured to the glass doors. "He was on the swim team in college. Came up against Cleaver more than once. Your guys plowed right over them," Armand said with a rueful shake of his head. "Shame what happened with Timothy Brice. How is he and his family doing?"

"Ah, fine." Keane swallowed around the sour-tasting grief and did his best to ignore the guilt. "Last I heard he was doing okay."

"Armand." A stunning woman with neatly arranged long blond waves rested a hand on Armand's shoulder. Had to be his wife. She and her husband had somewhat embraced the more casual look of the island with each of them wearing tropical colors, but the tailored slacks Armand wore and the silk fabric of her dress meant they needed another nudge in the relaxed-clothing department. "I'm sorry to interrupt. I'm going to give her another call. See what's holding her up. Keep an eye on Pippy, won't you?" She glanced back to the older woman sitting in one of the high-backed leather chairs.

"Certainly." Armand nodded. "Keane, Mano, my wife, Gloria."

"Aloha *ahiahi*," Mano said.

"Good evening," Keane followed up immediately to make certain the translation was understood. He glanced over to the elderly woman, his lips twitching as she pried open an extra-large wicker purse, pulled out one of the small bottles of rum from the hotel room refrigerator and twisted the cap open. "Mano, can I steal you away for a sec? About that issue we just discussed over the phone?"

"Yes. Excuse me a moment, won't you?" Mano and Keane walked over to the desk. "Koa," he said to the young woman behind the computer. "Call down to guest services, please, let them know Keane's here to pick up that order of supplies I asked them for."

"Yes, sir." She lifted the receiver as the elevator bell dinged in the distance.

"Akahi's health," Keane said under his breath. Only now did he let himself feel the concern that struck when he'd seen the older woman on her boat. "What do you know?" he asked Mano.

Mano guided him away from the desk. "The good news is the doctors ruled out multiple sclerosis."

Keane held back his relief. "And the bad?"

"Fibromyalgia," Mano said. "Which can be exacerbated by stress."

"Something she doesn't deal with at all as a small business owner," Keane suggested wryly. No wonder Polunu was worried.

"Her doctors have recommended retirement, but the money they're still bringing in covers her medication and treatment costs." Mano grimaced. "I offered to help, but—"

"Let me guess," Keane said. "Thanks, but no thanks."

"Their son and his family leaving for the mainland was a big blow, especially after their other two kids moved to Maui. Akahi and Polunu were hoping Jay would take over the business eventually, but he had other plans."

"Mainland life is tempting," Keane said.

"A lot of the young people, they have their eyes set on the horizon, not on the present and certainly not on the past. Most of the small businesses can't compete with the wages being offered on the more populated islands or even on the mainland, but people like Polunu and Akahi can't afford to match those salaries."

"You can match it though," Keane said. "I ran into Oliwa outside. He said you recruited him to come back."

"He needed to be home with his family," Mano said simply, but as usual in a way that told Keane there was more to the story. "As you say, I had a way to make that happen."

"But you don't have the means to do that for everyone."

Mano shrugged, his perfectly fitted suit sliding over broad shoulders. "I can invest money, time, offer a few positions here and there but the truth is, we have low turnover at the Hibiscus Bay. That's by design. I want my employees to want to come to work, to stay, to find a sense of belonging." It was a notion Mano had offered often, but this time when Keane heard it, he couldn't help but think he sensed something off in his friend's voice.

"Well, I'm glad you brought Oliwa home. He's always displayed a positive energy about Nalani and the resort. It's kind of contagious."

"That's what I'm counting on," Mano agreed. "A lot of his friends followed him to Honolulu. I'm hoping his return might entice them to return."

"Always thinking. Ah. This must be for me." He stepped away as two young men wearing the resort's trademark Hibiscus yellow-and-white-flowered shirts wheeled a substantial cart toward him. Keane spotted Oliwa headed their way, dangling a cart key in his hand, which he passed over to Keane after Mano's approving nod. "Whatever the cost for the alcohol, you bill me, yeah?" Keane told Mano.

"I'll bill you for half," Mano confirmed. "I'll cover the rest. As I said, I'm happy to help Polunu and Akahi however I can." He grinned. "Especially if they don't know about it."

"Don't worry." Keane had always appreciated Mano's generous—albeit secretive—nature. "I won't tell them."

He took a step to the side and collided with someone attempting to move around him. He reached out and grabbed hold of the woman's arms, keeping her on her feet. "I'm so sor—" He straightened, shock shooting through his system as he looked into an all-too-familiar pair of dark brown eyes. "Marella." Just the sight of her lightened his already good mood. "I was hoping to run into you again and here you are." He wondered if he'd ever not be transfixed by her pretty, if not cautious face. Or tempted by those incredibly kissable lips. Lips that instantly opened in shock.

"Keane." The color that flooded her cheeks was both familiar and entertaining. And more than a little concerning considering the panic that also rose. "Hello." She tugged herself free of his hold. She was flustered, obviously, and had changed into a simple coral summer dress that accentuated her lush figure and offset her beautiful thick, brown hair that tumbled around her shoulders. She had a matching sweater draped over one arm, and that small bag strapped across her body.

Her eyes wide, she scanned her surroundings even as Keane felt a boost of confidence. She'd remembered his name. "Um."

"Not that you care," he said in lieu of an icebreaker, "but I just saw Craig get into a cab with his luggage."

"He's gone?" She sighed, touched a hand

to her chest. "Ha, that's a relief. I'm glad he took the not-so-subtle hint."

"Oh, he took it." Keane found himself grinning at the memory. "Canceling his room was a good move, but changing his plane ticket? That's a new one."

"Took me more than a couple of supervisors to make it happen, but I tend to get what I want." Her smile seemed to fade before it widened. "I didn't realize you worked here."

"I don't, but I'm beginning to wish I did." Keane pushed his right hand into his pocket and felt the watch he'd been carrying around all day brush against his fingers. "I have something—"

"Marella." Armand Benoit and his wife approached. "There you are. We're going to be late."

"Yes, I know, Dad. I'm sorry." She darted nervous eyes in Keane's direction and for a moment, looked like an uncertain sea turtle pulling into its protective shell. "I was catching up on some work—"

"We had a deal, remember?" her father scolded. "This week isn't for work. It's for family."

"Says the man who was on his laptop less

than an hour ago," Gloria chided. "Don't mind him. You look lovely, Marella."

"Thanks, Gloria." Marella's smile warmed. "And I know I said I'd leave work at home, Dad, but someone needs to keep those company fires burning. Speaking of fires. I need to talk to you about one I just put out."

"Whatever it is can wait," Armand insisted. "Ah, Mother." He faced the older woman Keane had spotted imbibing by the trio of potted palms. "How are you doing?"

"I'll be doing better once we're rocking and rolling on that dinner cruise." The woman had a look of impatience about her, along with a spark of naughtiness one might see in the eyes of a troublesome child. "Hoping to get some boogie time. Marella, did I hear you say you've been working?"

Keane couldn't stop grinning at Marella's obvious mortification or the disapproval in her grandmother's voice.

"Yes, you did, Pippy." Marella reached out and grabbed hold of the older woman's hand. "I'm sorry I kept you waiting. We can go now."

"No need to apologize. Saw you chatting up these handsome men and couldn't resist a closer look." And look she did, her brown eyes magnified behind the biggest framed lenses Keane had ever seen. The elderly woman barely reached Marella's shoulder, hunched over as she was, and she shuffled a bit, but there was more than a spark of life in her. There was an entire inferno. "I'm Philippa Benoit. But everyone calls me Pippy." She moved past Marella to stand directly in front of Keane. Her hair had a bit of lift around her face and the silver highlights in the fading brown shared by her granddaughter no doubt camouflaged her age. "You've got eyes for my granddaughter."

Now it was Keane's turn to blush. "Um."

"Pippy." Marella's mortified whisper only widened Keane's grin even as Mano half coughed and half chuckled.

Recovering quickly, Keane decided to go with it. Pippy seemed enchanting. "I appreciate beauty when I see it, Pippy." He caught her free hand and squeezed it in greeting. "I'm Keane Harper. It's very nice to meet you."

"Keane. What an absolutely charming name," Pippy said. "She's free now, you know? Marella. Totally single and unattached."

"Pippy!" Marella's gasp only entertained him more. She swung on Keane, silently pleading with him to stop playing along. "I'm so sorry. Sometimes her filter doesn't work."

"My filter's got nothing to do with anything," Pippy insisted and stepped away from Marella. "I've simply reached the age of not giving a—"

"That's enough, Mother," Armand warned. "We need to get—"

"She gave that slug of a boyfriend of hers the old heave-ho." Pippy's eyes narrowed and stared straight at Keane, unblinking. "Saw him just a few minutes ago, scampering off with his tail between his suitcases. But I'm guessing you already knew that, didn't you? About time too."

"What's this?" Gloria asked Marella. "You and Craig have broken up?"

"He failed to meet my expectations of fidelity." Marella crossed her arms over her chest. "That fire I mentioned," she said to her father, who looked as if he'd rather be having this conversation anywhere else.

"But that means you don't have an escort to the wedding," Gloria said.

"I don't think that even cracks the top ten of things to worry about," Marella told her.

"Never met a more useless hunk of potato in my entire life," Pippy went on. "And I've got eighty-three years of dealing with all kinds of people. Po. Tay. Toe." She angled a look at Marella, ignoring the muffled snickers coming from the staff. "Smartest thing you've done in years, Marella, dumping him. So." She stepped closer and peered up at Keane. "Is this him?"

Keane couldn't help but look to Marella for guidance, but she'd closed her eyes and pinched the bridge of her nose.

"Mother, what are you talking about?" Armand asked with such strained patience Keane had no doubt this wasn't the first time a conversation like this had taken place.

"I think maybe we should be going?" Gloria tapped her diamond-encrusted watch.

"I saw the way you two reacted just now to each other," Pippy said without missing a beat. "Sparks! My cataracts might be a problem, but some things I can see a mile away.

You're the hunk she kissed on the beach, aren't you?"

"Where's a moat of quicksand when you need it?" Marella muttered. "Pippy, this is inappropriate—"

"Nah, this has to be him. I heard Crystal talking about it at the pool." Pippy winked at Keane.

What an absolute delight Pippy was. Not to mention a font of information.

"They thought I was sleeping," Pippy went on. "But I hear everything. Craig and that bridesmaid, what's her name, Amazonia?"

"Alexis," Marella said.

"Right. Alexis." Pippy rolled her eyes. "Marella here caught Potato Boy and Amazonia hot and heavy on the beach and do you know what your girl did, Army?"

The color that exploded onto Armand's face was evidence that the blushing tendency was a Benoit family trait. "It's Armand, Mother, please."

"Your girl dumped him," Pippy declared. "Right there in front of everyone and their uncle. Splat!"

"It wasn't exactly—" Marella began.

"And then as an exclamation point, she

kissed *him*." Pippy poked a finger into Keane's arm. "Just to make her point. From what I hear you two have quite the chemistry. Va-va-voom! Want to come to a wedding?"

"Someone kill me, please," Marella pleaded. "There was no...voom. Or any va-va-ing. And no, he doesn't." She looked to Keane, eyes pleading, but what could he do about it?

From his perspective there had been a plethora of both. As a result, his smile only grew.

"Now that's what I call a sudden life change," Pippy confirmed. "Wasn't so sure I believed it, hearing it come out of Crystal's mouth—"

"Pippy, please," Gloria pleaded. "Not in front of strangers."

"Oh, hush," Pippy ordered. "Nothing strange about either one of these fine men. You know, when they told me the wedding was going to be in this little town I'd never heard of, I wasn't so sure I'd find anything to enjoy." She turned around and linked her arms through Mano's and Keane's and tugged them close. "I do believe I've been proved wrong. I know his name." She squeezed Keane's arm, batted her lashes at him, then nearly fell over when she looked up at Mano. "What's your name, young man?"

"Mano Iokepa, ma'am. I run the Hibiscus Bay."

"Oh, a man of power." Pippy did a little butt wiggle and eyed Marella. "That's two for you to choose from, Mari. No potatoes here, that's for sure."

Instead of Mano extricating himself, he patted Pippy's hand as a porter came around the corner with a stylish transport chair. "I believe we've got some top-of-the-line assistance for you, Pippy."

Pippy's hold on Keane's arm tightened. "That looks like a wheelchair."

"I believe it is," Mano said easily.

"I don't need a wheelchair." Pippy stepped closer to Keane, pulled her arm free of Mano's. "I've got two good pins." She kicked up one of her feet, putting her shiny silver sneakers on display below the jade green velour track suit. "They still work. I'm walking."

Keane took a hint from Mano and covered Pippy's trembling hand. She clung to him like a barnacle.

"Mother, it's quite a distance to the dock—"

"I'm not putting my scrawny backside anywhere near that thing," Pippy insisted. "If anyone needs it, you do. You're the one who had the heart attack and was in the ICU for three days. Last time I was in the hospital was when you were born, so mind."

Armand sighed heavily.

"Pippy," Marella said. "Dad's just trying to—"

"You've gotten yourself in enough trouble today, young lady," Pippy said to Marella. "You want to deal with me too?"

"No, ma'am." Marella huffed. "Dad, it's okay. I'll walk with her. Or we can just stay here. How about that, Pippy? We could do dinner at the hotel, maybe take a walk on the—"

"Why don't you both ride down to the dock with me," Keane suggested. The anticipation of having Marella on board wasn't something he was willing to give up. He hadn't been this intrigued by a woman in a long time. "I have some supplies I need to drive down to the *Nani Nalu*. There's plenty of space for you two in the cart."

"What do you mean you have supplies

for the boat?" Marella blinked so quickly he was surprised she didn't take off in flight.

"Keane's part of your crew for the evening," Mano explained as the shock in Marella's eyes rose once more. "They were short staffed and he volunteered to assist. Sydney Calvert will be on board as well. She's the owner of Ohana Odysseys."

"The company that's arranged all of our excursions and tours?" Gloria said. "Oh, how lovely. Crystal's been so complimentary about working with them on all the arrangements. It'll be nice to meet her in person."

"Brita didn't do that?" Marella asked.

"No." Gloria's eyes sharpened. "No, we thought it best she only focused on the wedding."

"I'm glad to hear Ohana's been working out well for you," Keane said.

"We're all about Ohana here in Nalani," Mano said. "Pippy? Will the cart work for you?"

"Depends." Pippy narrowed her eyes at Keane. "What kind of cart?"

"It's like a golf cart, only cooler," Keane whispered loud enough for the others to hear.

"Hmm." Pippy seemed intrigued. "Can I drive?"

"No, you cannot—"

"Dear." Gloria cut her husband off and took hold of his arm. "Why don't we let Marella handle things from here? We'll see you down at the boat," she told them.

"I guess it's settled then." Keane turned his smile on Marella. He didn't think she could be more beautiful than in that moment right after she'd kissed him, but he was wrong. That temper flashing in her eyes was a stunning sight to behold. "You two can come with me."

"Perfect!" Pippy announced. "I just need to visit the little *tutu's* room." She poked a finger in the air and stepped back. "Be right back."

"*Tutu…*?" Gloria asked.

"It's *grandmother* in Hawaiian," Marella explained. "Apparently Pippy's been reading that information packet Brita gave everyone."

"I feel the need to apologize for my mother," Armand said to Mano and Keane. "I don't know what's gotten into her."

"No apology necessary," Mano assured

him. "I haven't been this entertained by a guest in a very long time. Go. Have a good time. Housekeeping will have all of your beds turned down by the time you return. Oh, and, ma'am." Mano stepped back to the desk, spoke again to the clerk and accepted a neatly folded zip-down sweatshirt. He handed it to Gloria. "It gets quite chilly out there on the boat. In case you need it."

"Well, thank you." Gloria rested a hand on the yellow fabric. "I suppose I should have remembered that myself. Or checked in with Marella. You seem to have thought of everything today."

Marella offered another smile. "I'm just going to go check on Pippy." She backed away, her eyes nervously looking over at Keane before she scampered off toward the lobby restrooms.

"We will see you on board then," Armand said to Keane with something akin to confusion in his eyes.

"See you there, sir." Keane waited until Marella's parents disappeared out the lobby doors before he rocked back on his heels. "Something tells me this evening is going to be anything but boring."

"Keane." There was warning in Mano's voice. There was also concern. "Be careful."

"Don't worry." He slapped a hand on his friend's shoulder. "I'm aces on a boat, remember?"

"I'm not talking about the boat. Or tonight." He glanced at the hallway Marella had disappeared down. "And you know it."

"It's just a little harmless fun." Even as he said it, he wasn't entirely sure it was true. "I'm not going to go breaking Pippy's heart."

Mano didn't laugh. "You and I both know Pippy isn't a factor in any of this. I'm talking about Marella."

"What about her?" But Keane already knew. He'd felt his heart flip over the second he locked eyes on her again. The moment he'd seen her, had her in his arms, everything inside him had shifted, as if he'd taken a step onto a completely unknown—yet tempting—road. "Don't go getting all worried, Mano. You know me. I don't do serious."

"No. You don't, do you?" Mano's brow furrowed and he ducked his head. "But you know what they say. There's a first time for everything."

CHAPTER FOUR

DESPITE THE PROMISE of a relaxing getaway—as if anything involving Crystal's wedding could be considered relaxing—Marella's limited time on the islands had so far consisted of one embarrassing moment after another. It was all she could do not to book a ticket straight back to New York City. But that would mean breaking her promise to her sister. The Benoit family might be chaotic and at times a bit…eccentric, but when push came to shove, they always had each other's back.

Besides, someone needed to stay close and keep an eye on Pippy, who was clearly having far too much fun already. Normally Marella enjoyed her grandmother's antics and running commentary, but when she was the topic of conversation? Yeah, not so much.

At least Craig was officially out of the picture. Not that his absence felt anything other than a relief. Just another piece of evidence that proved what she knew to be...true.

She looked at Keane, recalling their impulsive kiss. Maybe *knew* was too strong a word where her belief about passion was concerned. Or maybe it was her definition that needed to be adjusted? Either way, Craig had definitely done her a multitude of favors behaving as he had. Now she could focus on what was really important. Keeping the family business running while making certain everyone survived Crystal's wedding.

Pippy's laugh had Marella's lips twitching. There were times Crystal's jokes and comments shone a spotlight on Pippy's younger years, or at least what Marella had heard of them. It only went to show that family was dictated by love, affection and attention and not necessarily by blood.

For all her determination to remain mostly invisible this week, not a difficult task when she had a spinning disco ball of a younger sister as a distraction, Marella needed to stop adding to the pile of moments best forgotten or ignored. Now she was dealing with a filterless grandmother with delusions of being a matchmaker of some sort. Marella could only hope that thought passed quickly and without result. Better yet, she needed to find another distraction.

It didn't help that Keane appeared to counter Marella's lifelong insistence that the perfect man did not exist. He'd been utterly unflappable. First at the beach, then in the lobby of the resort. Was there nothing that knocked him off balance?

Keane. Marella tightened her arms across her torso as the cart bumped its way off the resort property. How she wished she hadn't known his name. Or seen him again. Thinking of him as anonymous, as a onetime encounter, made the attempt to keep this afternoon's dalliance in the *I hope I forget this* portion of her brain.

He'd been a sight to behold then with his bare chest, cool tattoos and charming smile that lit up the entirety of his far-too-handsome face. It really wasn't fair to the rest of the male population that he looked even better dry, cleaned up and dressed to impress.

She was fascinated by his hands. Strong, gentle, never hesitating. Something inside her had softened at the way he'd patted Pippy's hand when she'd become agitated about the wheelchair. His caring nature appeared to be part of who he was and showed a protective element that warmed even her skeptical heart.

"You okay back there?" Keane, hands firmly on the steering wheel of what was indeed a kicked-up golf cart, glanced over his shoulder at her. "You're awfully quiet."

"I'm always quiet." She grabbed hold of the side railing as they drove over a speed bump. Despite the lack of speed, the ride wasn't exactly smooth. "Just not really looking forward to tonight."

Her stomach was already pitching and roiling, and they'd only just taken the final curve that put them on the dock of the Hibiscus Bay Resort Harbor. Since it was later in the day, there weren't a lot of people about, but the ones who were, automatically moved to the side as they buzzed past at… She leaned forward to look at the dash. A speedy twelve miles per hour. This evening hadn't really even gotten started and she was already thinking it wasn't ever going to end.

"Why not?" Keane asked. "Because of

Craig? You aren't going to let what happened with him ruin your whole trip, are you?"

"It's not Craig," Pippy blurted. "Marella hates the water."

"Pippy," Marella warned even as she figured it was futile. Her grandmother was in rare form this evening. "I don't hate it, exactly," she felt the need to explain. "I just don't trust it." And what she didn't trust she went out of her way to avoid.

"Smart woman." Keane surprised her by nodding. "I've all but lived in the water ever since my dad threw me in a lake when I was three. Family swimming lessons," he added with what she interpreted as a bitter smile. "First lesson I learned was to be ready for anything."

Marella's mouth dropped open. His father had thrown him in a lake? How…why…and Keane actually turned it around to the point he loved the water? She shook her head. How was that even possible?

"The water is all about respect as well as recognizing and accepting that it has all the power." He grinned at Pippy. "My father probably thought he was playing a joke on me, throwing me into the water like that, but doing so helped me find my path in life. I consider that a bit of justice, actually, considering he was hoping I'd follow in his footsteps and be a mechanic. Instead, I ended up training and almost never leaving the pool."

"I suppose that's the silver lining then," Marella said when she couldn't think of another response. "You finding your own path."

"Speaking of paths." Pippy straightened in her seat to peer over the front of the electric cart. "We're really booting along here. I could do with one of these cart thingies back home."

"I don't think—"

"Can you imagine if we'd had one of these when I was growing up on the farm? Now that would have been a hoot and a half."

Marella nodded but was glad it hadn't been the case. Her grandmother's upbringing in rural New York often reared out of Pippy's mouth in interesting ways and at even more interesting times.

"Back then cars were a lot bigger than they are now. My father drove a Monte Carlo. You ever seen one of those?" she asked Keane.

"I have. We have a pretty big contingent

of automobile fanatics here in Nalani. The Monte Carlo is definitely a big car," Keane said as he slowed down and took an easy left turn while Marella placed a steadying hand on the box of bottles on the seat beside her. "They don't make them like that anymore. Bet it was fun to drive."

"You'd win that bet," Pippy confirmed.

Marella looked up at the mirror over her grandmother's head and saw a flash of joy on Pippy's face, enough that her own sourness melted away. Even as her trepidation over the boat remained.

"That car was this dark, shiny sort of green. My father would let me sit on his lap and steer sometimes. When my mother wasn't around of course," Pippy clarified. "I miss that car. Miss my father too, even though he's been gone nearly sixty years now."

"We never completely stop missing the people we love." Keane's voice was tinged with authentic understanding. "As long as we remember them, they're never gone. There she is." He pointed ahead and off to the right. "Best boat you're going to step foot on in Nalani. Pippy, while I love those sparkly shoes of yours, you can't wear them on the—"

"I know, I read the instructions," Pippy interrupted him. "Got myself a pedicure just for the occasion. Bright pink even though Crystal's color is yellow. No one wants yellow toenails, right, Marella?"

"No, I don't suppose they do." Marella was shocked she could squeeze any words out of her throat, which had gone so tight she could barely breathe. She really, really didn't want to get on that boat. Catamaran. Whatever the thing was called. It didn't look like any boat she'd seen back east, with its dual hulls and what looked like a platform connecting them. Parts of it seemed, well, normal, but…

Stop it! There will be no sinking. Nothing bad is going to happen. That's what she kept telling herself, anyway.

She would not surrender to something as annoying as fear, and on the bright side she didn't have a parent throwing her into the water as a joke.

And that, more than anything, had her counting her blessings as she stepped down from the vehicle and onto the dock.

"Ah, just in time, Keane, as always." A hulk of a man made his way around the side of the boat, casting an amused look to her family and sister's friends who had clearly already gotten the party started. "Aloha! You must be Ms. Pippy. I'm Polunu. One of your hosts for this evening. Welcome to the *Nani Nalu*." He stepped off the vessel and opened his arms in welcome. "We are happy to have you this evening."

Pippy beamed. "What a lovely boat."

Marella had to agree. It wasn't a millionaire's yacht by any stretch of the imagination, but there was a quaintness about the catamaran that brought a surprised smile to her lips. An unexpected surprise, rather than the image she'd built up in her mind. It also evoked a feeling of…home.

"It won't be so bad," Keane told her as Polunu helped Pippy with her shoes and then escorted her to one of the empty seats at the table, all the while answering her numerous questions about the vessel. "I've been riding on the *Nalu* ever since I was a boy. It's perfectly safe, I promise."

Marella eyed him and got out of the cart. "Nothing is one hundred percent safe."

"No, I suppose not." Keane inclined his head as if the thought had never occurred to him. "But what's the point of life if you aren't living it?"

She narrowed her eyes. "If I didn't know better I'd think you were in cahoots with my sister. I've already had that lecture today."

"No lectures from me," Keane assured her, that smile of his firmly in place as he reached behind her for one of the boxes. "Just straight up knowledge. Question, though." He leaned close and she felt his warm breath in her ear. "Craig might be gone, but are there any other paramours I need to be made aware of? If so, feel free to kiss me again anytime to get them to back off."

She couldn't help it. She laughed. "Noted for future reference."

"There you go. Laughter cures everything." He brushed a finger down the side of her face and every thought in her head vanished. "Oh, before I forget," he said. Keane reached into his pocket. "I found this after our…encounter on the beach." He caught her hand, turned it and deposited her lost watch into her palm.

She blinked. "You found it." Relief swept through her, as did gratitude. "Thank you.

Oh, I thought it was gone for sure." She set her sweater down. "Would you help me put it back on?"

"I think I can manage that."

She hadn't meant for the request to be anything but innocent, but when his fingers brushed against her wrist, as they worked the clasp and fastened the bracelet, her body warmed. There was such gentleness in him, but also a steadfastness that took her aback. He was a man who defied explanation or expectation. Hers at least. And wasn't that something...remarkable.

"I don't think that'll fall off again." He flipped her hand over, and before she could take a breath, lifted her fingers to his lips and pressed his mouth to her knuckles. "I love making you blush," he murmured as the color and fire rose in her face. "The sight rivals the most beautiful sunsets in Nalani."

She couldn't help it. She rolled her eyes even as slumbering bits of her awakened. "You must have women lined up around the block with lines like that."

He shrugged. "Just because it sounds like a line doesn't mean it isn't true."

"Hey, Keane." The female voice that called

to him had them both looking to the boat. Marella recognized the woman from the beach, the one who had been with Keane. "We're ready to cast off whenever you're done…commiserating." The smile the woman offered erased any unease in Marella. "I'm Sydney Calvert, by the way. Nice to officially meet you, Marella."

Marella's eyes went wide. "Officially? Right. From earlier." She flashed a shaky smile. "Nice to meet you as well. Thank you," she added as her confidence returned. "For your kindness at the beach. And for all your help wrangling this group. I have no doubt it's been a challenge."

"One Ohana Odysseys was up for," Sydney said with assurance. "Keane? You need help with those boxes?"

"I've got them, thanks, Syd. But first…" Keane shifted his hold until his fingers slid between Marella's. "Let's say we get you settled on board."

She took a deep breath, willing the butterflies swarming in her stomach to take a breather. "I really don't like boats."

"But you love your sister." Keane's voice was oddly calming. "And you certainly wouldn't want anyone thinking your issues with Craig are the reason you're backing out of the cruise. Or any other festivities for the week."

She narrowed her eyes and glared at him. "That's low." But people would think that. Especially if she didn't give them another reason for her caution.

"Perhaps. Or just consider it a challenge." He took the final few steps toward the catamaran and stopped at the edge. "Up for it?"

She ignored the eyes she felt on them, and the fact that the waiting guests seemed to have gone suddenly quiet. She didn't know why, but something about Keane Harper erased the trepidation with water she'd spent a lifetime building.

Routine and schedules and doing the expected had gotten her this far; but they'd also shoved her so far into a corner of boredom that it was only now she recognized it. She thought about the woman who a mere few hours ago had been in her hotel room, trying to come to terms with the fact that she'd been played by a man who had little to no interest in her as a person and mostly as a means to success at her father's company.

Now she had the chance to embrace something new, something different and unexpected. And in the form of a man who had, from the instant they met, set himself apart from anyone she'd ever known before.

Tired of thinking, exhausted from fighting herself and set-in-stone expectations, she lifted her foot and stepped onto the boat.

"Been a while since I saw you get flirty with any of the customers," Polunu teased Keane as they unloaded the bottles and placed them on the back bar. The trench allowed the bottles to stay easily accessible and on display and not become projectiles while the boat was underway.

"She just broke up with her boyfriend," Keane explained easily even though his own pulse was giving indication of being in overdrive. "I was only helping—"

"Stoke the fire of rejection?" Polunu suggested. "Very honorable of you, Keane. Always looking out for the ladies in distress."

"Nothing distressing about Marella," Keane confirmed. "She can take care of herself." Didn't mean he wasn't feeling protective. Or interested. Had it only been a few hours since he'd first seen her on the beach?

It felt longer. Surely it took time for someone to become engrained in one's memory. Or thoughts.

"Yes, so I heard." Polunu laughed. "I heard a lot about how you spent your afternoon, actually."

Keane stashed the empty boxes under the sink of the bar. "I thought we were ready to cast off."

"We are." Polunu hesitated. "Would you mind taking her out? The boat. Not the bride's sister."

"Ha ha. You sure?" Keane wasn't used to the request. Polunu liked to do all the casting off and piloting himself.

"I'd like to stay close to Akahi to be safe. She's putting the finishing touches on dinner, but I don't want her—"

"Serving when she's reliant on that cane? Sure." Keane nodded. "You man the bar and keep an eye on your wife. Sydney, Daphne and I have the rest."

He left Polunu at the bar and made his way out the double-wide doors to the main seating area of the catamaran. The long wooden table had been made especially for the *Nani Nalu*, carved out of an old rainbow eucalyptus tree that grew on Polunu and Akahi's property. After a hurricane knocked the tree down, they'd repurposed it thanks to the talent and skill of a local craftsman who had carved various Polynesian and Samoan imagery and symbols onto the side. The piece was a solid work of art, with natural red and green streaks, and was front and center of every dinner cruise they operated.

Keane would be lying if said he hadn't been keeping watch not only on Pippy, who sat at the head of the table, and appeared to be holding court among her family and her granddaughter's friends, but also on Marella, who was currently sitting stiffly on a bench on the starboard side of the boat.

Her hands were clenched around the edge of the bench, her knees locked together as she scanned every inch of space in front of her. It wasn't until Gloria Benoit came over to sit beside her and pushed a plastic glass of Akahi's special rum punch into her hand that she seemed to relax.

Keane gave Marella credit, facing her phobia, and okay, maybe he had been a bit callous playing Craig against her, but the truth was, he liked being around her. Sure, she was tightly strung, but it couldn't be easy being part of a big family like hers. A loud family like hers, he added, as he cringed at the rising noise level.

Grateful that Polunu had given him the option of captaining the cruise, he made a quick pivot around to the left where Sydney and Daphne were busy organizing the various menu offerings for those with food issues or allergies.

"Hey, Daph? Help me cast off?"

She set her slips of paper down, placed one of the paperweight rocks on top. "Sure. Be right back, Syd."

"No worries," Sydney said. "I've got this."

"You piloting tonight?" Daphne asked as they went around to the front of the boat, unwrapping the mooring lines.

"Polunu's worried Akahi's doing too much."

"Syd is too," Daphne agreed. "We should be able to make things easier for her."

"You've been crewing for them quite a bit lately, haven't you?"

"Last couple of weeks." Daphne smiled. "I might be more at home on land and in the rainforests, but I have to admit, I'm beginning to understand your affinity for the ocean. Not enough to take surfing lessons though," she quickly added with a stern look.

"I'll never stop trying," Keane told her, almost chuckling. Keeping out of the way of the guests, the pair of them strode to the bow of the boat, down the deck until they reached the ladder to the second level. "One left."

"I've got it." Daphne offered him one of her soft smiles. *"Makani 'olu a holo malie." Fair winds and following seas*, an often uttered wish of good luck to sailors.

He touched a hand to his heart. "Mahalo."

Keane grabbed hold of the railing and made quick work of the ladder, stepping into the pilothouse. Besides the navigation equipment and captain's chair, there was extra seating and storage. There wasn't a bad view from the catamaran, but he had to admit, there was something special about being behind the wheel.

He started the engine, let it warm up as he did a quick check of the operating system, checked in with the harbormaster and flipped the overhead lights on. The weather report was favorable with light winds and clear skies. Once the sun began to set, it would provide a spectacular show for their passengers.

Keane picked up the handset for the intercom and opened the speakers. "Good evening, everyone. On behalf of the *Nani Nalu* and Polunu and Akahi Tatupu, this is Keane Harper, and I'll be your skipper on this voyage. We're estimating approximately a ninety-minute sail up to Hilo before we head back and circle around to the Cape Kumukahi Lighthouse off Kapoho." The historic lighthouse was a metal tower that predated a number of lighthouses back on the mainland. It was definitely a must-see for those visiting the Big Island.

"Just as a reminder," Keane continued. "The restrooms are located on the bottom deck. We also have a first-aid center if you're having any issues. We'll do our best to assist. If we run into an emergency, please be sure to follow the instructions of your crew. This evening, Akahi and Edena are responsible for the exquisite and authentic Hawaiian meal you're about to eat." He smiled at the cheers and applause that announcement earned. "Polunu is manning the bar and will keep that rum punch dispenser full. Your servers this evening are Sydney and Daphne, who you'll all be seeing quite a bit of in the coming days as we are all a part of your tour company, Ohana Odysseys. Our goal, as always, is to give you a close-up and personal look at our island and introduce you to a number of delicacies and traditions. So, please, sit back, enjoy the scenery and your food and if you have any questions or concerns, don't hesitate to let us know. Mahalo."

He hung the receiver up on its hook and, with a shake of his head and an appreciative glance at the horizon, pushed forward on the throttle and eased the *Nani Nalu* out into the waves.

CHAPTER FIVE

"YOU MIGHT WANT to slow down on those, Marella."

Marella looked to her father as he slid onto the stool beside her at the cozy bar in the main cabin of the *Nani Nalu*. "Hi, Dad." She straightened, pulled her drink—complete with not one but two little pink umbrellas—closer and toasted him. "Don't worry." She sighed and sipped. "I stopped after one rum punch." That one had been enough to turn her bones to Jell-O. "This is just pineapple juice with some nonalcoholic accents." The punch had taken the edge off her anxiety and while she might not be buzzed, she was definitely on her way to a serious sugar high.

She looked back over her shoulder out the double-wide doorway to the table where the majority of their group were gobbling up the appetizers almost as quickly as they were glugging the punch being dispensed from a giant faux pineapple on the buffet counter. Thankfully, everyone was on their best behavior and seemed to be oohing and aahing over the truly mesmerizing sights around them as the boat made its lazy journey over the ocean.

"Good thing no one scheduled any activities before noon tomorrow." Her stomach rumbled, but she wasn't so hungry as to insert herself into the noisy festivities. She glanced at her watch. Slowest. Night. Ever.

"Your sister and brothers definitely know how to have a good time." Armand signaled to Polunu. He held a five-dollar bill between his fingers and dropped it into the tip jar. "I'll have whatever she's having. No umbrellas though."

"You've got it, Mr. B."

Marella's lips twitched even as her heart tilted. "Mr. B. I like that." She nudged her shoulder against her father's arm. "How are you doing? Feeling okay?"

"I'm fine, Marella," he assured her. "It's been months. You can stop asking me that every time you see me. I've got a stent in place and the prognosis of a long, healthy life ahead of me. Stop worrying."

She shook her head. "I'll never stop worrying about you."

"Hmm." Armand nodded. "That's supposed to be my line. My time away from office gave me an opportunity to think a lot about the business and the future of Benoit & Associates." He glanced at her. "About you."

"About me?" She winced, took a long drink and longed for the tongue-loosening false courage alcohol often provided. "I'm sorry, Dad. The situation with Craig. I made an error in judgment dating him in the first place. He just…ugh. He seemed, I don't know, a safe bet. Emotionally speaking. Not worth a tremendous amount of investment, if you know what I mean."

"I don't know what to say to that," Armand admitted. "That you quantify relationships in terms of being emotionally safe. All love is risk, Marella. But it's a risk worth taking, I promise you."

She wanted to say she believed him. That she understood. And she did. As far as he was concerned. But she'd also been old enough to witness the utter grief her father had struggled with when her mother had died. She'd been terrified when he'd had his heart attack. Terrified of being left alone. She wouldn't have been, of course. She'd have had her stepmother and her step-siblings, but if she'd lost her dad…

She wished she hadn't said anything. "I'll take your word for it. But I am sorry about almost putting you in a difficult position about Craig. He was hoping for an interview."

"Yes, I know," Armand said. "He'd have gotten one eventually." He shrugged. "Even though I wouldn't have hired him. He may have thought dating you would get him in the door, but your relationship would have prevented me from giving him a job."

Marella thought on that. "Wish I'd known that sooner. Maybe he'd have ended things before I'd had to. He did see that Phoenix Coffee was a good client to go after."

"But you did the work," Armand said. "Did he help with your proposals? From what I heard, you're the one who went out to Seattle to meet with them in person. Where was his initiative? Bringing that company to us would have been a solid calling card for someone looking to get hired. Not using your girlfriend's personal connections." Her dad was always good at telling it like it was.

"It was your show from beginning to end and you performed brilliantly."

"Thanks." The frank talk eased the pressure she felt in her chest, allowing her to fill her lungs with invigorating, fresh ocean air. "That means a lot."

"Never were one to toot your own horn. I'm so proud of the way you handled things while I was out of the office. You just stepped right in and did what needed doing. No hesitation. No doubt."

Oh, there had been doubt. But doubt was why she kept most of the staff on speed dial.

"I'm sorry for how he treated you, Marella. No one deserves that. Especially my little girl."

"Dad," she warned in a tone not dissimilar to how she'd warned Pippy to behave. "I haven't been a kid for a very long time."

"Yes, well, father's prerogative. You'll always be my little girl."

"Can I ask you something?" The question was bothering her, lodged in her mind as a constant reminder of what she may be doing wrong with her life. "Do I strike you as cold? I mean, am I too logic-minded? Too...I don't know...stodgy?" She couldn't stop wondering if her lack of passion for, well, anything, was part of the reason Craig had slipped through whatever defenses she might have.

"No." The fact that he answered so quickly eased her mind a bit, but then he continued, "I think people in your case mistake cold and logical for straightforward and practical. You know what you want and you go after it. Emotions have never entered into it for you, Marella. You've always been very… accepting. Matter-of-fact. Levelheaded for sure. Very much like me."

"Dad, that's about the nicest response you could have come up with."

"I didn't particularly mean it as a compliment." Armand drew her against him and pressed a kiss to the top of her head. "You are many things, my beautiful girl, but you are not now nor have you ever been cold, stodgy or boring."

"I never said anything about being boring," she grumbled when he sat back.

"Like I said, I've had a lot of time to do some thinking. And since you've opened the door, I think it's time we had a conversation about the future."

"You're retiring, aren't you?" She glanced around, wished for the first time there were more people around so as to delay the talk she'd known for weeks was in the offing. "I—I don't know if I'm ready to take over the agency."

"All evidence to the contrary," Armand argued, but he held up a hand. "But no, I'm not retiring. Not yet," he added in an imitation of her tone. "Much to your stepmother's consternation. That said, I now see a future when I do and it's not too far away."

She wasn't certain if his confirming her suspicions was a good thing or not.

"Now that I've had some time off, I can see a few changes that need to be made. Lance and Tag for starters. Your stepbrothers have both expressed interest in working at Benoit & Associates."

"They have?" Marella couldn't hide her surprise. "But I thought Lance was happy at that financial firm on Wall Street?"

"He was." Armand inclined his head. "He's also twenty-six and on two blood pressure medications."

Marella's mouth dropped open. "I didn't know that."

"No reason you should have. Gloria's concerned about him. As am I. Maybe my recent heart issues have given him something to think about. While we have our share of stress, it certainly isn't at the level he's been working at for the past few years."

"Lance would be a great fit for the agency." It wasn't lip service. Her brother had an amazing mind for figures and strategy, not to mention a gut instinct when it came to investment opportunities. In a lot of ways, advertising lined up with what he'd been doing as a broker and trader.

"I'm happy to hear you say that, Marella." Armand took a deep breath. "And I look forward to your input as far as what division he'd do best in. As for Tag." He shook his head and laughed into his drink. "Tag has decided he wants to go to culinary school."

"Ah, okay." Marella frowned. "How does that fit in with the agency?"

"Given his mother and I just shelled out a substantial fortune for him to spend six years at a four-year college—"

Marella offered a sympathetic smile. Poor Tag. Being the youngest in an odd collection of siblings, he'd just never found where he fit in. He was a throw-spaghetti-at-the-wall kind of guy who was still waiting for something to stick.

"I've told Tag that if this is what he wants to do," her father continued, "then he needs to foot half the tuition costs. That means he'll need a job. One where he'll be held accountable."

"And where you can keep an eye on him," Marella added. "He's a good kid, Dad. He's just…a bit aimless."

"Believe me, Gloria and I count our blessings he's never gotten into trouble, but he needs to find his way sooner than later. College is behind him. He's going to be twenty-three and he's still spinning like a top. A job with responsibility should go far to instilling that, and if he's serious about becoming a chef, he's going to need to develop a very strong work ethic. Speaking of work ethics—"

"Crystal." Marella nodded. "I know what she does seems a bit flighty and superficial, but she's good at what she does, Dad. She's made ButtercupDoll a pretty substantial brand."

"I'm aware. Actually, Crystal's the one

I'm not worried about. I am, however, quite worried about you."

"Me?" She had the feeling she shouldn't be surprised, but she was. "Why are you worried about me? I'm financially stable, I've got a job I like. I own my own apartment and my portfolio—"

"I'm worried about your heart. No, not in that overstressed, heading-down-the-road-to-an-ER-visit sort of way. Well, not only in that way."

"I work out every day, Dad. Just ask my treadmill. In fact, I can pull the app—" He caught her hand when she turned her wrist over and started to tap the screen.

"You don't give yourself any time to relax. Even after I told you I didn't want you doing any company work while we were here, you've still been banging away on that laptop of yours."

"Hey, you bought it for me, so that's partly on you." Her attempt at humor fell flat. "Dad, work makes me happy. Why can't any of you accept that?"

"Because I don't believe you know what happiness really is. A job shouldn't be the only thing you have in your life. You think of a relationship as an obligation, and then look who you choose to have one with. Someone you consider emotionally safe." He frowned. "You've always known what you wanted, always had your goals firmly in place and you never once deviated. Whatever risk may have been involved was conquered early on. Everything has been very…safe."

"Since when is safe bad? Most parents would consider a daughter playing things safe as reliable and dedicated." Definitely not someone they had to worry about.

"And others, like me and Gloria, think it makes for a very lonely life. Marella." He covered her hand and stopped her from climbing off her stool. "I know how hard it was for you, losing your mother. You were so young, but I saw her loss in your eyes every single day. I still see it. Like a ghost hovering around you. She'd have hated that."

"Of course, I miss Mom." Marella scrunched her nose. "Dad, I don't really want to talk about—"

"I did my best to help you cope with the loss, but I was dealing with my own grief. I loved her so much." He spun his glass on the bar. "In a different way than I do Gloria. But I made myself get out there and live again. I had to. If for no other reason than to show you that life goes on. In every possible sense."

"Dad, if this is your way of asking me if I resent Gloria, let me be absolutely clear. I don't." She turned her hand over and squeezed his. "I love her. Better yet, I like her. She's been good for you, good for both of us. And no, she's not Mom, but she's always been someone I felt comfortable with."

"That's good to hear."

"She also made sure I didn't go through life with only-child syndrome," she added. "She gave you three more chances to be a dad. Something you happen to be extraordinarily good at. You've always, always given me everything I've ever wanted. More importantly, you made certain I had what I needed."

"I'm relieved to hear you say that because as of now, I'm putting you on sabbatical."

Marella was shocked. "I'm sorry, you're what?"

"You heard me. Effective immediately, until after your sister's wedding, consider yourself off the job. No work. No phone calls. No client talk. No doing anything other than having fun and taking some you time."

She tugged her hand free. "Dad, this is ridicu—"

"I asked Mano Iokepa if he'd personally retrieve your laptop from your room. It's being kept in his office safe until you check out of the resort. I've also instructed your assistant, Julian, not to accept any calls from you."

She sagged back in her chair. "That's not possible." Her head was spinning.

"I'm his boss, and yours, Marella, remember? I assure you, it is possible."

"I don't understand." Her chest tightened and her skin went clammy. Was she having a panic attack? "Dad, I'm not going to agree—"

Armand signaled to someone behind Marella, and Gloria joined them.

"You told her?" her stepmother asked as she touched Marella's shoulder. "Marella, are you all right?"

She blinked up at the woman who had been in her life for the past nineteen years. "I—I don't actually know." She folded her arms.

"Seven days, Marella," her father said.

"You unplug and live seven days without an iota of work. Or…"

That dangling *or* felt like a hatchet over her head. "Or what?" she croaked.

"Or I'll have to reconsider where this company is going and who's leading it and why. I won't have you—or any employees—forgetting there's a world out there beyond our offices. You need to find a balance in your life, Marella. Before you're faced with the reality of what I've had to deal with these past months."

She swallowed hard. "Dad, you can't mean this." Panic had the words flooding out of her mouth. "You need me. Benoit & Associates needs me." Marella glanced back at the table filled with the rest of her family and their friends. "Especially now with Lance coming to…and Tag. Dad, we have to get things ready for them, not to mention deal with the issues that come up while we're gone. We have nearly two dozen clients to think of. You can't manage all this alone."

"I don't intend to. We have a crack staff back in New York, Marella. A staff you're pretty much responsible for assembling, so it's time we both put our faith in them and let them do what they were hired to do. Training wheels off. It's time."

"This will be good for you, Marella," Gloria insisted in what Marella could only describe as a maternal tone. "When did you last have a day off or do something you *wanted* to do?"

"I don't need a day off and work is what I want to do." She gaped as her father stood up and slid his hand into his wife's. "Dad, please. I don't think you've thought this through."

"I have. I would rather shut the company down than have it end up hurting you. That's where we're headed if I don't make a change." She couldn't argue when he used that tone. There were no magic words that would change his mind. "Seven days," he repeated. "And yes, I know it's going to be a challenge, but I'm doing this because I love you, Marella. Because I need to know, down the road, when Benoit & Associates is yours, that you'll understand that work is not all there is. Am I understood?"

She was shaking, more from uncertainty and maybe a little fear. Suddenly being on a boat in the middle of the ocean didn't seem all that bad. But seven days with nothing to do but live in her own head?

"So what do you say, Marella? Do you agree to the deal?"

"No." Inspired, she looked at Gloria, who looked as surprised as Marella's father. "No, I don't agree. But I will counter."

For a moment, she could have sworn she saw a spark of admiration in her father's eyes. "All right. Let's hear it."

"I'll give you the seven days. I'll take off work and I'll join in the wedding festivities and I'll even try to have some fun." Even the word *fun* seemed to get caught in her throat. "And then? At the end of those seven days." She took a deep breath and stepped into the deep end of the ocean. "If I meet your requirements and fulfill your bargain, you retire. At least, partially. Enough that you turn Benoit & Associates over to me to run."

Tears glistened in her stepmother's eyes as a sad smile of gratitude curved her lips. "Marella," she whispered.

She'd surprised her. Surprised them both, and the doubt she saw in her father's eyes was likely reflective of the same expression she'd been wearing for the past few minutes. "Well, Dad? What do you say?" She stood and stretched out her hand. "Is it a deal?"

Her dad glanced at his wife, then over Marella's shoulder to where Sydney and Daphne were bringing out aluminum trays filled with fragrant, stomach-rumbling offerings.

"Dad?" she pressed. "No more counteroffers. No more discussion. You offered, I countered. Deal's on the table. Yes or no?"

"All right." Armand accepted her hand and shook. "It's a deal."

ONE OF THE perks to captaining the *Nani Nalu*, aside from getting some serious one-on-one time with the ocean, was having a couple of his best friends waiting on him. It was a joke, of course; Keane appreciated it when Daphne arrived shortly after castoff with a selection of appetizers. The small refrigerator installed under one of the bench seats beside the helm provided plenty of bottled water and energy drinks.

The sun had yet to disappear completely into the horizon, but the light was dim enough to warrant flipping on the lights so he could see where they were going. He could hear the muted conversation from the lower deck. Near as he could tell, fun was being had by all. As much as he enjoyed a good party, he preferred where he currently sat, surrounded by the sights and sounds of the island that, in Remy Calvert's voice, had called him home.

He also heard the distinctive squeak of someone grabbing hold of the side bars to the ladder leading into the pilothouse.

"You're a little early with dinner, aren't you, Syd?" Keane glanced over his shoulder, expecting one face, only to find another looking not at him, but out the windshield with something akin to awe in her eyes. "Marella." His hand tightened on the wheel. "Either you've gotten over your fear of boats or—"

"Funny enough I'm under the influence of something that negates fear."

"What's that?"

"Anger." She frowned. "Confusion. Or maybe it's some new emotion like angusion." She had her feet planted firmly apart, had yet to release the death grip she had on the railings, but she looked determined about something. "Confunger? I don't know. Up here seemed a good place to be. At least, until they finish setting out the food." She sniffed and inched forward, clearly struggling to keep her balance. "I missed out on the appetizers."

"Have plenty to share. Come on." He reached out one hand and felt a surge of triumph when she grabbed hold and allowed him to tug her toward him. She plopped onto the padded bench next to the steering console and eyed the plate, her back to the ocean. "Help yourself," he urged at her hopeful glance. "I'm waiting for the main course. I could eat an entire tray of Akahi's luau stew all by myself."

She plucked up a garlic chicken drumstick and bit in. "Oh, my goodness." She licked her fingers before taking another bite. "That's amazing. It's both sweet and zingy." She polished off one and reached for another. "I wasn't sure I'd feel like eating while I was on board."

"Got your sea legs under you then?" He kept one eye glued to the waters ahead. The slanted windshield and the boat's rather slow speed kept the wind at a minimum. So far the weather reports had been accurate and the waves had been mostly calm.

"Didn't really have a choice, did I?" She made quick work of the chicken before her gaze landed on one of his particular favorites. "Is this the Spam thing I've heard about?"

"Musubi," Keane confirmed. "It's sushi rice with a slice of Spam wrapped in seaweed. You got yourself on a boat," he teased. "I think you can handle *musubi.*"

She lifted the flat, oval rice cake and took a tentative bite. "I guess this evening is full of surprises." Around another mouthful, she managed to say, "I left my drink downstairs."

"There's a fridge right here." He pointed. "Nothing alcoholic though."

"Don't need anything else clouding my head. Thanks." She took out a water, twisted off the lid and drank. She turned around, looked at the ocean ahead of them. "You got the best seat in the house, didn't you?"

"I did luck out," Keane confirmed. "I was twelve the first time Polunu let me pilot this baby." He ran a free hand over the top of the console. "One of my favorite places to be in all of Nalani."

"Are you from here?"

"No." Keane followed her lead and grabbed a water as she nibbled on a carrot. "No, my grandparents had a home here a long time ago. I came out during the summers. It's how I met Sydney and her brother, Remy, who became my best friend. We went off to college together, started making all those big dreams happen. After graduation, I lived here for almost a year before I headed back to the mainland for work."

"What kind of work? I mean, other than competitive swimming."

Keane glanced out the side window. "I did do that for a few years. Wrangled endorsement deals. Then I turned to coaching at Cleaver University."

"Is there money in competitive swimming? I mean, does it earn you a good living."

"If you're good at it," Keane said.

"Were you?"

"Some say I was." He shrugged. "I think of myself as a bit of a candle. I glowed brightly for a little while then got snuffed out. Rotator cuff injury. Wreaks havoc with certain strokes." Even now, despite not having any serious issues, the phantom pain of disappointment and change shifted through him. "Fortunately the success I did have opened up other employment opportunities."

"You're only here for the summer then?" She drew one leg under her and faced him more directly, still focusing on his appetizers.

"My plans are a bit fluid at the moment." This wasn't a topic he wanted to delve too deeply into. "Kinda just going with the flow." He grinned at her. "I bet that idea doesn't sit well with you at all."

"Funny." She plucked up one of the fried meat wontons. "If you'd said that a half an hour ago, I might have said you were right."

"Oh? What's happened since then?" He'd meant to tease her but even in the dim light of the cockpit he saw her jaw tighten. "Sorry. None of my business."

She shrugged. "No reason not to confide about my life to a complete stranger."

"We're not complete strangers," he reminded her. "You have kissed me. And we've taken a lovely bumpy ride together with your grandmother."

Her lips twitched. "Touché. It seems I've been put on a forced sabbatical from work."

"It seems?"

"My father told me if I didn't take time off from the business he'd... Well, I'm not sure what." She popped a second wonton into her mouth and sat back, pouting.

"Obviously you don't agree that you need a break."

"I do not. I thought countering his offer might make him change his mind, but..." She frowned. "Maybe he wants to retire and couldn't find the right way to tell me. But I honestly thought that's where the conversation was first headed. He had a heart attack six months ago. A pretty big one," she added.

"Sorry to hear that." Keane checked the compass, made certain they were staying on course. In about twenty miles he'd be turning around at Hilo and they'd be making their way south, past Nalani toward the lighthouse. "He seems to be doing okay now."

"Oh, he is. New lease on life. He seems happier even. I don't know, lighter. Can people look lighter?" She tucked her hair behind her ear just as the breeze caught a different strand and pushed it across her face. "He thinks I don't have a life. Or rather, he doesn't think work should be my life."

"Not going to get an argument about that from me," Keane offered. "But then, I'm lucky right now. My life and the job I'm currently in are pretty much the same thing. As long as I'm on or near the water, I'm where I'm supposed to be."

"Makes total sense. And for me, that's my office. It's about finding solutions to problems, finding new ways to bring attention to our clients' products. It's where I feel useful."

"Maybe what your dad is trying to tell you is it's okay not to be useful for a while."

She scowled at him. "Sounding boards shouldn't talk back."

He found her sourness amusing. "Sorry to disappoint but this sounding board always has an opinion. Or at least a word or two of advice. He's worried about you. That can't be good for his heart."

Her scowl deepened. "Is this supposed to be helpful?"

"I'm just saying maybe doing as he asks

will ease his mind a little. Do what he suggests. Take the next seven days here in Nalani and just…be."

"Be. What does that even mean?"

"It means you turn off everything you're supposed to and take the moments as they come. You said you countered his offer."

"I did." She smirked, looking a bit proud of herself for an instant. "If I make it the seven days without working—or think about working—he gives me control of the business."

Keane whistled. "Wow. That's some counteroffer. So you're saying in a week you could be running…" He glanced at her.

"Benoit & Associates," she supplied. "It's an advertising agency. He started it right after he got out of college, shortly before he met my mother."

"Your mother. Gloria?"

"Gloria is my stepmother."

"Ah, okay." He nodded. "I was wondering why you called her by her first name."

"My mother died when I was eight. He married Gloria a few years later."

"And Crystal and your brothers—"

"Steps." She shrugged. "Don't know why I always refer to them that way."

"Family's more than just blood," Keane said. "I considered Remy a brother. I'm closer to Sydney and Daphne than I am to anyone in my actual family." But this conversation wasn't about him. "So running your family business, that's what you want, yeah?"

"Of course."

To his ear, it sounded like she was forcing the answer. As if she was trying to convince herself of the fact that she did, indeed, want to take over the agency.

"And you're sure your dad is okay with retiring?"

"You mean did he accept my counteroffer because he thinks I can't make it seven days without working? No." She shook her head. "No, retirement's definitely coming. Especially where my step… Where Gloria is concerned."

"Do you want my take on it?"

"Sure, why not." She looked over the now nearly empty plate.

"I think your father believes you taking time off is important enough to give up the business he's spent a good portion of his life building. You know what that sounds like to me?"

"Desperation?"

"Love." He gestured to the horizon. "He wants the best for you, even at the expense of his own achievements. I'd say you've been given a pretty special opportunity, Marella. Not only to make your goal of running the company come to pass, but to show your father you understand what he's after."

"Huh." She sat back again. "I didn't really think of it that way."

"Consider it part of the service." Keane paused. "So now that you're seeing your father's deal in a different light, you going to embrace the challenge?"

"I don't particularly have a choice, do I?" She still didn't sound enthralled at the idea. "I'm supposed to just turn everything off? And, I don't know, relax? Sit out by the pool for hours on end? I'd need a book, at least." She poked a finger against her temple. "This doesn't just turn off because I stop working. It's like a hamster wheel in here."

Keane chuckled. He'd never seen anyone so utterly flummoxed at the prospect of taking a week off.

"Sounds to me like you need a coach."

"A coach? For fun? Is there such a thing?"

"If there isn't there should be." Given people's lives these days, he couldn't imagine Marella was the only one clueless as to how to go about it. "It would be a challenge, teaching someone how to loosen up and not take things so seriously." He glanced at her. "Learn how to go with the flow."

"You volunteering?"

He knew she meant it as a joke, but it wasn't a horrible idea. He liked her. He'd liked her the second she'd stormed past him on the beach, before she'd even noticed he was there. He'd been excited at the prospect of her being on the cruise tonight and thoroughly entertained watching her interact with her family—a family he could tell was filled with love and concern for one another. Marella's current predicament acted as prime evidence in that case.

"Maybe I am."

She sat up straight. "You want to coach me in how to have fun."

He shrugged.

"What would that entail exactly?"

He laughed. "You really can't turn it off,

can you? The whole idea is to embrace the un-expected. I don't do play-by-plays, Marella."

"But, by definition, you'd be choosing what you consider to be fun. What would that be?"

"Ah." His mind raced and ended up think-ing of the list of activities offered by Ohana Odysseys. "Okay, ever been on a helicopter tour of the islands?"

"No." She shuddered. "Aren't those dan-gerous?"

"Not statistically and definitely not with Sydney flying." He put that on the possi-ble list. "I take it you weren't planning on going with your sister's group for zip-lining. There's volcano exploring—"

"Like with lava?"

He wanted to believe she was joking. "We do have active volcanoes on the island. One here on the Big Island, in fact, but no, we'd choose a dormant one. There are rain forest hikes. Horseback riding—"

"I like horses."

"Swimming under a waterfall. Oh! I could teach you to swim."

"I know how to swim," she said patiently. "Okay, I know how to doggie paddle well enough to save my life. I think. I just don't enjoy it."

"Surfing, then. Or parasailing. Now that would get you over your fear of water real quick."

"All of this is moot." She shook her head. "I'm not hiring myself a fun coach." She narrowed her eyes. "That would be humiliating. 'Oh, look, Marella's so clueless about life she needs help having fun.' Dragging you around trying to get me to do different things. Geez, I could just imagine Christmas. I'd never hear the end of it."

"Then don't hire me as a coach," he suggested on a whim. "Hire me to be your boyfriend."

CHAPTER SIX

"EXPLAIN THIS TO me again, Keane," Sydney said to him before the others arrived for their monthly Ohana Odysseys employee meeting at her home. "And this time—" Sydney set the now-empty coffeepot back on its stand and got a second brew going "—do so as if I'm a five-year old."

Keane sat back, a mug of steaming coffee in his hands, and gave a sweeping glance to the spacious kitchen in the house Sydney and Remy had grown up in. It was different from how he remembered it as a kid, when Sydney and Remy's parents had lived here. It was more modern now with its rich earth tones and without the hideous wallpaper that their mother had insisted should stay put because her husband—their father—disliked it so much. The Calverts were always doing silly pranks on each other. The old linoleum floor had been replaced with recyclable gray-tinged bamboo and begged those who arrived to ditch their shoes at the front door and revel in the smooth natural texture.

The back door opened and he and Sydney turned as tall, slightly gangly and regularly befuddled Theo Fairfax strolled inside, sans shoes and wearing the most hideously green-gecko-covered Hawaiian shirt Keane may have ever seen. The recent transplant looked as if he'd just returned from the beach. Hard to believe a few short months ago the man had never even put his feet into sand. He had yet to ditch his glasses though, which gave him that perennial geeky look Sydney had fallen hard for.

"Morning." Being a smart man, Theo made a quick detour on his way for coffee and planted a kiss on Sydney's upturned face. "Sorry I was asleep when you got in last night." He kissed her again and had Keane grinning behind his mug. "How was the cruise?"

"Ah, entertaining?" Sydney hedged. "The bride and her two bridesmaids nearly went into the ocean trying to get selfies with the lighthouse."

"Didn't they read—"

"The excursion instructions?" Keane asked. "Apparently they considered those more as guidelines for other people, rather than rules. The bride's father adding a substantial tip helped smooth things out."

"Poor Polunu," Sydney said. "He was stressed to begin with by Akahi's health issues. I think the young women got the message. Especially after Marella was done with them."

"Woman does have a way with words," Keane agreed.

Theo winced. "I really need to get over my tendency toward seasickness. I miss all the good stuff."

"Thankfully, the antics stopped there." Daphne slogged into the kitchen looking less than half-awake. She quickly sank into a chair near Keane and all but collapsed on the table. "Thanks for letting me crash here last night, Syd," she mumbled into the scarred wood. Her red hair looked as if birds had been nesting in it and the sleep mask she'd worn was now crookedly stretched across the top of her head. "Never again will I accept leftover rum punch from Akahi as a parting thank-you gift. Never. Again."

Sydney snort-laughed. "I've still got some in the fridge if you want, Theo."

"Ah, if that's the endorsement—" he pointed at Daphne "—I'll pass, thanks." Instead, Theo lifted the lid to the all-too-familiar bakery box on the counter and plucked out a passion-fruit-filled *malasada*. "And here you thought it would be smooth sailing with this group."

Keane chuckled. "Nice one. But you know what they say. It's not a wedding until some-one gets—"

"Let's not finish that thought, please," Sydney advised. "I would not be surprised if the punch was no longer a part of future sailings." She grabbed a bottle of lemon-lime soda out of the fridge, poured a glass and dropped some morning-after fizzy tab-lets into it. Once those settled, she set the glass in front of Daphne and touched a gen-tle hand to the back of her head. "Drink up, sweet'ums. You have an afternoon rain for-est hike to lead."

"Bad employee. Bad tour guide," Daphne groaned.

"Don't think anyone's going to argue with that point," Keane teased and earned a one-eyed glare when she lifted her head. "You've always been a lightweight. Why would last night be any different?"

"Hope springs eternal," Daphne grumbled, then stared at Theo's sugar-coated cream doughnut. "That looks gooooood."

"And she's back." Sydney retrieved the box of delectable pastries and set it on the table along with napkins. "I already went over this with Tehani so she didn't have to get up at the crack of dawn to join us."

"Lucky Tehani," Daphne grumbled.

"But back to Keane's new job," Sydney said.

"You got another job?" Theo frowned. "I thought you were sticking with Ohana as their water activity specialist?" The slightly panicked look on his face only added to Keane's amusement. "Syd, I love you. And I love Ohana, but there is no way I can—"

"Don't worry, Theo. I'm not about to put you anywhere near the water. Yet," she added with an arched brow at Keane. "I'm thinking you can manage to do both jobs adequately, don't you, Keane?" Sydney went on before he could explain. "He's gone and hired himself out as the maid of honor's boyfriend for the week. On the bright side, it means

Daphne will have backup on the hike seeing as Keane will be along for the ride, or in this case, walk. Or are you doing this for the fun of it?"

Daphne blinked sleepy eyes at him. "You did what?"

"You know any other hangover cures?" Keane asked.

"Is this some kind of Nalani or island code I'm not understanding?" Theo asked.

"Okay, long story short," Keane tried again. "Marella's been told she needs to put work aside for the week and focus on having fun."

"And this is a problem because?" Theo asked.

"Marella's out of her comfort zone when it comes to fun," Sydney said. "Completely out of her league where anything impulsive is concerned, and while she'd agreed to attend all of the prewedding festivities—"

"She'd been secretly harboring a plan to do work in order to get out of everything," Keane said. "Her father told her to either take a vacation this week or she can kiss her job goodbye. See?" He plucked up a *haupia malasada* and bit into the coconut-pudding-filled fried dough. "I really wish Maru would lose her touch with these. I'm obsessed."

Sydney smiled and joined them at the table. "Therefore, Keane volunteered to be Marella's fun coach. Under the guise of being her boyfriend. Because, why not?"

"I see." Theo nodded. "Is this the woman who kissed you on the beach?"

"You told him?" Keane asked Sydney.

"Honey, the entire town is talking about it. And you just fanned the rumor flames by offering to be her plus-one for the next six days." She shook her head. "I can't wait to see what you wear to the wedding. Didn't you say you're allergic?"

"To weddings? Yes, I am. I break out in a run." But he was willing to stick this one out if it meant giving Marella a bit of cover with her family. He had nothing to lose by agreeing to the deal. If anything, he had a chance to spend more time with a woman he was finding extra appealing by the minute.

Why exactly he felt that way he couldn't precisely pinpoint, but that was a concern for another day.

"Well, now that we've had our employee updates," Sydney said. "The rest of this meeting will be short and sweet."

"I can make it even shorter, Syd," Keane

assured her. "I will fulfill all my obligations to Ohana and fit Marella activities around those obligations. Does that ease your mind?"

"Yes, it does. Not everyone in the bridal party plans to do everything on the schedule. I've confirmed with Brita—"

"The wedding planner, right?" Keane asked. "Or coordinator. Is that what she calls herself? I haven't seen much of her."

"According to the bride," Sydney said, "she's been holed up in her room getting the itinerary down for the ceremony. And it's coordinator. She thinks being called a wedding planner makes her sound like an extra in a romantic comedy," Sydney said. "I did manage to connect with her at the hotel yesterday to get the signed waivers for the helicopter tours. We've got one going up at sunrise for the next three mornings. FYI, Marella isn't on the list for any of them, so you don't have to worry about that."

"Bummer," Keane said. "I love getting into that bird and flying with you. It's a spiritual experience."

"Yes, well, I heard you trying to talk her into changing her mind about that last night."

She chuckled. "You're lucky you didn't get pitched into the ocean."

"She got on the boat last night, which means anything is possible."

"Today they have the rain forest hike," Sydney said.

"Trek," Daphne corrected her. "Call it a hike and people chicken out. I checked in with the guides at Manoa Falls to make sure there's enough runoff that the waterfall is a payoff of a destination."

"Nothing worse than a ninety-minute hike… trek," Sydney corrected herself quickly, "only to see nothing more than a drop of water on the rocks."

"Should be fine," Daphne confirmed. "I'll pick up the boxed lunches from Little Owl Bakery on my way to the hotel to collect the guests who are participating."

"Okay then. Tomorrow morning, surf lessons for four," Sydney told Keane. "You've got the bride, her two brothers, and one of the groomsmen."

"Understood." Keane toasted her with his mug.

"What's in it for you?" Theo's question silenced the table. "Sorry." He frowned and glanced up. "I'm still stuck on you playing Marella Benoit's boyfriend. Why?"

Keane shrugged, unwilling to voice the fact that he couldn't explain anything where Marella was concerned. She flummoxed him. Confused him. Entertained and amused. But mostly he just liked being around her. "She needed help with something and I had a way to do that. It's not a big deal."

"If you say so," Daphne sang in a way that illustrated she was clearly feeling better.

"Look, I like her, okay. I'll admit it."

"Shocker," Sydney teased.

"And I like her family. Especially her grandmother."

"I'll second that," Daphne piped up. "Pippy and Polunu hit it off after dinner when he was playing the ukulele. Syd even taught Pippy some hula moves."

"In answer to your question, Theo," Keane said. "I don't need to get anything out of it except knowing I helped someone achieve their dream." It didn't occur to him that was the case until he'd said it. "If she does as her father asks and checks out of work for the week, she gets to run the company.

That's important to her. It's her dream. If I can make that happen, then I've done something worthwhile. I'd like to make a positive difference for a change."

"Keane." Sydney reached across the table and caught his hand. "What happened with Timothy Brice wasn't your fault."

"Maybe." He cringed, not wanting to get too in-depth with the topic. He didn't know how much Theo knew, and Keane certainly didn't want to go through the details now. "Maybe not. I didn't see it coming though and I should have. I can see everything where Marella's concerned." Near as he could tell she was an open book. "There's little risk with this." But there was potential for a huge payoff.

"There's always risk when you put yourself out there for someone," Daphne said. "Be careful, Keane."

"What's with these dire warnings? First Mano, now you?" Keane got to his feet. "You can all stop worrying I'm going to take some kind of romantic fall. I don't do romance, remember? And as far as a lot of people are concerned, I don't even have a heart. Are we done?"

"Ah, sure. We can be." Sydney shrugged. "I've sent an updated itinerary to each of your phones, which you'll need to turn on," she added for Keane's benefit. He'd mentioned to Syd that he had shoved his phone in the nightstand drawer when he'd checked into the Hibiscus Bay.

"Great. I'll take a look and be where I'm needed." He glanced outside. "I have to get back to the resort and check out before I head over to the cottage. I'm going to try to catch some waves after and clear my head."

"Of course. Keane—"

He walked out the door, hating how he left things, but not wanting to hear, yet again, that he wasn't to blame for a student in his charge almost dying.

"I'M NOT GOING to make it." Marella stared at the hotel notepad in her lap, clenched her pen and contemplated ordering another pot of coffee. She needed to start the day like this—without checking email, without making a schedule, without making notes of what needed to be done and by when—for another six days. "There is no way I can do another morning without work and not lose my cool."

She'd been up since five, even though she hadn't gotten to bed until after one in the morning. She might have been asleep sooner if she hadn't had to remind Crystal and her pair of flighty bridesmaids—Alexis, the boyfriend snogger, and Shawna, the groom's younger sister—that they weren't teenagers, and that their behavior on the boat had been both unacceptable and embarrassing.

In hindsight, she might have been taking her inner frustrations out on them.

That said, it didn't matter how much sleep she got or didn't get; her eyes always popped open at the same time every single day. Some routines couldn't be forgotten or ignored. That was why she'd ended up visiting the resort's gym and running five miles on a treadmill. Given the pace she'd set, she was surprised she hadn't set the gears to smoking.

To avoid temptation and ensure she'd stick to the deal she'd made with her father, she'd rearranged the apps on her phone and kept safe ones on the homepage, which allowed her access to her music and the heart-pounding tempos she'd needed to make her sweat.

She'd hoped the music would also help

her forget the fool she'd made of herself last night with Keane. The very idea of hiring Keane Harper as her fun coach— disguised as her pretend boyfriend—was so far out of the stratosphere of her experience and reasoning, she couldn't quite wrap her head around it. Fortunately the chaotic end to the evening hadn't left her and Keane much time to chat about what had to be an impulsive offer on his part. She'd been back in her room by six to shower, change and… do what?

She stared at her to-do list that earlier felt like an adequate response to boredom. So far she only had one thing listed: find a bookstore. As attached as she was to electronics, she was still a physical-book girl at heart. If for no other reason, the printed page gave her eyes a break from staring at a screen for hours. Right now she had nothing else to occupy her brain unless replaying her moments of mortification counted. Yep. She definitely needed a bookstore.

She couldn't help but think she was having a physical withdrawal from not using her personal electronic devices. Sure enough, after her deal with her dad, she had gotten back to her room and her laptop was nowhere to be found. In its place, she found a beautifully handwritten note from Mano Iokepa explaining how she could retrieve the computer when she and the rest of the party checked out.

The note had, in some odd way, cemented her father's ultimatum and reminded Marella of her subsequent counteroffer. Her mouth twisted. She should have known her dad would call her bluff. He knew her tells, she reminded herself, and how to play her.

Guilt wrapped around her heart and squeezed. It wasn't as if she wanted to put him out of a job. She liked working with her father. It was one of the perks of her job as far as she was concerned, but either he had absolutely no faith she could fulfill her end of the bargain, or he was looking for the means to ease them all into his eventual retirement. She couldn't very well stand in his way.

"Or Keane is right and Dad's willing to do what he thinks is best for you," Marella told herself. Even walk away from the job he loved.

Whatever the reasons, Marella hadn't felt

this out to sea in…she couldn't remember how long. She needed something to do! Her fingers and toes were tingling with anticipation or frustration. She wasn't entirely sure which.

Now that the sun was up and her coffee was gone, what was she going to do with her time? Not just now, but for the rest of the week? She checked her watch, found herself smiling a little at the idea of Keane returning it to her. He'd carried it around with him, which meant she'd been in his thoughts. Maybe as much as he'd been in hers.

"Don't really think that's possible." But she had to admit, his presence on the dinner cruise last night had made the evening not only bearable, but enjoyable. He had an ability to distract her from the fear she'd always felt about the water. Or he'd made it less scary, at least. He'd even let her take the helm for a few minutes, although he hadn't been far away.

Holding on to the wheel almost felt as if she held everyone's destiny in her hands. There was something almost powerful about that. But not nearly as powerful as the water that surrounded them.

She still didn't like the water. But after last night, after looking out into the vast darkness that occasionally tipped up to kiss the rising moon, she maybe understood it a little bit better. As if she might be able to see it how Keane did.

But there was no boat, no ocean and no Keane to distract her this morning. She got up to call the front desk and ask if there was a bookstore anywhere nearby when someone knocked on her door.

Her heart lightened at the thought it might be Keane and she did a little hop on her way to the door. "Lance. Tag." She frowned, leaned out to peer down the hall. "Hey. What are you two doing here? Is Pippy okay? Is it Dad or Gloria?"

"They're all fine as far as we know," Lance said. "We could hear Pippy snoring through her door. We're here to rescue you." Her stepbrothers exchanged a sheepish look that reminded her of when they'd been caught sneaking down to secretly unwrap their Christmas gifts that had been left under the tree.

"Rescue me?" She stepped back to let them in. "From what?"

"From yourself." Tag, wearing down-to-the-knees cargo shorts and a loose-fitting palm-tree Hawaiian shirt, strode inside. Lance, a bit less casual with khaki slacks and a navy polo shirt followed, only to stop short when Tag grinned at him and held out his hand. "You owe me twenty bucks."

Lance grumbled something as Marella scooted around them. She moved in time to see Lance slap a twenty-dollar bill into his younger brother's palm.

"What's that for?" Marella asked.

"I bet Lance you'd made your bed," Tag boasted.

"I forgot you don't know how to vacation." Lance's sigh was overly dramatic and made her smile. "Someone should have told you one of the best parts is not having to make your bed."

"Why wouldn't I make my bed?" She shrugged.

"Hang on." Tag held up a finger and ducked into her bathroom. "Yep. No towels on the floor."

"I didn't take the bet about the towels," Lance argued.

"They aren't on the floor because I don't like mess," Marella explained. "Housekeeping has enough to deal with picking up after guests like you two. I'm not about to add to their load. That reminds me." She elbowed past them and opened one of the dresser drawers. Marella pulled out an envelope she'd written "thank you" on and set it by the television. "You remembered to leave tips, didn't you?"

"Last night really put you into mom mode, didn't it? Yes, we did." Lance plucked up the envelope and peeked inside. "Although I might be a little light comparatively speaking."

"My roommate in college used to clean hotel rooms during the summer," she told them. "Tips sometimes paid for her books. It's something I've always remembered."

"You're a good person, Marella," Tag said and sat on the edge of her perfectly made bed. Despite his being an adult, she could still see the curly-headed, blue-eyed little boy he'd been once upon a time. "A bit of a control freak, but—"

"I'm still waiting on an explanation for your early-morning visit," she purposely interrupted him. "I thought you two were going to sleep this week away."

"That was before we received our revised wedding itinerary and schedule," Lance said. "We want to make the most of any free time we've got."

"We heard about the deal you and Dad struck last night," Tag said. "Thanks to you, we didn't need an alarm clock this morning."

"What—"

"We could hear you gnashing your teeth all the way at the other end of the floor."

"When we couldn't hear Brita doing the same," Tag added.

"What?" Marella frowned. "What's wrong with Brita?"

"She's in over her head evidently," Lance said. "Don't worry though. It'll be fine. Or so Crystal keeps sayings. Just a few... hiccups."

Marella pressed her lips together to stop from inquiring further. She'd offered her help, more than once where the wedding plans were concerned, and been turned down, not only by Crystal but by Brita. The last thing she wanted to do was add to the tension, so she backed off. If and when they needed her, they knew where she was.

"Hence the rescue," Tag finished. "Grab

your key. We made reservations for breakfast at the restaurant downstairs."

"Okay." She did as they asked, pocketed her room key card and followed them out the door. Alexis and Shawna emerged from their room, bikini clad and oversized woven bags slung over their shoulders. "Guess everyone's getting an early start. Have you two seen Crystal or Chad this morning? Wonder where the soon-to-be happy couple got off to."

They walked down the gold-patterned carpeted hall toward the elevator bank.

"No. Chad seemed a bit out of sorts last night when we got back." Tag punched the down button. "I don't think his mother was impressed with the antics on the boat last night."

"Yeah, none of us were," Marella muttered.

"There's a lot Mom will put up with, but a lack of respect is not one of them. I haven't heard Mom that angry since she caught you smoking in the rose garden," Tag reminded Lance.

"She was mad because I'd accidentally set fire to her favorite bush," Lance said as if that was a defense. "Heard you had a fun first day in Nalani, sis. Interesting payback against Craig, kissing a total stranger."

"From what I understand the entire town knows about that." Funny enough, she'd moved past her humiliation and embarrassment and straight into I-don't-give-a-hoot territory where the kiss was concerned. She was embracing her impulsivity. Or her first attempt at it.

Chances were Keane had a lot to do with her reset, but if that was the case, she could claim credit as well. She was the one, after all, who had kissed him on the beach. Marella pushed her hands into the pockets of her black linen shorts, scrunched her toes in the strappy sandals that were completely impractical but screamed, *I'm on vacation*.

"Dad told me you're coming to work at the agency," she said as the elevator headed to the lobby. "You're going to be a good fit. And I'm looking forward to working with you."

"Yeah?" Lance gave her a hesitant smile. "That's nice to hear. I hope you have a lot of patience because it's going to be weird, getting used to a completely different kind of career."

"Not all that different," she assured him. "We work with numbers almost as much as you did as a trader and broker. Just consider it an offshoot. And don't worry about the adjustment. We give you at least six, maybe eight weeks before we stop allowing for mistakes." She laughed at his sour expression. "I'm kidding. I'm sure Dad will be happy to fill you in on all the errors I made when I first started."

"This is providing you're still working there yourself," Tag reminded her.

"Don't worry," she assured him. "I'm not leaving. You all are stuck with me." She elbowed him playfully. "Permanently."

The doors dinged open and they stepped out into the breeze-filled lobby. The fresh air almost made her cough and she wondered if she'd ever get used to the beauty she found whenever she stepped outside.

Southern Seas, the only restaurant on resort property, sat across from the registration desk. With its giant glass windows, passersby could see straight through to the patio and ocean-side seating. Once more, the open-air decor and use of living plants made for a tempting sight.

She'd all but memorized the menu included in her information binder in her room, a sure sign she had nothing else to do. She knew the food was a bit on the fancier side, with unique takes on Hawaiian staples, but she'd been intrigued.

The fact that she smelled fresh roasted and brewed Kona coffee—they only served the best of the best at the Hibiscus Bay—got her stomach to rumbling even after the carafe she'd drunk this morning.

"Good morning. You must be the Benoit party." The young woman at the hostess stand wore a pale yellow knee-length dress and a solitary hibiscus flower behind her right ear. Her name badge identified her as Aolani and the smile she offered was as warm as a summer day. "Welcome to Southern Seas. Would you like to sit indoors or out on the patio? We have a lovely ocean view."

"Patio sounds great, thanks. I'm Tag, by the way." Tag turned on his million-watt smile, causing Marella and Lance to exchange a knowing look. Tag was nothing if not charming. "What do you recommend?" Tag asked her once they were all seated.

"I'm partial to the macadamia-nut pancakes."

"Well, then, that's what I'll have."

"I'll be sure to let your server know," Aolani said easily. "I'll send Turi right over to get you started with coffee, if you'd like. Aloha." She bowed her head. "Enjoy your meal."

"Is it me?" Tag said slowly as he watched her return to her podium. "Or—"

"It's you." Marella and Lance spoke at the same time before they laughed. They both knew Tag's weakness for pretty young women. "This is nice," Marella said as she looked beyond her brothers to the gentle tide of the ocean. "The quiet. The mood. I can see why Dad said I needed to remember what it feels like to relax."

"You haven't begun to relax until you've experienced a stone massage and visited the resort's rain forest room," Tag said.

"Didn't waste any time, did you?" Lance teased. "Me? I'm looking forward to exploring Nalani, see what kind of businesses are around here. Start to appreciate their marketing approach."

"Uh-oh." Marella sat back. "Sounds like work to me."

"More like homework," Lance confirmed. "Which I am allowed to do. Dad said that's how you got started in the business. By going on research trips, examining stores' approach to publicity and branding. Can't be a bad idea to follow your example."

"He used to take me on long walks down Fifth Avenue and quiz me on company logos." She'd forgotten about that, how those walks had started shortly after they'd lost Marella's mother. Looking back, that might have been one of his coping mechanisms. Spending time with Marella but also remaining focused on his job and career. How lucky she'd been, that he'd brought her into his world rather than shutting her out of it.

"Hello and good morning, you three." The perky, high-pitched voice was instantly recognizable. Marella looked up to find Brita, the wedding consultant, standing before them. She was tall, slender, and her dark blond hair was knotted at the back of her neck. The simple summer dress she wore was an explosion of flowers exhibiting just about every color of the rainbow. The dark circles under her eyes were new. "You all set for the afternoon rain forest adventure?" She tapped her ever-present tablet computer. "Crystal asked me to check in with each of you as she has you down as participating."

"Looking forward to it," Tag said in a far-too-happy tone. Marella kicked him under the table and earned a glare, but his smile barely slipped. "We're supposed to meet in the lobby at noon, right?"

"That's right. A light lunch will be provided by Ohana Odysseys and the van will be transporting you both ways. Be sure you wear comfortable walking shoes," she added. "No sandals and no flip-flops. I hear those trails can get a little muddy."

"Will you be coming with us?" Tag asked innocently.

"Um, no." Brita's laugh sounded a little like a donkey's bray. "No, me and nature are not a good mix. But Crystal had it on her list as a must do. It's a nice way to explore other parts of the Big Island." With that said, she dashed away, making a beeline for Mano.

"Is it possible she has actual springs in her shoes?" Lance murmured. "And for the record, Crystal isn't the least interested in exploring Nalani."

"But it will make an absolutely fabulous next installment on ButtercupDoll," Tag suggested. "Here's hoping she doesn't do a header into the waterfall when she takes a picture. Hey, there's a company for you to examine, bro."

"I've been up close and personal with Crystal's online venture long enough, thanks. And don't think you're getting out of homework, Tag," Lance said. "You're coming to work for Dad too."

"Ah, yes, but I'll be in the mail room. Or something equally inoffensive and unimportant. I don't want to take work home with me. I'll have plenty of that with culinary classes."

Lance looked skeptical. "A chef. What on earth triggered that idea?"

"I like food," Tag said with a shrug. "And I like to be creative. Plus I'll always be employable."

"Sure about that? Thank you." She smiled up at the middle-aged man who filled each of their coffee cups to the brim. "You guys ready to order?"

She followed Tag's lead and indulged in the short stack of macadamia-nut pancakes that came topped with a sprinkling of toasted coconut and a passion-fruit-infused syrup.

"Have you ever worked in a kitchen, Tag?" Marella already knew the answer. "You do realize professional chefs work long hours, standing on their feet, right? That aside, there's a lot of repetition and scullery work. You'll be washing more dishes than you create for a good long while before you can get established."

Tag sipped his coffee. "You don't think I can do it."

"I happen to believe you can do anything you set your mind to. I just hope you know what you're getting into. Working in a kitchen around other cooks and staff, it takes…"

"Focus," Lance said. "The word you're looking for is *focus*, Marella." He glanced at his younger brother. "Something you've never possessed a large amount of."

"I know." Tag shrugged. "But in answer to your question, Marella, no, I've never worked in a kitchen per se."

"Try at all," Lance muttered.

"It's something I'm interested in," Tag insisted. "You think I don't know Mom and Dad see me as the Benoit sibling screwup?"

"No one thinks that," Marella insisted.

"Speak for yourself," Lance countered. "At some point you're going to have to figure out a career, Tag. You're going to be twenty-three next year. Pick something already."

"And you don't think it'll be cooking." Tag didn't look hurt exactly, more like disappointed. "Dad's not footing the bill this time, Lance."

"He's not footing the entire bill," Lance corrected. "There's a difference. You're still using a safety net, Tag. And the more you do, the more worried Mom gets that you're never going to find something you can run with."

"Okay, this conversation's getting off track." Marella held up her hands. "This was supposed to be about you two rescuing me, not assassinating Tag's chosen profession."

"Latest chosen profession."

"Says the man who just tanked a career on Wall Street," Tag told Lance. "We aren't all picture-perfect like you and Marella. Some of us have to take a little extra time to find out what we're meant to do."

"None of us is perfect, Tag," Marella said. "I would have thought last night's ultimatum over my career and job would have proved that."

"It might have taken a little polish off your shine," Tag said with a slow nod. "But there's a difference between being told you work too hard and being thought of as lazy and unfocused." He accentuated *focused* for Lance's sake. "I don't hear either of you complaining about Crystal's so-called job taking photos and posting them online when something goes sideways."

"And you won't." Lance clearly wasn't amused. "Not from me, anyway. Do you guys know how much Crystal made last year?"

"Uh…" Marella, hopeful, eyed Tag, who shrugged. "No. Not really," she said.

"Would it surprise you to learn she made double what I did working on Wall Street?" Lance glanced at each of them.

Marella gaped. "You can't be—"

"Serious?" Lance finished. "Ever known me to exaggerate? She's also got herself a top financial adviser and accountant. So how about you two stop with the assumptions about her ability to earn a living?"

Marella sagged back in her chair as Tag busied himself taking a large swig from his coffee cup. "She has a top financial adviser?"

"A team of them," Lance said. "And before you go assuming that Dad's been footing the bill for the entire thing, he's not. Other than paying for the family to come out to Hawai'i, this is Crystal's show. One hundred percent."

"How do you know all this?" Marella demanded.

"Because she talks to me," Lance said. "More than she does to either of you. Probably because I don't treat her as if she's someone who only wants to look pretty for the camera. She's good at what she does, Marella."

"I never said she wasn't."

"Maybe not in words," Lance stated. "But as someone who's looked up to you, I can assure you it's really hard to be thought of as less than by your big sister. Just something for you to think about."

Marella had never been so grateful for

food to arrive. She hadn't made Crystal feel that way, had she? Sure, she'd thought along those lines over the years, but she didn't want Crystal to think Marella believed her incapable of self-reliance.

But she had.

"I'm beginning to understand why we don't have these sibling breakfasts very often," Tag said as he stuck his fork into the pitcher of syrup to taste. "It requires far too much thinking on all our parts."

"It seems it does," Marella agreed, although she felt inspired. "However, that tells me we should do it far more frequently. What do you say? We do this again before we head home. Same time. Same table. Only next time we'll include Crystal."

"You really think talking to her about this kind of thing in public is the way to go?" Lance arched a brow.

"No, I don't, actually. But don't worry. It'll be okay." Because as soon as she got the chance, she was going to have an overdue heart-to-heart with her sister.

CHAPTER SEVEN

"YOU AREN'T LEAVING because of me, are you?"

Keane retrieved his credit card from the reservation clerk and found Marella standing behind him. He had a better understanding of her now and knew that the way she was standing, her brow slightly furrowed, her arms wrapped around her torso, indicated she was feeling uneasy. The idea she was uneasy about him both intrigued and worried him. Outside, the bells from the church across the street clanged in early-morning welcome.

"I guess it does look as if I'm making a break for it." He cast a glance to his stuffed duffel. "Don't worry," he said with an easy smile. "I'm not going far. Just to more permanent accommodations at the other end of town."

"Oh." Her smile was quick before she ducked her chin. "Of course it's none of my business where you go or what you do, I guess, I just—"

"Didn't like the idea of your new boyfriend taking off before you could ask him to be your date at your sister's wedding?" Not even the perfect wave on the perfect summer's day brought him as much joy as watching Marella's face flush. "I'm kidding. Thanks, Koa." He turned from the counter and drew Marella with him to retrieve his bag. "Did you think I forgot our deal?"

"It wasn't really a deal," Marella said. "I mean, I don't know what you're going to get out of this. Not entirely sure I'd want to wish my family craziness on anyone."

"Must be the question of the day."

"What?"

Keane shook his head. He wasn't sure what it said about him that people didn't understand his motives. Considering he didn't really understand them himself, their confusion made some sense. Was she looking for a way out? Or a confirmation they were still moving forward with his "fun coaching" her? "First reason, I've got a lot of hours to fill in a day and since your sister is Ohana Odysseys's only client for the week,

I have spare time. Also, gives me a chance to check out a lot of the excursions Sydney's made available to our clients. I'm usually relegated to water activities." He didn't continue. Something told him she wasn't in the right frame of mind to hear he liked her and wanted to spend time with her. He hoisted his bag over his shoulder. "You had breakfast already?"

"Yes, with my brothers." She pointed behind her to Southern Seas. "It was delicious."

"Did you go *loco moco* or pancakes?" He narrowed his eyes. "No, wait. Don't tell me. Pancakes."

She smiled and seemed to relax a little. "I indulged. Figured it was a good toe in the water toward having fun."

"I'm now headed into town to pick up the keys to my new lodgings. You want to come with? Won't take me long to drop off my stuff. I can give you all the gossip about Nalani along the way." He glanced at the clock over the registration desk. "You're signed up for the hike this afternoon, right?"

"I am, yeah." She looked down at her sandals. "I'm not sure I've got appropriate shoes though."

"We can take care of that. One of the benefits of having friends on the island. You good to go?"

"Sure." She shrugged. "Nothing else on my agenda."

And didn't she sound simply thrilled about that. "Okay, great. Well, good morning, Pippy."

The sight of Marella's grandmother leaving the elevator bank and heading their way was one to behold.

Her stark silver hair was piled high on top of her head. She wore a gauzy swimsuit cover-up and a bright blue one-piece that had some serious sagging issues. Her knobby, very white legs were so thin he wondered how they supported the rest of her as she walked around in orthopedic sandals. Hooked over one arm was that same wicker purse out of which she pulled an extra-large pair of sunglasses.

"Morning, handsome." Pippy beamed at him. "I'm headed to the pool to catch some sun." She looked down at her feet. "Don't want anyone thinking I'm my own ghost at the wedding on Saturday." She eyed Marella, then Keane. "You two eloping?"

Marella rolled her eyes.

"We are not." Keane slipped his free arm around Marella's waist and drew her close. "I'm about to give your granddaughter a private tour of Nalani."

"Good." Pippy nodded so hard the big blue bauble earrings she wore bounced against her cheeks. "Glad to see you living, kiddo. And taking your father's advice to heart."

"It wasn't advice," Marella said. "It was an ultimatum."

"Potato, potahto. How early do they start serving mai tais at the pool?" Pippy asked Keane.

"They'll serve them anytime you'd like," he told her. "In fact, how about we get you all settled pool-side before we take off? Be right back." He dropped his bag at the desk, said he'd return for it in a few minutes, and rejoined Marella and her grandmother. "Allow me." He crooked his arm for Pippy to grab hold of.

"You're going to be a hard one to leave behind," Pippy told him as they followed the signs to the main pool area. "I was hoping to get down to the beach, but last night really wiped me out." She clung tightly to his arm as they walked slowly through the busy lobby. "Slept great though. That ocean air is something."

"One of the main reasons I keep coming back," Keane agreed and glanced over his shoulder at Marella. She was looking at him with something he wanted to interpret as gratitude, not that it took much effort to be around Pippy. "You got some sunblock with you?" he asked. "I know you want to get a little color, but we don't want you to burn."

"Don't you worry about me. I'm not so far gone I don't know how to prevent getting roasted like a chicken. Speaking of chicken." Pippy looked up at him as they approached the sliding glass doors that led to the pool. "I heard someone talking about Hula Chicken? What's that?"

"Hula Chicken might just be the best place to eat in Nalani," Keane told her. "Open spit-roasted spicy chicken, lots of traditional side dishes. It's a picnic table, eat-with-your-hands kind of place, but you won't be disappointed."

"That's my kind of eating," Pippy announced. "I know Armand puts on his airs about fancy schmancy eats. Sometimes the boy forgets he grew up in Brooklyn, where something simple but tasty was always cooking on everyone's stove."

"Then we'll make sure you get to Hula at least once while you're here," Keane assured her. "How does this spot look?" As it wasn't even eight in the morning, the pool area was almost empty except for a young woman swimming laps and the bar-and-snack hut that was getting ready for day-long service.

"I don't know." Pippy frowned and stared at the chairs closer to the hut. "A little far away from all the action, I'd say."

"It's too early for any action," Marella told her grandmother. "I think this looks great."

Personally, Keane would have suggested one of the half-dozen tented cabanas across the way, but if Pippy was determined to get some sun, those wouldn't be of help. "How about you take a seat here and give it a test?"

He indicated to Marella he'd be right back and made his way around the pool to the hut. The front of the seemingly innocuous structure had counter space for up to ten customers. Three to four employees manned it, two of which were on the other side of the bamboo wall in the kitchen that offered everything from ahi poke nachos to big bowls of *saimen*, an island version of ramen. There was also homemade ice cream and a long selection of drinks to make any guest happy.

"Hey, Keane! Aloha, brah! Howzit?" a voice he knew called out to him.

"Aloha, Maka." Keane fist-bumped his longtime friend and former surf partner from before he competed in San Diego. "You catch any good waves lately?"

"Nah, brah," Maka replied, his hair revealed hints of gray beginning at the temple. He'd also bulked up a bit, stretched a couple of buttons on his Hibiscus Bay shirt, but the gregarious personality of his was firmly in place. "Don't like to stray too far from shore. Got three little ones to worry about at home. But they'll be ready to start surfing soon." His face went from serious to blissful at the statement. "I'm hoping at least one of them's a fish."

"One can hope." Keane gestured to Pippy and asked, "Hey, can you do me a favor today?"

"Sure thing."

"The older lady in the lounge chair over there, she's part of the Benoit wedding party."

"Right. Big to-do this weekend, yeah?"

Maka leaned over the counter. "Who's that with her? Is that the woman who kissed you on the beach?"

Keane couldn't remember the last time he felt his face flush. Marella really was rubbing off on him. "It is, actually. That's Marella. Sister of the bride. And that's her grandmother, Pippy."

"You want her *tutu* to get the star treatment?" Maka asked. "Sure, brah. No problem."

"She's looking to try your special mai tais. And make sure she eats something."

Maka nodded. "I got ya, brah. Hey, I'm going to be bartending at the wedding. You, ah, planning on coming to the wedding as your Marella's date?"

"Depends," Keane said. "Why? You aren't starting up a betting pool or anything, are you?"

"Maybe." Maka shrugged far too innocently.

"I'm not a fan of weddings, Maka. You know this." But if anyone could change his mind, it was probably Marella.

"I do. Or I did." His gaze shifted to Marella. "Maybe something's changed. Puts the idea up in the air, doesn't it?"

And makes for a lucrative betting pool. "Let's just say my attendance is on the table." It wasn't that he didn't like weddings. They were fine, he supposed. Not that he'd ever been to one. It was marriage that didn't sit well with him. The commitment it took, the promises that were required—promises that in his experience, weren't so easily fulfilled. He never wanted to be someone else's disappointment. More to the point, he didn't want to walk down any path that could possibly turn him into his father. "I'll check in with you when we get back. I want to give Marella a look at Nalani."

"Go," Maka said. "Take your girl out. We'll take care of her *tutu*."

Before Keane was out of earshot, Maka was giving his fellow servers Pippy-dedicated instructions.

"You all set here, Pippy?" She'd unloaded her bag as if she was setting up camp. He couldn't help but chuckle. Two pairs of glasses. One very large bottle of super-strong sunscreen, her phone, which was a newer model than what Keane owned, lip balm, a large-print Harlequin romance novel and a pair of headphones. "I see you got towels in case you want to take a dip in the pool."

"I am all ready." Pippy beamed at him, her eyes going wide when she looked over his shoulder. "Oh, what's this?"

"Tutu Pippy." Maka arrived with one of the resort's fresh coconut drinks loaded to the brim and topped with multiple skewers of pineapple. He set the coconut down amid her belongings and accepted the oval plate from the employee who had followed him over. "I'm Maka. I'm going to be taking care of you today."

"You are?" Pippy eyed Keane. "This your doing?"

Keane grinned. "I thought you might enjoy being treated like a queen and no one does that better than my friend Maka."

"You need anything, you just ask," Maka confirmed.

"Well, I wouldn't want to stop you from doing what you do best. Pleasure to meet you, Maka." She waved at Marella and Keane. "Okay, shoo now you two. I've got some sunning and chatting to do. Maka, tell me about yourself. You married? Any young Makas running around?"

Keane guided Marella away, amused by the fact that she kept looking over her shoulder as if Pippy was about to float out into the ocean with no paddle.

The guests were beginning to emerge from their upstairs rooms, mingling and wandering about the property as the morning settled in. Across the way, he spotted her brothers, Lance and Tag, exiting the restaurant.

"That drink will have her under the table in ten seconds flat," Marella said. "I don't think—"

"Maka's using his special tonic for her drinks," he said. "It tastes almost the same, but there's almost no alcohol."

Marella caught his arm.

He turned, concerned he'd said something wrong. "What?"

"I—I don't know." She shook her head, frowned. "Thank you, I guess? For taking care of her. For taking pity on me," she added with a forced laugh. "I don't know. For being a nice guy? I guess I got pretty lucky kissing you yesterday." It was the first time she'd mentioned their kiss without blushing and while he missed that sudden rush of color to her cheeks, he was glad to see it wasn't something she regretted.

He stepped closer, lifted a hand to stroke her cheek. "Is that such a surprise? That there are nice guys out there?"

"Maybe." She shrugged and leaned into him. "I mean, my brothers are nice guys. And my dad. But—"

"But then there are the Craigs of the world." He pulled her closer to him. "Believe me when I say there are more of us, than there are of him." Keane paused, thinking again of how much he like spending time with her. "Hey, I just realized what's in this deal for me."

"You did?" Her lashes fluttered as if she was in a kind of daze. "What?"

He knew what he wanted to say. He wanted to say, *You're what's in this for me*, but that wouldn't be fair. Not when he knew there wasn't anything for them beyond this week. He liked her. From the moment he'd first seen her on the beach, it was as if he'd been caught up in her spell—and maybe he had been. But spells weren't real. Instead, he said, "You experiencing everything you can about Nalani while you're here. If that means I'm your private tour guide, then that's more than enough in exchange for my time." His kiss on her forehead was quick and innocent, but a hint of what could be, and a public display of affection that would no doubt be making its way through the resort's rumor mill in no time. "Are you ready to see my Nalani?"

She nodded and for a moment he considered she might be caught in a spell of her own. A spell of his making that he hadn't realized he'd cast. "Let's go."

MARELLA HAD GOTTEN a taste of Nalani yesterday in the hours following her encounter with Keane on the beach. She'd walked up part of Pulelehua Road, the main thoroughfare that stretched from one end of Nalani to the other, but she'd stopped short of exploring beyond the central stores and eateries.

She'd spent most of her time in Luanda's, but also poked her head into The Hawaiian Snuggler, a shop that offered stunning handmade quilts and other fabric creations. She'd even taken a detour to the quaint church located across the street from the resort and stopped to browse the collection of market stalls where people were selling soaps, lotions, woven crowns accented with tiny hibiscus buds and some seriously tempting sweet treats.

She'd found the architectural style simple and charming. The tongue-and-groove siding on most of the buildings was painted in varying colors, each complementing the backdrop of the ocean in surprising ways. There were no dark, earthy tones, but rather vivid, cheery ones that seemed to make the sun shine brighter.

"Sorry to drag you through town before we stop anywhere," Keane said as she slowed down to look into the window of a jewelry shop. "I just really want to off-load my stuff and then have us get on to more fun things."

The window display was a mesmerizing mix of island-made jewelry from local stones and gems. "What's this?" Marella asked. "This stone here." She pointed to a simple, silver pendant with a polished green stone in its center. "I don't recognize it."

"That's olivine. It's native to the islands. You've heard of our black sand beaches, right?"

"Sure." Only now was she wishing she'd done a bit more research into the islands before she'd arrived. Of course at that time she hadn't realized she'd have so much free time to explore.

"Well, we also have some green sand beaches thanks to this stone. Just a bare hint of it, mind you. I've seen elaborate, sparkly kind of jewelry pieces made with it."

"I like simple things." She loved the way the stone looked as if it had waves of green moving across it. "Sorry. I'm not usually a jewelry person, but that caught my eye."

"I don't blame you." She and Keane resumed their walk, passing by a small pharmacy that also boasted a post office, and a storefront offering shave ice. She frowned as they passed by, wondering if the sign was misspelled.

"It's not." Keane's statement had her thinking she'd spoken out loud without realizing. "Spelled wrong. Shave ice was brought to the islands by Japanese immigrants. The Pidgin dialect translated it to *shave* instead of *shaved*." He shrugged. "It actually comes from the Japanese tradition of *kakigōri*."

"Interesting. I never thought of snow cones being cultural. I just figured it was fair or carnival food."

"Oh, it's definitely cultural around here

and I can guarantee it's nothing like what you have back on the mainland, unless it's specifically a shave ice shop. Here we use things like condensed milk and fruit juices. Most of it's all natural. After all, we grow the best sugar in the world on the islands."

"I'm going to have to start making a list of things to try to check out on our walk back." She looked at her watch.

"Stop that." If he meant to distract her by taking hold of her hand and slipping his fingers through hers, job well done. Every time he touched her it was as if dormant cells in her body leaped to life. "I know what time we need to be back. We won't be late."

"Don't begrudge me the one electronic device I can still use without penalty," she accused. "Besides, you aren't wearing a watch."

"Don't need one. It's coming up on nine." He pointed to the sky. "The sun tells you when we are. If you know how to read it."

"That sounds like a challenge." She kept her hold on him light; not so light as to show disinterest, but not too tight that she came across as desperate.

"Maybe tomorrow I'll teach you?" That

smile of his widened. "If you're up for a morning walk on the beach? Either before or after the surf lessons your brothers and some of the others have scheduled."

She shuddered. "Surf lessons. Nope. Nothing you can say will convince me to take that on. No offense."

"None taken. But you don't know what you're missing."

"I'm missing getting smacked down by the ocean," Marella told him. "Seriously, I'm passing."

"How about a helicopter ride?"

"Are you purposely choosing things you know I'm going to say no to just so other stuff doesn't sound as dangerous?"

"Not intentionally. Or maybe it isn't so bad to face new kinds of challenges. But FYI, Sydney's one of the best pilots on the islands. Until she moved here, she was an instructor and a search-and-rescue specialist. You couldn't be in safer hands if you did decide to take a chance on one."

"Hmm." She had to admit, he made it sound tempting. "I'll put it in the maybe column."

He stopped walking, faced her. "You'll

give a helicopter tour some thought but it's a hard pass on surfing."

"I know." She sighed dramatically. "I'm an enigma. Keep trying to puzzle me out. Oh." She looked up the staircase to the charming bamboo-sided building above them. "This is Ohana Odysseys?" She looked back and saw how far they'd come from the main stretch of downtown Nalani. They'd arrived up a slight hill, curved away from the thorough-fare. Other than the rustle of the coconut and banyan trees and the roar of the ocean on the other side of the building, she didn't hear a thing.

She loved the tropical hut with enormous leaves lining the roof that rustled in the breeze. The gentle plink of bamboo wind chimes added that last touch of authentic-ity that had her marveling that a place like this existed.

"There's a whole track of houses across the street there. It winds around and through the forest. And farther up there." He pointed up to the top of the hill. "That's where the landing pad is for the helicopter. If you keep going around it, it curves off toward more houses, which is where I'll be living for the foreseeable future."

"How long are you staying?" It occurred to her the question could be considered rude. "I mean, I thought my dad said you're a swim coach at a college on the mainland. That must mean you get summers off."

"I do. And I was. Am." He flinched as if the admission brought him some kind of pain. "Remains to be seen. Come on. I'm ready to dump this duffel." He had yet to relinquish his hold on her hand, something she found she didn't mind as they climbed the steps and crossed the rather large front porch to the open door. "Hey, T. You decent?" He grinned back at Marella. "That's code for—"

"Never you mind what it's code for." The woman who stood up from behind a tall desk aimed a warning look in Keane's direction. "Just for that I'm not going to show you the picture from my sonogram yesterday." She approached, and only stopped long enough to elbow Keane in the stomach. "You must be Marella. Aloha. Welcome to Nalani. I'm Tehani Iokepa."

"Nice to meet you." Marella accepted the

traditional island greeting of brushed cheeks and inhaled the intoxicating fragrance of island flowers. She'd heard the phrase *island beauty* before, but she'd never seen someone who exemplified it. With her straight black hair that reached to the base of her spine, her beautiful bronze skin spoke of countless hours beneath the sun. Marella looked for signs of the woman's pregnancy, but couldn't really see any beneath the blousy orange tank top and beige shorts. "Congratulations on the baby."

"Thanks." Tehani's smile came across as a bit sad. Marella glanced at Tehani's hand and noticed there wasn't a wedding band. Or any sign there had been one recently. "I'm only five months so far, so the adjustment's slow in coming. In another month or so I might not be so eager to move. Or be able to see my feet."

"Okay, I'm sorry I teased you. Really sorry. Let me see." Now Keane did let go of her hand as he leaned over and dropped his bag on the ground. "Gimme." He flexed his fingers like a three-year-old after a treat.

Marella couldn't help but laugh at his infectious excitement. Tehani retrieved a small square photograph from her desk and brought it over. "No teasing the baby," she ordered when she handed it to him.

"I'd never tease my honorary niece or nephew," Keane said, feigning offense. He squinted at the photo, looked closer. Turned it around. Then around again. "What am I looking at?" He tilted his head, then again in the other direction. "So...you're having a blob."

"Oh, good heavens." Marella snort-laughed. "Forget what I said earlier. You're hopeless." She stepped beside him to get a look. "Okay, that's an arm, I think. And here's a...leg?" She glanced to Tehani for assistance.

"I'm beginning to see the attraction between you two," Tehani said. She poked her head in between them. "You're right, Marella, that's an arm. And a leg. And that—" she indicated something else "—makes him your nephew."

"It's a boy..."

Marella wasn't certain what she was hearing in Keane's voice. Wonder? Amazement? Or...sadness? Tehani nodded, tears pooling in her eyes.

"Oh, T., it's a boy." He wrapped an arm

around Tehani's shoulder and pulled her in close, pressed his lips to the top of her head. Keane squeezed his eyes shut but not before Marella saw a sheen of tears in his gaze. "A little Remy. You doing okay?"

"I'm fine." Tehani nodded, sniffled a little and wiped her eyes. "I'm fine. Marella must be thinking we're both overreacting too much."

"No," Marella insisted despite being curious about the story Tehani clearly had to tell. "This is a lovely moment between friends who clearly care about each other." Another tick in Keane's good-guy column. "I'm sure your baby boy is going to be absolutely gorgeous, Tehani."

"How soon can I buy him a surfboard?" Keane demanded.

Tehani laughed and shook her head. "Anyone else, I might have said that offer only came because it's a boy but I know good and well it wouldn't matter if I was having a girl. This one's all about creating ongoing generations of surfers," she told Marella.

"Yes, he's already tried to convert me," Marella confirmed. "I already promised him, he's not getting me out in that ocean."

"You did tell me that," Keane confirmed. "And yet last night we cruised the seas and gazed at a glorious sunset and lighthouse."

"That's right, the dinner cruise." Tehani waved them both over to sit at the large round table at the back of the open office space. "Syd said there was some excitement toward the end."

"Just a bit too much overexuberance on the part of some of the guests," Keane said the words in such a diplomatic way that Marella's heart instantly warmed. "You would have enjoyed Pippy's attempt at the hula far more, believe me."

"Pippy's your grandmother, right?" Tehani asked Marella. "Oh, I can't wait to meet her. I wanted to go last night, but me and boats aren't getting along at the moment."

"It was a great evening for the most part," Marella confirmed. "The food was wonderful."

"I'm sorry, I should have offered you something to drink." Tehani walked over to the coffee-and-beverage station, which included a small 1950s-style sky blue refrigerator.

"I'm good, thanks, T.," Keane said.

"Me too. I've already had a pot and a half

of coffee this morning." Which explained why she felt like a squirrel that had overdosed on nuts. "Iokepa." It only just dawned on her. "Are you related to Mano Iokepa?"

"Depends." Tehani threw her a look. "What did he do?"

Keane laughed. "Mano's her brother."

"Older brother," Tehani clarified. "Why do you always forget to say that?" She turned on the electric kettle for hot water and sorted through a clear plastic box of tea bags. "Seriously though, I lucked out in the big brother department. In fact, I ended up with four of them."

Keane straightened in his chair as if he'd just been knighted. "That might be the nicest thing you've ever said to me."

"No, it's not. Mano and I grew up here in Nalani," Tehani explained to Marella. "Fifth generation to do so. Sydney and her brother, Remy, were born here as well. We all went to school together." She touched a hand to her stomach. "Remy and Mano and Keane, then later after college with Silas and Wyatt, they all kind of came together like a family."

Marella noticed the warm smile on Keane's lips. "Remy." Marella frowned.

That was the second time the name had been mentioned. "I don't think I've met—"

"Remy died earlier this year," Tehani said in a way that finally locked the puzzle pieces into place. "Ohana was his pride and joy." She looked from one end of the hut to the other.

"Not his only pride and joy," Keane reminded her.

"That's sweet," Tehani said. "He built Ohana Odysseys pretty much so he had an excuse to show Nalani off to everyone who came here. He made the business a success and had a lot of plans for the future. Now Sydney runs it."

"Ah, not quite," Keane said. "Sydney couldn't do half of what she's done without Tehani. It's a family business. Always will be."

"Provided no one else tries to steal it out from under us. Sorry," Tehani said and poured the water for her tea. "Don't know why that whole buyout offer is still bothering me. Anyway." She sighed. "Marella. You must be excited about your sister's wedding."

"Sure." Marella shrugged. "Haven't really had much to do with it, I mean, I threw her a bridal shower before we left New York. Or rather, I hosted it. Crystal pretty much made all the arrangements. So…I guess my main role is walking down the aisle ahead of her? And making sure her veil is straight." And staying out of the way.

"You being here to support her is what matters," Tehani said. "Certainly the activities and excursions you all have booked should be an excellent way to ease into the festivities of the weekend."

"Sure." Marella wasn't sure she could sound less enthused. "It's all a bit…I don't know…whirlwind. Crystal and Chad have only been dating for a few months. Not that much longer than me and—" She cut herself off, shook her head. "Sorry. Don't know why I keep thinking about Craig."

"Craig would be the cheating weasel, right?" Tehani dunked her tea bag a few times and winced. "Sorry. That's what Syd called him this morning."

"Sydney would be correct in her description," Marella agreed. "I'm just glad he's gone so I don't have to worry about possibly working with him when I get back to New York."

"You're in advertising, right?" Tehani carried her mug over to the table. "You know, I've been trying to figure out new opportunities we can take advantage of where Ohana Odysseys is concerned. I don't suppose you—"

"No," Keane cut her off. "She can't." He gave Marella a hard stare. "Not for the next six days. No work, remember? Only fun."

"As I told my father last night." Marella could feel her patience straining. "Work is fun for me. But, unfortunately, Keane's right." She twisted her mouth. She had to prove to her father she could find room in her life for more than work. That was her surefire path to running the company one day.

Keane, however, was obviously going to be a stickler for the rules her father had set forth. She also wouldn't put it past him to go tattling to her father. "If I have a chance after the wedding and before I head home, I'd be happy to consult with you. Otherwise, we can do it over a video chat. Free of charge," she added at Tehani's shocked look. "As a thank-you for everything you all are doing for my family while we're here."

Marella glanced around the office. She really liked the vibe of the place. Yes, it was a business, but it also felt…comfortable.

The long, wide windows were propped open and allowed for that ocean air to come through the surprisingly spacious interior. There was the carved oak reception desk that displayed artistic renderings of island activities. It was enchanting.

"I will absolutely take you up on that," Tehani said. "But I am curious—"

Marella knew exactly what she was going to say. "My father doesn't think I'm having enough fun in my life."

"Any," Keane corrected. "He doesn't think you're having *any* fun in your life. Workaholic." He jerked a playful thumb in her direction.

"He told me to take the week off and enjoy myself. So this one…" Marella jerked a playful thumb in his direction.

"Is showing her how to have fun," Keane filled in the rest for her.

"Just waiting for the fun to start," Marella ground out. "It helps that he's so gregarious and…"

"Immature?" Tehani's eyebrows went up. "Whimsical? Irresponsible? I'm kidding.

No, really, Marella." She reached over and covered Marella's hand with her own. "I am kidding. You couldn't be in better company. Especially if you're looking for a fun time." She waggled her eyebrows.

"Thanks," Keane said, then frowned. "I think. And on that note, Syd said that you have the keys to the cottage, T.?"

"Oh, right." Tehani pushed to her feet. "Rewa was out there yesterday. Gave the place a quick tidy. Clean sheets and towels are in the bathroom closet. Kitchen is re-stocked. Anything else, you know the drill." She retrieved a set of keys from her desk and tossed them to Keane. "You heading up there now?"

"Just long enough to drop off my things. Then we're going to take our time walking back to the resort."

"Sounds good." Tehani nodded. "You've got the waterfall hi—I mean, trek," she said, switching words at the last second.

"That reminds me." Keane snapped his fingers and left the table to dig into a small cabinet in the wall. "Yep, knew she had some stashed in here. What size shoes do you wear, Marella?"

"Um, seven and a half. Or an eight. Depending. Why?" Her eyes went wide at the hiking boots he dragged out. They were sturdy, looked heavy and had her second-guessing her decision to go on the afternoon excursion.

"These are eights." They thunked on the floor where he dropped them. "We'll grab you some extra-thick socks at Luanda's."

"Thanks?"

"Hang on." Tehani rolled her eyes, and grabbed a large wicker bag off the wall. "You can't go dragging those around Nalani with you like that."

"Thanks," Marella said and dropped the shoes inside the bag. "I've got six and a half days to kill," Marella reminded Keane. "But for the record, I'm okay if today's the only day I need these."

"Well, you are scheduled for the volcano and zip-lining," Tehani said. "Can't hurt to keep them handy."

"Since you're coming with me to the cottage," Keane said, "I could use your help carrying something."

"You mean the bag that almost made you topple over?" Marella teased.

"No." He retreated into a small corner room and came back with the orange-and-white surfboard he'd had with him yesterday on the beach. "This."

It was taller than she was, but not, she discovered when she grabbed hold, as heavy as she anticipated. "I can manage this." She tried to tuck it under one arm, but bashed the back end against the door. "Oops, sorry." Only then did she notice the horrified look on both Keane's face and Tehani's. "What?" She checked to see if she'd caused any damage. "Is it bad?"

"Just…be careful with that, please," Keane pleaded, then seemed to have second thoughts. "You know what? Let's just wait—"

"Keane, she'll be fine." Tehani walked over and touched his arm. "It was Remy's board," she told Marella gently. "So it's—"

"Special." Mortified, she offered an apology. "That was careless of me. I apologize. I'm so sorry." She ran her hand over the smooth surface. "I'll be very careful with it from here on. I promise."

Keane didn't look completely convinced, but he nodded.

"It'll be fine," Tehani repeated in a low whisper to Marella as she followed Keane to the door. "Some things are too strong to break."

CHAPTER EIGHT

"OKAY, I MIGHT have cottage envy."

"Yeah?" Keane passed by Marella and stepped from the gravel path onto the wrap-around porch. With summer just about here, the flowers were in full bloom and nearly obscured the side of the white bungalow. "It is pretty great. Sydney's guy, Theo, was staying here up until recently, but now that it's free, I took a chance. Come on in. Oh, watch your feet," he advised. "We've got a pair of geckos who also call this home. Don't trip over them."

When he glanced over his shoulder, he saw Marella taking slow, deliberate steps across the porch, avoiding the corner of the house and railings. She was most definitely keeping her earlier promise.

"You can just leave the board out here, by the door." He pointed to a spot next to one of the two rocking chairs Theo had bought during his stay. Keane made quick work of the lock, ducked inside, leaving the door open for her to enter.

He walked through the galley-style kitchen and eating area, detoured at the living room and carried his bag into the bedroom. He liked the cozy feel of the place, and the calming yellow paint on the walls fit in nicely against the backdrop of the ocean. Knowing the water was only steps away, waiting for him to jump in at any time, filled his heart.

He stood at the elevated window in the bedroom, rested his hands on his hips and took a long, calming breath. Closing his eyes, he focused on pushing all the confusing thoughts he'd brought with him from the mainland down, far away where he couldn't reach them.

"Feel free to put a few things away before we go. You must want to settle in," Marella called out from the living room.

At her suggestion, Keane made quick work of unpacking. He'd always traveled light. A few sets of clothes; more than double that in board shorts. Flip-flops, a sturdy pair of hiking sandals, his own pair of hiking boots and a plethora of T-shirts. Everything he owned could be washed in the stackable washer/dryer unit in the closet between the bathroom and bedroom.

He paused, looking at the polished wood box that came along with him wherever he went. He cracked open the lid, looked at the scattering of photographs inside. He'd learned early in life not to be sentimental. Things were easily lost. Easily destroyed. He touched a finger to the image of the four children huddled together on the front steps of one of his childhood homes. Memories on the other hand...

"Hey." Marella knocked softly on the doorframe. "Sorry to interrupt."

He flipped the lid down, then set the box on the small dresser across from the bed that was draped with a soft sea green blanket. "You're not." But it took a bit of extra effort to ignore those memories. "What's up?"

"I think your roommate is hungry." She pointed behind her, an amused smile on her pretty face.

It struck him how whenever he looked at her all he wanted to do was smile back. She had an amazing effect on him. An effect that left him feeling strangely antsy the more he thought about it.

"Let's see what's in the fridge." He went on ahead, ducked into the kitchen. "Don't need the fridge. This works." He plucked up a mango out of the fruit bowl beside the coffee machine. "We can split it with him."

Marella joined him. "He's still there, sitting on the table outside. Like he's waiting to be served."

"Because he is." Keane expertly sliced off the bright green and yellowed mango skin, then chopped the fruit into tiny chunks. He opened the cabinet overhead, and let out a cry of disbelief.

"What? Something wrong?" Marella asked, coming up beside him.

"Theo has lost his mind." He reached up for the two tiny plates. "He keeps dishes, like plates and bowls, for Noodles and his girlfriend." Shaking his head, he slid a good amount of mango onto each of the two plates, then handed one to Marella using two fingers. "So you can make a friend."

Keane went outdoors and Marella followed him and set the plate down in front of the little gold-speckled green lizard.

She bent toward the gecko. "Hello, Noodles. You are handsome, aren't you? Look at those bright blue rings around your eyes. Like itty-bitty glasses."

Noodles inclined his head, scampered forward a bit, just far enough to bump his nose against Marella's finger, then shoved his face into the mango.

"I think I'm in love." She rested her chin on the table. "Is that other plate for his paramour?"

"Zilla. She's still shy around humans. Hey, Nood, chew your food or you'll get a tummy ache."

Marella's laughter filled the air and that, along with the breaking waves, soothed Keane's soul.

"You want to be out there." Marella stood, faced him, hands in her pockets. "On the water. On that board."

He shrugged. "Always."

"So why don't you? Show me what surfing can be. Maybe I'll change my mind about it." She nudged him with her hip.

"You wanted to see Nalani and—"

"I've got plenty of time to check out Nalani. I—" She stopped, as if uncertain of what she was about to say. "I get the feeling that you need it, some time out there on the water. Or am I wrong?"

"You're not." The fact that she saw that, that she felt it, he wasn't entirely certain how to process it. He always enjoyed getting to know people. But people getting to know him? That was another thing entirely. "You sure you don't mind?"

"I want to see you on the waves. Noodles and I will hang back here. I'll finish the mango," she added. Marella caught his arm, tugged him to the door. "Go. Change. Then show me what you've got."

He touched her cheek, overwhelmed and confused at the same time. She was a woman supposedly so consumed with her work that she didn't have any connection to the outside world. How wrong that was.

He resisted the temptation to brush a kiss across those amazing lips of hers. Lips he knew were smiling for him. "Okay, thanks. Won't take me more than a minute to get changed."

MARELLA HAD NEVER understood the concept of a calling. The idea that destiny or fate somehow played a part in one's life and the choices they made always sounded more myth or fairy tale than reality.

But that was before she watched Keane Harper step into the waves, board tucked under one arm, leash tied securely around his ankle. His shorts—decorated with various cartoon birds doing the hula, rode low on his hips, the hem skimming the tops of his knees.

It would be difficult to find a more perfect male body, she told herself, doing her best to keep her thoughts observational. Analytical. Controlled. He moved gracefully, like a dolphin smoothly gliding the water. Something about his mood, his stance, his energy shifted the moment she'd suggested he go ride the waves.

Waves that sounded louder to her now than they ever had before.

And yet he stood there, the waves lapping up around his calves as he stared out at the horizon, as if mesmerized by a sight that he must have seen a million times before.

She moved one of the deck chairs around the table for a better view, set down her own plate filled with leftover mango from the kitchen and joined Noodles as he slurped his way through his breakfast.

"What do you think about this surfing thing, Noodles?" It didn't occur to her that she was talking to a lizard. It seemed, strangely enough, the natural thing to do. It made just as much sense as Marella, on a weekday, sitting on a porch in Hawai'i, watching a man pretending to be her island boyfriend, willingly walk into a wall of water.

Noodles peeked up at her, then over at Keane. In her island-foggy mind, Marella was convinced the lizard shrugged before he went back to his feast. Movement out of the corner of her eye had her looking down. A smaller, more delicate lizard had stopped right at Marella's feet as if to say, *Who are you and what are you doing with my man?*

"You must be Zilla." Marella bent down, but didn't reach out a hand. She merely softened her voice and smiled. "You are so pretty. Look at all that blue on your nose. You just glow."

Zilla took a few steps back, looked at Marella, then scampered up and around the porch post before dashing across the table.

She stopped, eyeing the small plate that still had mango. "He made that for you." Marella nodded. "It's okay. Go ahead."

The joy she felt watching this tiny creature begin to nibble at the food left for her had Marella fighting to catch her breath. She sat up slowly, fanning her face to rid the tears blurring her eyes. Her breath caught again when Keane placed his board on top of the waves, stretched out on it and began to paddle.

"Well, there he goes."

Transfixed, she sat in her chair. His arms moved so fluidly, in strong, smooth strokes. He bounced up and down, over the waves, again and again, until he was so far gone she was afraid she'd lose sight of him.

Farther down the beach, she could see other surfers and swimmers jumping and all but dancing in the tide, so completely unafraid and free of this majestic force that, in all honesty, terrified her.

But Keane... Keane held a power of his own, a command she could feel pulsing back to her on the beach. He turned and twisted, lying prone on the board, just as the water rose behind him.

She covered her mouth, eyes wide as he pivoted, leaped onto the board, feet planted. The higher the wave grew, the more easily he seemed to skim its surface. Arms stretched out to his sides, he all but flew to the shore, as the curling, frothy curve of the wave chased him.

There was an instant, just before the wave broke, that she lost sight of him. But then there he was, exploding out of the crescent, his legs bending as the board weaved up and down, until he skidded across the once-again-calm waters. She heard him whoop and holler as he dropped down and straddled the board, waved his arms at her as if she hadn't been watching him the entire time.

She waved back; the tears she'd attempted to keep at bay were there full force. His laughter carried on the ocean wind to where she sat, calmer now, before he turned his board toward the rolling waves and began again.

Never in her life had she seen such a sight or encountered a man like Keane. So self-assured. So certain in who he was that it resonated even through the elements, like the wind, the light and, definitely, the ocean.

All thoughts of time, schedules and the emails she'd been mentally counting up since she'd first opened her eyes this morning… they all vanished as she sat there.

And watched him ride his waves.

CHAPTER NINE

"WHY DO THESE lessons have to be so early?" It wasn't the first time Crystal Benoit had asked the question. It wasn't even the second. For the third morning in a row, Keane shook his head and crouched in front of where she was lying flat out on her borrowed board. "It's not even 7:00 a.m. Only Marella is up at this hour."

Keane had images of the young woman as a little girl, kicking and pouting until she got her way. As if the sun and surf were her domain.

"We are early because I don't want you, our guests, crashing into other surfers on the water. And because the waves are more manageable in the morning." He tapped his knuckles on her board. "Come on. Time to get back in. You still have twenty minutes to go."

He looked out to where her fiancé, Chad,

brothers, Lance and Tag, and groomsman Beck were wobbling and struggling on their boards. Keane stood up, excitement and pride swelling as Tag swooped low, stayed on his feet and coasted almost effortlessly to the shore.

"Now that was awesome," Keane yelled and pointed at Tag, who beamed in response. "You going to let your brother show you up, Crystal?"

That seemed to do the trick. She shoved herself up, shimmied a bit in her wet suit— she'd been irritated she couldn't surf in her meticulously chosen bikini—and picked up her board before she stomped toward the waves.

"I did good, right?" Tag called out as he ran over to Keane. "That was incredible, man!" He bent over, shook his head to get rid of the excess water. "I can't believe you chose swimming over surfing. This is such a rush."

"Swimming afforded me educational opportunities," Keane said with barely a twinge of bitterness. "No one offered me a surfing scholarship. Swimming got me my degree. And my job."

"And almost a trip to the Olympics." Tag and Keane watched the others maneuver their way around the morning tide. "I might have googled you. Must have been rough when you missed the cut."

"It wasn't great." Missing out on being part of the US Olympic team a little over ten years ago was something he never thought he'd get over, but then his alma mater offered him a job as their head swim coach. It took most of the sting and disappointment away and left him feeling as if he was bringing along the next generation of aquatic athletes. At least for a time. "Your dad told me you swam competitively for a while. You went up against my guys?"

"Once or twice." Tag grimaced.

"You ever rank?"

"Nah." Tag shrugged. "Swimming was more of an outlet for me sports-wise, rather than a career choice. I'm lacking the Benoit drive. Just ask my dad. Or Lance." He paused, as if he'd said too much. "They have no trouble reminding me I'm often at sea. Directionless."

A familiarity rang loud to Keane's ear. How many times had he heard those words growing up? Although he couldn't imagine the ones Tag heard had been spoken with the harsh disparagement Keane had to listen to. "What about Marella?"

"Marella's different. Always has been. She's driven, for sure, but she's never judged or criticized me. Her observations are more, I don't know. Tactical." His lips twitched. "She always thinks before she speaks. Or acts. You've been spending an awful lot of time with her the past few days. You must have a pretty good idea as to the kind of woman she is."

Keane had more than an idea. Marella Benoit, in her determination to prove to her father she could indeed find ways to have fun, had not only surprised Keane by being surprisingly athletic when it came to their rain forest hike a few days ago, but also, she'd become incredibly adept at avoiding any attempt he made at getting her to the beach.

He couldn't predict what she was going to agree to next. She'd filled every single day that followed with laughter and adventure she hadn't known she was capable of having. The deluxe three-and-a-half-hour ATV tour that had them exploring the southern parts of the Big Island left him holding on for dear life as her driving proved she was most definitely from New York City. He'd caught a glimpse of Armand Benoit, who'd been in a different vehicle with his son Lance, staring disbelievingly as Keane and Marella had zoomed right past them, Marella yelling in triumph.

Zip-lining? The nine-line course Sydney had chosen for the group had proved entertaining. Not only because Crystal had gotten some impressive footage for her latest YouTube channel update, but Marella had accepted her brothers' challenge to attempt it in the first place.

Keane hadn't been convinced it was the right choice for her.

At least three of those lines went directly over water and near as he could tell she was still in serious avoidance mode about the waves. Clearly, sibling rivalry loomed somewhat large in the Benoit house. Although, before leaving the platform she'd looked back to where Keane was setting up and asked him to give her a shove. "Before I lose my nerve," she'd clarified.

He'd done as she'd asked, but indulged himself with a quick kiss that took her by surprise and made him feel a bit better about her launch off the platform. She didn't start screaming until she reached the first stop.

This morning had Marella's father and stepmother along with Orla Harrington, the groom's mother, on a sunrise helicopter tour of the island. Marella had yet to be convinced to climb aboard and was in fact the only one of the wedding party not to have participated.

"You have a great family, Tag," Keane told the younger man. "You are very lucky to have each other."

Tag nodded. "Mom hit the jackpot with my dad. Armand," he corrected quickly. "I was only three when he and my mom got married, so he's always been Dad to me. Never a step-anything, Marella, either."

Keane didn't respond. He had noticed Marella always referred to her siblings as steps.

"He's never treated me as anything but his own. I mean, I know I've disappointed him, but he's always loved me. Always had my back even when he disapproved or didn't understand. That's not something a lot of kids can say in that situation."

"It's not something a lot of kids have period. I didn't," Keane admitted. "With my dad. Sometimes I think everything I did when I was younger, all the training, all the tournaments...it was only so I could finally hear one thing."

"And did you?"

"No." Keane shook his head. "I didn't."

"We never stop trying to win our parents' approval, do we?"

"Or their respect." Or at the very least their good will. "Hey, I'm thirty-three and there are still days..." What good did it do to voice wishes that could never come true? "Chad seems like a great fit for your family. He looks totally in love with Crystal."

"He's been mooning over her since the first time they met. I brought him home for Christmas break and that was it for him," Tag said. "It's funny though. I think this whole wedding thing knocked him for a loop. He wasn't even thinking marriage yet. Lance and I tease him that Crystal had just run out of excuses for another party. A wedding was all that was left."

"She does strike me as the kind of person who gets what she wants."

"My sisters do not take no for an answer," Tag agreed. "Oh, man." He gasped as Crystal wiped out spectacularly. "That had to hurt."

"I bet it did." Keane was already sprinting into the water as Crystal surfaced. She yanked her leash back, grabbed hold of the board and smacked her free hand down hard on it.

"You okay?" Keane called out and waded to her.

"I'm fine." She continued to spit out water. Her blond hair was plastered to her scalp. He was impressed that there wasn't a trace of fear in her eyes, but rather irritation. And determination. "It's my pride that hurts."

"If you need a break—"

"No. It's just I'm a little distracted… Brita and I had this big argument last night and it's circling in my brain. I'll get it together. I'm not stopping until I slide into shore."

"Okay, go for it." Keane backed up. It would take her a long time to get to that point, but he didn't have anything else planned. It was a free day, until sunset, when he had a secret plan where Marella was concerned. "Come in when you're ready. Be sure to plant that back foot," he reminded her. "That's how you steer, remember. You lock that in place, you'll find your balance. Crystal?"

"Yeah?" she grumbled, hugging her board against her chest.

"You've got this. You can do it." He gentled his tone. "I have faith in you."

"Yeah?" Crystal brightened. "Thanks, Keane." Her eyes narrowed as she looked over his shoulder. "Is that Pippy?"

Keane turned, but it wasn't Pippy who caught his attention. Well, not all of his attention. It was Marella, standing beside her grandmother, holding Pippy's arm as she shuffled through the sand.

Keane's first instinct was to go and meet them, but he stayed where he was, with Marella's sister, waiting and watching to see just how close Marella would get to the water.

"Good morning!" he called when the two of them reached the damp sand. There hadn't yet been a time when the sight of Pippy Benoit didn't bring a smile to his face. Today's outfit consisted of a bright orange bikini and a matching goldfish-patterned cover-up. Her thick-soled orthopedic sandals were already covered in sand and those wide sunglasses on her face made her look like a caricature of herself.

Marella, on the other hand, looked more than a tiny bit perturbed at her current close location to the ocean.

"You coming in for a dip, Pippy?" he asked.

"Not if I have to wear a getup like that," Pippy said and pointed at his knee-to-neck black wet suit. "I don't think it's humanly possible for me to squeeze into rubber."

"It's neoprene," Marella corrected. "I don't know why I know that."

"This is a nice surprise." Now Keane did leave Crystal with her board and pressed through the water. "Didn't think I'd ever get you this close to the ocean."

"*You* didn't," Marella said cautiously. "This one tricked me."

"Pippy tricked you?" The disbelief in his voice had everyone except Marella laughing. "How'd she manage that?"

"She told me she had a date."

"I do have a date," Pippy announced with pride. "He's just not here yet."

Marella shook her head, telling Keane she wasn't buying it.

"Pippy found herself a boyfriend too?" Crystal plowed her board into the sand beside Keane as Tag joined them as well. "Must be a chain reaction of serious island romance going on around here." She nudged Keane in a very sisterly way. "You're wearing a suit," she accused Marella and pointed at her. "Come on in then."

"I was going to the pool," Marella said. "I was intercepted."

"You're here now." Keane stepped forward, held out his hand. "The water's just about perfect."

"When is the water not perfect for you?" The hesitancy remained in Marella's gaze, but for the first time he thought he saw a crack in her reticence. A crack too large to ignore.

"Give it a try," he urged. "I won't let you go. Promise. You'll be safe."

"I don't want to interfere with their surfing lessons," Marella said.

"We were done ages ago," Crystal piped up without hesitation. "Hey, Pip. You want to take a ride? Don't worry," she said to

Marella, who's jaw had dropped open. "I'm not going to send her out to ride the waves."

"She could," Pippy stated. "But I don't think I'd last long." The old woman caught her lip between her teeth, eyes assessing. "Would be nice to be in the waves again. My father used to take us to Coney Island every summer. I'd spend hours in the ocean. I miss it."

"Well, come on, Tag." Crystal pointed to their grandmother. "Help us out here, will you?"

"You got it. Come on, Pippy. I'll take your shoes and stuff and go leave them with ours."

Keane stepped away from the group and stood beside Marella, who looked far from convinced that this was a good idea. He slipped his hand into hers, held on tight and kept her in place when she looked ready to intervene.

"She'll be fine, Marella," he murmured. "She's happy and so are Crystal and Tag. Let them enjoy this moment." Because she still felt tense in his grasp, he released her hand and wrapped an arm around her shoulders, hugged her against him. "It's a memory none of them will forget."

"You always know how to win an argument, don't you?" Marella said quietly. He wondered if she realized how effortlessly she slipped her arm around his waist and held him close. He'd be lying if he said he hadn't noticed how comfortable they'd become with one another, how easily she touched him, held his hand. Cuddled against him. Every time she did, it felt like he'd broken through another emotional barrier, even if he reminded himself how long they had together. And time was running out fast.

"Just be careful," she whispered as if her family could hear her. "Oh, my goodness." She covered her mouth, but the laugh still escaped as Crystal held the board and Tag sort of scooped Pippy onto it.

Water splashed up and over them as the small waves lapped the shore. The board bobbed and dipped, but the smile on Pippy's face was an expression that, while Marella appeared a bit mesmerized by, Keane didn't think he'd ever forget. Memories of his own with Marella's family. What an unexpected gift.

"She's playing matchmaker between us, you know," Marella told him. "Making up stories about having a date. She knew I'd come with her, wherever she'd end up, even the water. I wouldn't want her wandering down here by herself."

"I don't think she would have been alone," Keane said. "Your dad and stepmom are right back there." He inclined his head to a small rocky area at the top of the beach. "Their helicopter tour must be over." And, Keane noted, Armand Benoit had his cell phone out and was recording Pippy's aquatic adventure. "What do you say?" He gave Marella a quick squeeze. "Want to give them a surprise show?"

Marella rolled her eyes. "You really aren't going to let this go until I put my foot in the water."

"I'm really not." It was perhaps his main goal, making sure she experienced everything these islands had to offer. Chances were she was going to fly away from Hawai'i and never look back, let alone come back. "Just think, you do this today, I may leave you alone when it's time for other water activities."

"I'm not signed up for other water activities," she reminded him even as she kicked off her sandals.

Yeah, that's what she thought. But he let her go and scooped up her shoes before she changed her mind.

With a heavy sigh, she pulled her baggy Hang Loose tank top over her head and shimmied out of her shorts. "What?" she asked him.

"What *what*?" The roaring in Keane's ears had little to do with the ocean and far more to do with the stunning emerald bikini Marella was wearing. Her suit was simple, practical, with the teasing hint of sensuality that set off curves that, up until now, he'd only suspected she possessed. "Oh, sorry." He blinked himself out of the fantasy. "I was, uh. trying to think of the best way to introduce you to the waves."

"We were introduced a long time ago." With a sour look at him, she took her shoes back and walked them over to the growing pile of belongings. "We just didn't get along. I do know how to swim, remember?"

"I know. It's more of a trust issue for you, which as I said means you're smart about the water." Focus, he told himself. Focus on her. Not on…*her*. This time when he took her hand, he wasn't about to let go until she told him to. He led her beyond where Lance and Beck were still having a wipeout competition, but he could feel eyes on himself and Marella.

Her steps beside him were short and hurried, as if she was struggling to keep up with him. But he felt her pulling back on his arm, as if she might stop his approach to the sea.

"Like dogs, the ocean can sense fear."

"No, it can't," she countered. "Can it?"

"I have an idea." He turned his back to the waves, something he rarely, if ever, did. But he wanted her to see him standing in front of that which scared her. He wanted her to see that he would be there for her, helping, guiding, protecting if need be.

"Listen to the waves, Marella." He gentled his voice. "There's a rhythm to them. They're your guide if you let it happen. They tell you everything you need to know about the world they come from."

"You're trying to hypnotize me," she accused, but she swayed a bit, squeezed her toes into the sand to keep from tipping into him. "I think it might be working."

"Good." He captured her other hand, lifted both toward his chest and took a step back. "There you go." Her feet moved toward him, her toes brushing against the gentle tide that swept over their feet. Another few steps and the waves reached her calves.

Her hands tightened and she pulled back, lifted her gaze to his. "I guess it's not so bad."

"I'll take that as a rave review. It's all good. Let's go farther."

She shook her head. "I'm fine here." The back tide tugged at them.

"Okay." He wasn't going to push it. She was already farther in than he'd expected her to go. It made him wonder what enticement might work to get her to take those final few steps.

"What's that look?" She narrowed her eyes. "You're thinking."

"I'm always thinking."

"How well I've learned that the last few days." Her brow arched and she smirked. "You're thinking about kissing me."

He seemed to smile automatically when it came to her. "Maybe. It is my turn, isn't it? When it comes to a kiss on the beach."

"Huh, if you're going to put it like that…"

He bent his head, his senses filling with this special woman who was utterly and completely unexpected. A woman who, if he wasn't very, very careful, could make him break every promise he'd made to himself.

"Thinking yourself out of it?" she asked, her breath warm against his face when she spoke.

"I just realized I've never felt time pass so quickly before."

"I know." One of her hands released his and she touched her fingertips to his cheek. "I've been trying to wish time would slow down."

"It's not going to," he told her. "After Saturday, all the fantasy and the make-believe of this place is going to go away. You'll return to your life in New York. You'll jump into those new challenges of taking over your family's business, and I'll be doing surf lessons in the morning and figuring out what the rest of my life looks like."

"Sounds like we both have a lot of work in the future." She rose up on her toes. "But the future isn't now. This is."

"I thought it was my turn," he murmured when she brushed her mouth against his.

"It was." She kissed him, a gentle press of her lips before she smiled again. "You took too long."

He slipped his hands down her sides, reveling in the feeling of her bare skin against his fingers. When he did capture her lips, when he did kiss her, he had to brace his feet to stop from tumbling into the waves.

Something inside him shifted, as if the earth had moved. She tasted like everything he'd ever wanted: hope, happiness and the promise of an endless summer. He did his best to keep them standing, but it was no use. He could feel the water battering against his hips, his back. But he didn't release her mouth. Didn't stop kissing her for fear that it could very well be the only time he surrendered himself to someone.

They only broke apart when the water crashed over their heads. He tightened his hold on her hips and kept her close. "The ocean takes what it wants," he murmured. "Are you okay?" He let the waves carry them and her eyes went wide.

Marella had a death grip on his shoulders. "Yeah." She managed a shaky nod, after which a small, nervous laugh emerged. "I'm okay."

Deeper into the waves, there was an unusual calm about the water. They bobbed up and down, Marella's body relaxing with every bit of movement.

"Don't let go." She looked over his shoulder. "There's a big w—"

"Marella." Her name sounded like the most beautiful word on his lips. "I've got you."

The wave came and tumbled them together, arms and legs tangling as they spun around. They both went under, but only for a moment before he swam up to the surface, bringing her with him.

She came up sputtering, shoving her long dark hair out of her eyes. He expected fear or anger that he had pulled her so far beyond the shore, but that wasn't what he saw. He saw...wonder. And joy.

But not at the ocean that surrounded them. It was all for him.

MARELLA COULDN'T BELIEVE she was laughing as they stumbled their way back to the beach. Her lungs burned. Her skin instantly cooled even with the sun beginning to beat down.

There was an odd tightness to her body, as the salt started to evaporate. She felt… She wasn't entirely sure what she felt. Exhilarated. And also reborn.

Weeks before, when Crystal's wedding destination had been planned, Marella had only one rule: she wasn't going near the ocean. Now she hadn't only gone near it multiple times; as of this morning, she'd been fully submerged in its riotous depths. And she'd done it without barely a moment's hesitation.

She'd done it because of Keane.

"So next up, surfing lessons, yeah?" Keane teased as they left the water behind.

"Don't get ahead of yourself, beach boy." Marella shook and sent droplets of water against his chest. "One tumble in the ocean does not a surfer make."

"Let's go get you a towel." He slipped an arm around her waist again, but before they started to walk, she felt his lips press against her temple. "Thank you. For trusting me. And for taking a step into my world."

She smiled. Truth be told, she felt as if she was the one who should be thanking him, but she couldn't very well do that without admitting she was wrong. And they hadn't become so involved she was willing to do that. At least, not yet.

"I didn't realize we'd come out so far." She could see the edge of the beach where she'd walked down with Pippy, and the Hibiscus Bay Resort in the distance, but she couldn't spot her family.

There was something off. Something different. Was it the quiet walk down the beach, looking at the people setting up for the day, munching on breakfasts from Hut-Hut or her new morning staple, Kona coffee from Vibe? Children were squealing and racing around, kicking up sand as they ran to and from the water. A pair of toddlers filled sand buckets and dumped them over each other's heads. One screamed while the other went back to scooping, and their parents scrambled off a blanket to offer aid and comfort and serve up a warning.

This entire week was feeling as if she'd stepped into another world. Everything seemed different. Brighter. Happier. She felt different.

She stopped walking and looked at Keane. "Do not tell my father this, but he was right."

"About?"

She wondered if he had any idea the image he presented, that beautiful, beach-boy face of his that looked as if he hadn't ever had a care in the world. Maybe it was the ocean's effects. Or maybe he was just that good at keeping himself to himself. Whatever it was, she could not believe this kind, handsome, funny man had strayed into her path at just the right time.

"About everything, I imagine," she said. "But about me needing to take some time and, I don't know, find myself? I feel like I've had this recharge that makes me even more capable of doing what I need to do once I'm back home." Home. At the moment she couldn't imagine returning to the nonstop hustle and bustle of New York. She didn't want to imagine it. Especially now. "But I'm not there yet." She tightened her hold on him. "You have plans for the rest of the day?"

"Not really, no."

"Not really?"

"Well, I was hoping my fake girlfriend might make me an offer as to how I can spend my time, but… Ah. There it is. My favorite sound in the world."

"What's that?"

"You, laughing." He seemed to surprise himself with the comment and he glanced away.

"I do have a date tonight. With Pippy," Marella told him. "She wants to go to Hula Chicken for dinner. You're welcome to join us."

"Dinner at my favorite restaurant with two of my favorite women?" He lifted her hand and pressed his lips to it. "Sounds like the perfect evening to me."

CHAPTER TEN

KEANE HAD JUST stepped out of the shower and tugged a clean turquoise shirt over his head when someone knocked on the cottage door. For once he glanced at the time. "Yeah! Come on in!"

After he and Marella spent the day exploring just about every inch of Nalani, he'd dropped her at the hotel with the promise of picking her and Pippy up for their dinner at Hula Chicken, but she'd countered—she was getting good at that—and offered to meet him at the shave-ice shop.

He put the rest of his clothes on, shoved his feet into his walking sandals and headed out. He wasn't sure who he expected to see pulling open the screen door, but it wasn't Theo Fairfax. "Theo. What's up? You missing the place already?"

"No, actually." Theo glanced at the sandy beach and grimaced.

Keane shook his head. Theo and Marella would have a lot to bond over should they meet. The aversion some mainlanders had to the ocean truly confused him.

"You left the office as your phone number." Theo handed him a folded-up piece of paper. "Tehani took a message for you from Cleaver University. She thought you might want it right away."

"Thanks." Keane tossed the note onto the kitchen table. "I was just about to leave. I'm meeting Marella at Seas & Breeze. I think she's gotten addicted to the *lilikoi* and guava...what?"

"You aren't going to read it?" Theo stared at the paper.

"Did you?" Keane asked.

"Well—"

"You can tell me." He refused to let the knots tightening in his stomach ruin his positive mood. "It is what it is. If I'm out of a job, great. If I'm not—"

"You're not." Theo shoved his hands into the pockets of his baggy shorts. "Out of a job. The board of directors of the college voted eight to one in favor of your reinstatement. They want you back for the fall semester."

"All but *one* of them does," Keane's attempt at humor didn't land.

"I guess this means you're going back."

"Don't know." Keane busied himself slicing up leftover fresh fruit to put out for Noodles and Zilla, who had taken to expecting their plates to be filled at least twice a day. "Maybe." He loved his students, his swimmers. He loved watching them exceed their own expectations and start to find their place in the world. "Maybe not."

"I think that's why Syd had me deliver the message," Theo told him. "She's afraid of what you're going to decide."

"I'm not going to leave her in the lurch," Keane assured him. "If I decide to go back, I'll make sure she has a list of suitable replacements to take over my duties here."

"I don't think she's interested in a list," Theo said. "I know it doesn't matter what I think—"

"Sure it does." Keane set his knife down and faced Theo, who he considered to be more than a new acquaintance. "You're going to marry one of my best friends."

Theo frowned. "Who told?"

"You did." Keane grinned. "I've caught

you coming out of Sky & Earth Jewelry three times in the past week. You're ring shopping."

"Maybe," Theo hedged. "You changed the subject."

"Did I?"

"I know it might not matter what I think," Theo said, resuming his previous train of thought. "But you belong here. Definitely more than I do."

"Oh, I don't know. You're coming along." Near as Keane could tell, the former California accounting manager had almost earned his first island tan.

"Remy wanted you here," Theo said. "Those emails he sent to you and to Silas and Daphne, he wanted you all to be partners in Ohana Odysseys."

Keane was beginning to understand how Marella felt when he found a way around her defenses. "That's true, I know." That email had been what brought him back to Nalani, although he'd stalled, even after Remy had died. He hadn't wanted to face what the island meant to him without his friend, but in the end, he'd been incapable of resisting what became Remy's final wish. "Syd doesn't need me, Theo. She's doing fine on her own."

"Maybe she doesn't, not for the business," Theo told him. "But you're her family, Keane. You and T. and Mano and Daphne. You are people she loves most in the world and she'd especially love it if you were around full-time. In Nalani. And not just because she lost Remy. Is it the money? Because if it's financial—"

"It's not the money." Keane didn't want anyone to think for one second that money decided any life-altering issue for him. "I'm perfectly okay on that front." More than okay. He'd managed to keep most of what he'd earned in sponsorships from back in the day locked safely in an investment account. "I just need time to think about what I want to do is all."

"Which brings me back to the message." Theo retrieved the paper and handed it to him once again. "The college wants an answer by the end of next week. In case the board has to find your replacement."

"Awesome." All the pressure he'd managed to off-load the past few days suddenly pressed in on him once more. He'd been lucky, he supposed, that he'd been able to keep it at bay for as long as he had. But he was quickly running out of time.

He had to decide his future. Soon.

"Okay." He took the paper, shoved it into his pocket. "I'll talk to Syd in the next couple of days. And I'll take what you said to heart." How could he not? Nalani was the only place that had ever felt like home to him. It should be easy to walk away from his life on the mainland. Why couldn't he cut those ties yet?

Because he'd made a promise. Not only to himself, but to his students. They counted on him. The job wasn't simply a route to stay connected to the sport, but to hopefully make a meaningful contribution to these kids' lives. If he were honest with himself, the last few years had given him far more than his years as a competitive swimmer. Helping his students discover who they were not only in the water, but out of it too, had meant so much to him.

How could he quit that?

The ocean roared around him, beckoning him as it always did with its beauty and power, asking a question of its own.

How could he not?

"How many calories are in a shave ice?" Marella sank her teeth into the now-familiar freezing-cold treat. "Or are they negated by the fact that I've eaten every one of these things standing up. That means the calories go straight to my toes, right? I'm so obsessed with them already, and I really need the sugar bounce after the day we've had."

She glanced over her shoulder at Keane, who followed her out of the now-familiar Seas & Breeze, one of Nalani's long-established locally owned shops. She'd come in here every afternoon and while the last couple of days she'd always chosen the tropical combination of *lilikoi*, otherwise known as passion fruit, and guava, today, thinking she might have gotten a bit too predictable, she opted for coconut and condensed milk. She'd nearly swooned at the first bite. It tasted like frozen coconut cream pie.

"Keane?"

"Yeah. Sorry." He blinked at her as if coming out of a trance. "What was your question?"

"Where's your—" She pointed to his empty hands.

"Right." Shaking his head, he ducked

back inside. When he returned, the yellow of his pineapple ice had Marella thinking about the bridesmaid dress hanging in her room back at the resort. That led to thinking about the wedding, reminding her she'd be going home in a few short days. "Okay. *What the*…?" Marella stopped abruptly, stared wide-eyed at the colorfully painted golf cart whizzing past them, heading along the winding roads up into the hills. "That was Pippy!" She pointed. "Did you see that? That was my grandmother in the passenger seat." She swallowed, trying to make sense of the scene. "Who is that driving? And… was that a pig in the back seat?" She looked to Keane for some answers. "That pig was wearing the same red-and-white-print Hawaiian shirt as the driver."

To Marella's mind, it seemed to be the first time Keane had smiled since they'd met up at the treat shop.

"So that's Pippy's mysterious boyfriend," Keane mused.

"Her…boy…? But who…?"

"That's Benji. And Kahlua, his potbelly pig. You've seen them around, surely."

"Um, I have." Off and on this week. The

last time had been on their way back to the resort when she thought she'd caught sight of a pig—Kahlua—on a miniature surfboard down by the shore.

"Benji's Nalani royalty," Keane told her. "He was town mayor back in the day. He's the one who got the ball rolling on the Hibiscus Bay. I guess this answers the mystery of where Pippy's been disappearing to." He chuckled and bit into his cone. "I think it's cute."

"Sure, yeah, cute." Marella almost glanced at her watch, a habit she'd been trying to break. "What's up in that direction, anyway? Beyond the helicopter pad."

"The older part of town where Benji grew up. There's some nice historical buildings and secluded beaches. They'll probably run into Daphne. She's been working on one of the mayor's pet projects, turning the old elementary school into a community center and garden."

"Up-cycling at its best," Marella commented as they wandered up Pulelehua Road. She'd all but memorized the line of shops, stores and business by now. Unique little places like the handblown-glass store, the sea-inspired candle shop, the florist whose window display changed every morning and offered fresh leis for sale, which definitely added to that small-town welcoming vibe. By the corner near the church, stalls were being assembled for the beginning of the summer market season. According to Keane, it would give the residents a chance to sell their home-made items, everything from crafts to jams and sauces to their own garden produce.

She regretted she wouldn't be around to experience the market herself and not for the first time she thought about how much she was going to miss this place. She quickly glanced at Keane.

"You've been awfully quiet," she told him as she finished her ice and tossed the paper cup into one of the nearby recycle receptacles. "Everything okay?"

"Just have a lot on my mind. Decisions I need to make." He flashed her a smile. "Nothing for you to worry about."

"You know the sounding board thing works both ways, right? I'm happy to listen, if there's something you need to get off your chest." Heaven knew he'd been listening to her enough these past few days. She hadn't realized how much she tended to complain about things that honestly didn't matter. Things that for the life of her she couldn't recall in that moment.

"I appreciate that."

"Keane." She slowed, caught his arm and turned him to face her. A group of students making their way down the hill from school presumably, bustled past them and beelined for the beach. Their-shirts and backpacks coming off the closer they got to the water. "What's going on?" she asked.

The frustration she saw on his face didn't concern her as much as the confusion. "You don't want to hear—"

"Yes." She stepped closer. "I do." She noticed the bench was empty near where Maru, the *malasada* queen had her morning stand. It was the perfect Nalani location, a little apart from the traffic and crowds and near enough to the beach so as to hear the comfort of the ocean. "Come on." She guided him over to the bench and sat down beside him. "Spill. What's going on?"

He shrugged. "I just have some decisions to make is all, about going back to work."

"At the college? Why wouldn't you go back?"

He stared down at his cone. "Because I'm not sure I'm doing any good there anymore."

She felt like she was doing a jigsaw puzzle but had only half the pieces. "Okay, I'm going to need more to go on than that. You coach the college swim teams. The mens' teams and the womens'?"

"Sometimes, but mostly the mens'." He leaned over, braced his elbows on his knees. "I pretty much fell into the job after I missed the cut for the Olympic team."

"You tried out for the Olympics?" How had she missed that? Because she hadn't taken the time to ask. She'd been so full of her own issues, her own drama about being forced to take a vacation, she hadn't stopped long enough to learn more about him—her fake boyfriend. She was a terrible fake girlfriend. "That's a big accomplishment. From what I know about it, it takes an awful lot of work to even be in contention."

"It does. Took me years to get there. I can't tell you how many hours I spent in the pool in high school and in college, getting my times good enough to qualify. I think those were the only moments I enjoyed hearing my father yell at me. Telling me to keep going. To swim faster."

"This would be the father who threw you in a lake when you were little?" She couldn't have hidden the disdain in her voice if she'd tried.

"Yeah." His laugh was harsh, a sound that until now, she hadn't heard. A sound she most definitely didn't like. "He was like that with all of us."

"You have siblings." She didn't know why that surprised her. Maybe because this was the first he'd said anything about his family. Or rather, his family on the mainland. "How many?"

"Two brothers." He seemed to have lost interest in his shave ice as he set it on the bench next to him. "Our family isn't close like yours is. I don't think I've seen either of them since our mother's funeral."

"It's never easy to lose your mom." She reached out and took hold of his hand. "Whenever and however it happens makes a lasting impact."

"The last thing she said to me was how much I reminded her of my dad." His smile was tight. "I know she meant it as a compliment…but to us, me and my brothers, he was a bully. Someone who never thought we were good enough. Who pushed us probably because he'd never really done much with his life." He hesitated. "The only thing he ever excelled at was cheating on my mother. I think that's the one thing I can never forgive him for. How much he hurt her."

"Some people aren't meant to be married," Marella murmured.

"Boy, is that the truth. One thing I learned early on. You live up to your commitments. No matter what." He seemed to be looking at nothing in particular. "You keep your word. My grandfather taught me that, out there on those waves. Without that, you have nothing. You are nothing."

"Your grandfather sounds like a good man. You were lucky to have him."

"I was. Everything I've ever done in my life, I've always stuck with it because I made a promise. When I joined the swim team in high school, I promised to do my absolute best. Not just for myself, but for everyone else. I earned the number one ranking in the state, then number three in the country.

I got myself to the Olympic trials on that promise and I planned to keep going. That was the last day my entire family was together. Cheering me on from the stands. I could hear them. And then…" He sat back with a sigh. "And then I blew out my shoulder. Happened just like that." He snapped his fingers. "I swear I heard that snap echo in my head for weeks afterward. The future I'd planned, the future my father had in his sights, was gone."

"I'm so sorry."

"Don't be." He shrugged and gave her a half-smile. "This wasn't meant to be a woe-is-me declaration, Marella. In a lot of ways, it was the best thing that happened to me because it showed me something. That people can't change merely because you want them to. They have to want to change and some people aren't capable of rising to that challenge. When I left the pool that day, after those trials, the first thing my dad said to me was that it had been a waste of six years. I'd failed. Failed myself and failed the family."

"But—"

"I know." He squeezed her hand. "Most days, anyway. It was a freak occurrence,

an injury that could have happened to anyone. But it showed me who my father really
was. An angry, bitter man who was trying
to live out his life through his sons. I was
his chance at success, the success he'd never
been able to achieve. And then I'd failed
him as well."

"I don't know what to say to that."

"Neither did I. That was the last time I
saw or spoke to him. He passed away suddenly five years later. My mom died a few
months after that. From a broken heart, can
you believe it? Even after all he'd put her
through. And all I can remember her saying is that of all his boys I was the most like
him."

It took Marella a second to clear the rush
of anger for a woman she'd never met. Love
was such a precious gift, one that was meant
to lift and encourage, not drag down and be-
rate or use as a weapon. "You think she was
talking about the man you knew. She wasn't,
Keane." Marella moved closer, lifted a hand
to stroke his hair from his face. "Given what
you've said, I think she saw in you the man
she fell in love with. The man she wanted
your father to always be. I think she saw

what must have been his good qualities in you."

"I didn't realize they sold rose-colored glasses in the resort gift shop."

"You know me better than that by now. And I know you." Impulse pushed the words out, not only because he needed to hear them, but because she needed to say them. "You are without a doubt the kindest, funniest, most gentle man I've ever met. You lead with your heart, Keane, that's special. Unique. Wonderful, in fact. Everything you do proves that. How else do you explain letting me kiss you on the beach that day?"

"Like most guys would reject a beautiful woman kissing them out of the blue."

For once his self-deprecating humor didn't land. But it did explain so much about him. "You've devoted most of your time this past week to making my family believe we're a couple." Not that it had been difficult to convince anyone. Keane, whether he wanted to believe it or not, was family material. He... fit. "Spending hours, days with my mom and dad, and everyone, couldn't have been easy."

"You really think so, after hearing about mine?"

Her heart cracked, for the little boy who had so much love to give yet he'd had few people to give it to. "Your first instinct wasn't to leave me to cope with my severe-lack-of-fun genes. It was to help me activate them." She rested her head on his shoulder. "You crewed the *Nani* because they knew they could rely on you. You came back to Nalani because Sydney could use your help and because Remy asked it of you. While I will agree it is sad your father couldn't stay who he was when your mother married him, I will happily say, that despite the odds against you, you turned out to be an incredible, admirable man."

"Careful." Besides the return of that playful spark in his eye, as he looked at her, she saw something she hadn't ever seen before in Keane Harper. She saw fear. "Don't go falling in love with your fake island boyfriend."

Too late. She caught the words before they slipped out. But that didn't stop the breath from halting in her chest. Or her heart from hammering so hard against her ribs she could feel it stutter. He'd proved her lifelong theory wrong. First about passion and now about love. Love she'd convinced herself she wasn't destined for or wasn't capable of feeling.

"Well." She cleared her throat. "Aren't you completely full of yourself," she teased instead, although a little piece of her heart broke. "So, what's this big decision you're torturing yourself over."

"I guess after unloading on you about my family there's really no point in not telling you. The school called. They want me back next semester."

"That's good news, isn't it?" She wrapped her arms around his and cuddled closer. "Why wouldn't the college bigwigs want you?"

He didn't hesitate. "Because earlier this year one of my kids tested positive for drugs and I had absolutely no clue what was going on. None. At all."

She wanted nothing more than to help him get through this, past whatever doubts he was feeling. She looked at him, stared hard into his eyes. "Tell me."

"Timothy Brice. Nineteen. Kid had so much talent. Way more than I ever did. And he had this intense passion for the sport." Keane's fists clenched. "He just kept winning and winning and I'm telling you, he would have made it right to that top podium at the next Olympic games. That's…all I saw. What he could be. Not what he was."

"And what was he?"

"A scared kid with the weight of the world on his shoulders. He'd earned a great scholarship and made his way up the rankings. Marella, you wouldn't believe what this kid was capable of in the water. He was a natural. And he was always pushing himself to do better. That he could be better. And yet, he didn't think he was living up to anyone's standards, and for a release, or a chance to switch off, he turned to drugs. I suppose it was an escape from the pressure. From all the pressures. One night at a party he accidentally took too much and almost OD'd."

"Oh, Keane." She could feel his pain, saw it in how he kept clenching his fists. "I'm so sorry. Is he all right?"

"Yeah." Keane nodded but seemed a bit shaky. "He's doing okay. Put his studies on hold and the competitive swimming too, of course. He's got a good doctor and his parents are real supportive. I only wished I'd seen what he was doing to himself." He shook his head. "Especially since I was once where he was. Having to worry about school, relationships, competing."

"Well, that's good he's okay."

Keane let out a bitter laugh. "I missed it, Marella. I missed it completely. What kind of coach does that make me? I'm not sure I'll ever forgive myself."

"Keane—"

"The school was right to suspend me. I let them down. I let everyone down. If I go back, what if it happens again? How do I make sure I see it next time? Or…was it that I didn't care enough to look for it?"

"That's not true, Keane, obviously you do care because you've been thinking about it ever since. But you were only a small part of that young man's very big life. How many kids are on your teams? Two dozen? More? They're all okay, aren't they? No other problems like this?"

He took her hand. "No. We've made special counseling available to anyone who's feeling too much pressure and isn't sure how to handle it. The kids are open to it."

"I bet you are the kind of coach the students can come to. If they did have a problem."

He shrugged as if it didn't matter. "My door is always open. Over the years, several swimmers have confided things and we've worked those out. I just… I can't help but think that something I said, or something I did, made Timothy think drugs were his only solution."

"Keane, you aren't all-knowing and all-powerful, despite what I've seen you do on a surfboard. At some point you're just going to have to forgive yourself for not being perfect." It was the truth but she poked him nonetheless, trying to lighten the mood.

"Easy for you to say. From what I've seen you're about as perfect as they come."

"You can't be serious." She let go of his arm and scooted away. "Have you been paying attention during the last few days? The first time you saw me I was verbally lambasting my ex-boyfriend, then I had to be negotiated by my father into learning how to have a life. Would you like to know when I last slept through the night without waking up in a blind panic, looking for my phone or laptop? What? What are you laughing at?"

"*You.* You're right. You are a bit of a mess but still…you're pretty great." He slid closer to her and slipped his hand in hers again. "And I still see the perfect woman." He kissed her. Maybe because he needed to. Maybe because he realized she wanted him to. But when he did, she clung to him, not wanting the moment to end. Wanting instead to create a memory for herself that she could carry with her back to New York. Back to her real life.

"You don't have to decide right now about returning to the college," she murmured, once he'd pulled away. "And you don't have to worry if you do decide to go back. What happened with Timothy changed you. It had to have. But you'll make more adjustments where necessary and avoid repeating any mistakes you might have made. It's called life, Keane. Or, maybe you don't go back because you've found where you belong after all. You'll know it when you see it—the right thing to do. Because you know to be open to it when it happens."

"I never want to be a disappointment to anyone ever again."

"Believe me when I say this, Keane Harper." She caught his face between her palms, stared so deeply into his eyes she could see her own reflection. "That simply is not possible. If you believe nothing else I say for the rest of our time together, believe that. Because I do. With my whole heart."

CHAPTER ELEVEN

"MAYBE WE SHOULD go look for her?" Marella stood on her tiptoes and stretched her neck, looking down Pulelehua Road.

"You said dinner at Hula Chicken was Pippy's idea, right?" Keane wasn't about to admit Pippy's tardiness had him a bit concerned. It wasn't that he didn't trust Benji, but his golf cart was known for running out of power. The older man had a tendency to forget to plug it in at night. "We'll give her another ten minutes before we raise the alarm."

"Okay." Marella nodded and stopped pacing. "Yeah, that's good."

Typical, Keane thought. As soon as she had a plan, any plan, she relaxed. Routine and schedules reassured her. One of the many differences between them. Differences he needed to focus on if he was going to stop himself from falling completely in love with her because as things stood now...

He turned away from her, took a deep breath and let it out. As things stood now, he was beginning to have a very difficult time imagining even an hour in Nalani without her.

Now Keane was the one pacing. His heart-to-heart conversation with Marella had been surprisingly eye-opening. Her comments and advice had made him realize that where his job as a coach was concerned, he'd neglected to do the one thing he'd done with everything else in his life: listen to what his gut told him. Probably because everything surrounding Timothy Brice had left his gut twisted in a tangled mess of knots. Ones that only now were beginning to loosen. Maybe it was time for him to stop blaming himself. Timothy's drug use had been a secret, one his closest friends hadn't known about.

Keane knew his suspension had more to do with appearances than anything else, but still, one of the college's top athletes had gotten into trouble on his watch. That was something he wouldn't forget, nor was the flawed drive for success that some colleges and programs encouraged in their student athletes. He should be thinking about making the system better, shouldn't he? He shouldn't be considering walking away altogether.

And this, he reminded himself, was why his mind kept spinning.

It was also why he wasn't paying attention to where he was walking. He crashed right into a woman hurrying toward the hotel entrance. "Sorry." Luckily, he caught her before she toppled into a pile of suitcases waiting by the bell desk. "Brita. Hey. Haven't seen you around these past couple of days."

Crystal's wedding planner looked up at him with a deer-in-the-headlights expression. She seemed harried and stressed out. "Hi, uh…" She snapped her fingers. "Keane. Right. You're Keane. You've been hanging around with oh, hey, Marella." Brita smoothed a hand down her mussed hair. "Just heading up to my room to make more calls about the wedding."

"Okay." Marella smiled as she joined them. "No problem. Did the dresses get here?"

"The dresses. Right." Brita glanced behind her as if she was looking for someone. "Yes, they're arriving today. Don't worry. Everything is under control. If you'll excuse me, I'll just be…" She pointed to the doors before she darted off.

"That was weird, right?" Keane asked.

"Very," Marella said slowly, her curiosity piqued. "I wonder if I should talk to—"

They both turned at the sight of a speeding golf cart whizzing around the circular drive, Pippy holding on to her hat with one hand and the side safety bar with the other. "We're here!" Pippy announced, fumbling with the lap belt at her waist. "Late. But we're here. Thanks, Benj. You're a doll."

Keane approached the cart and rested a hand on the top while he helped Pippy climb out. "You two have fun today? Looks like you caught some sun."

"We had an early picnic on the beach," Pippy said, smiling from ear to ear. "Best macaroni salad I've ever had in my life. He's a good cook!"

Benji immediately shot Keane a warning look. "I might have had a little help with the salad."

Keane had no doubt. If it was the best Pippy had ever eaten, chances are it was Sydney who had made it, not Benji. But Sydney did keep Benji in constant supply of the tasty dish, the recipe for which her mother had made famous.

Keane motioned discreetly to Benji that his lips were sealed and earned a grateful smile from the older man. It reminded Keane once more that he hadn't spent much time with him. Benji was walking Nalani history. He'd been around during Pearl Harbor and frequently spoke at the schools about his experiences growing up in the islands, and his connections to the royal bloodlines. "See you tomorrow, Philippa." Benji leaned back when the pig began to whine. "Hang on there, Kahlua. Keane, give her a hand, will you? Bring her up front?"

"Uh, sure." Keane ignored Marella's giggles as he struggled to get his arms around the substantial animal and heft her into the golf cart's front seat.

Kahlua shoved her wet snout in Keane's neck and oinked a thank-you.

"Never would have imagined a pig had a personality," Pippy announced as Benji sped off. "He's teaching that animal to surf. I think it's safe to say I've lived long enough to see it all. You two ready to get your feedbags on?" She looked up at the sun. "'Bout dinnertime, isn't it?"

"If you're ready, we're ready, Pippy." Keane held out his arm. "May I?"

Pippy grinned at him, her large sunglasses taking up most of her face. "Like I'm going to say no to a polite, good-looking escort. Oh, there you are, Army, Gloria." She tugged Keane back as Marella's parents emerged from the hotel. "We're about to go get some chicken. Want to join?"

"Hmm." Armand glanced in the other direction. "We were thinking we might eat at the Blue Moon Grill."

"Well, think different," Pippy ordered. "'Bout time we all got to know Keane a bit better, don't you think? He's practically a member of the family. You coming to the wedding, young man? Marella's without a date, you know."

Marella shot him a look that clearly said "it's not so funny now, is it?"

"Yes, I am aware," Keane said easily. "And to be honest, we haven't discussed it. By the way, if you haven't had Hula Chicken yet, you're missing out," he told Armand and Gloria, who both looked tempted to accept. "Come on. It's not far." Close enough he could smell the outdoor roasting from here.

"Where are Tag and Lance this evening?" Gloria asked.

"They signed up for one of those midnight snorkeling tours," Marella told her stepmother. "They even talked Chad, Crystal and Orla into joining them."

"Chad's mother is going snorkeling?" Gloria seemed both surprised and impressed. "I hope someone takes pictures."

"Crystal's there. Plenty of photos will be taken," Marella reminded them. "She's good at memory making."

She wasn't the only one, Keane thought as he and Pippy led the way into town. Marella was getting pretty good at making memories herself.

"HE'S A LOVELY young man."

"Hmm?" Marella pulled her gaze away from the end of the table where Keane and her father were discussing the myriad number of sports they followed. "Sorry, Gloria." She shook herself and focused her attention. "My mind was wandering."

"I know where it was wandering to," Pippy sang.

"Eat your chicken, Pippy," Marella told her.

"He's a lovely man," Gloria said again, wiping her fingers on a towel after setting her drumstick onto her biodegradable paper plate.

Marella had to admit, she liked the sight of her parents enjoying a casual meal outside, as the sun began to set and the air began to cool. Gloria was on her second mai tai, Pippy her first and her father had knocked his bottle of beer against Keane's in a toast to making new friends.

The table was covered by platters and bowls filled not only with the sweet and tangy *huli-huli* roasted and grilled chicken the islands were known for, but a multitude of delicacies from salmon poke to roasted purple sweet potatoes, steamed rice and a spicier take on the luau stew they'd eaten on the dinner cruise.

Their server was a young woman named Vivi, who was yet another example of the exemplified hospitality of the town of Nalani.

The outdoor seating—the only seating Hula Chicken offered—was filled to capacity, with every picnic table bursting with hungry customers.

"Is there a reason you haven't invited Keane

to the wedding?" Gloria asked. "You've been spending enough time together and we have an opening now that Craig's left."

"Oh, it really hasn't come up." Truth be told, she hadn't brought it up because she didn't want to take the chance he'd say no. Pretending to be her boyfriend for a week was a lot. Asking him to be her date to a big family event? That might be one step too far. "We still have a few days. I'll ask him later tonight. Or tomorrow."

"Don't know what you're so uptight about," Pippy said. "I've already asked Benji to be my date. We're going to get matching shirts, just like him and Kahlua wear."

Marella almost spit out her drink. "Tell me he isn't bringing the pig," she choked on the words as she mopped up.

"I told him he could," Pippy announced. "But he didn't think that was a good idea."

"Smart man," Gloria said and surprised Marella by laughing. "I can only imagine Crystal's reaction if you asked to bring the pig, Pippy."

"I think we'd witness the first human to space launch without a rocket ship," Marella laughed in return.

"Although a pig would add a bit of character to the festivities," Gloria mused. "Your father and I were saying only this morning how rigid Crystal seems to be with all the plans."

"She is?" Marella frowned. "I barely know what's going on. She keeps telling me Brita is handling everything."

"I'm sure it'll be lovely once we're underway but at this point, honestly? I just want it to be over," Gloria said and signaled Vivi for another drink.

Marella rested her chin in her palm, surprised and more than a little entertained at her stepmother's lack of filter. "On that we can definitely agree." Marella lifted her glass to toast Gloria. "Why didn't you ever ask me to call you Mom?" It was a question she'd had for years, one she'd never been particularly brave enough to ask. "I mean, it's okay that you didn't, but—"

"I wanted to." Gloria set her empty glass down and rested her hands in her lap. "I talked to your father about it a number of times. He said when the time was right, I'd know it. I, well, I suppose I was like you asking Keane to go to the wedding with you. I was afraid you'd say no." Her smile was tight and just a little bit sad.

Marella's response caught in her throat.

"Do you remember your thirteenth birthday?" Gloria asked her. "You didn't want a party. You only wanted a cake with the family and a quiet day at home. You've always been a fan of quiet," she added in a way that brought tears to Marella's eyes. "We had a lovely day and that night, after I'd tucked Tag in, I stopped outside your room. You were talking to your mother, telling her everything that had taken place and that you had only wished for one thing. For her to be there with you, celebrating."

"I—" Marella swallowed hard. "I don't remember that. I remember you gave me a beautiful bracelet with my mother's and my birthstones on it. I still have it in my keepsake box."

"That's nice to know." Gloria smiled. "I think that's when I realized that she would always be your mother and that I'd have to be something else. A friend. A guide, perhaps. I might not have earned the right to be your mother, but I hope you don't mind that I consider myself so."

Marella couldn't help but glance back down the table to where Keane sat, laughing and chatting with her father. A father who had never once made her feel anything less than absolutely perfect. She should have realized before now, she'd had a stepmother who had done the same.

"I think," she began, then stopped, held out her hand until Gloria took it. "For a long time, I didn't let myself believe you weren't going anywhere. All of you. Losing my mother, it was the hardest thing I've ever gone through, until Dad had his heart attack. Keeping you, keeping everyone at a distance, it was a way to protect myself, I guess. Now here we are, almost twenty years later, and I'm just now realizing I robbed myself of a second chance." Tears blurred her eyes. "You've been my mother, if not in name, certainly in spirit. And maybe, if you don't think it's too late—"

Gloria let out a soft sob, slipped out of her seat and stood, pulling Marella into her arms. "It would never be too late." Gloria held her close for a long moment, then caught her face in her hands and leaned back to look into her eyes. "What a gift you've been to me. To all of us, Marella." She pressed her forehead against hers. "I love you so much."

Marella blinked the tears free. "I love you too. Mom."

"Hey, how about that." Pippy slapped her hands on the edge of the table and nudged her son with her knobby shoulder. "Took near twenty years for that to happen, but it was worth the wait. I haven't been this choked up since you two got hitched."

She and Gloria sat back down, each wiping the tears from their cheeks. Marella glanced first at her father, who looked at both her and Gloria with such love Marella wondered if her life had ever felt so full.

Then she looked at Keane, who toasted her with his bottle and smiled. A smile that now represented real strength, caring and affection. He'd opened her eyes that first moment on the beach when he'd welcomed her retaliatory kiss as if she were giving him a gift. And yet she was the one reaping the rewards. How could she ever thank him enough for that?

How would anyone ever, ever live up to this man named Keane Harper?

"Well, enough of this sniffling and weeping," Pippy said. "One would think none of you knew all of this love existed before today. But I did. Of course, I did. You're all mine, aren't you? Now, where did that Vivi get to? I'm ready for another drink. And dessert."

"WHERE ARE YOU taking me?"

Keane kept Marella's hand firmly in his—something he planned to do for as long as she would let him—as they headed to the marina. They'd walked her parents and Pippy back to the resort and spent more time talking before they finally said good-night.

The moon was on its way to its zenith, the sun having set a while ago. Marella had pulled on one of her new Nalani sweatshirts and happily agreed to an after-dinner stroll. Little did she know he had something else in mind.

"I want to show you something." He waved at friends as they passed, his pace increasing the closer they got to his planned destination. "There she is."

"There who is?" Marella looked around at the various boats bobbing in the night tide.

"*Kalei*. Happiness," he explained and pointed

to the forty-two-foot catamaran Remy had bought for snorkeling excursions for Ohana Odysseys.

"Yup, it's a boat," Marella laughed. "What else would you be so excited to show me? Wait, where are we…? Keane…" She only resisted for a moment before she sighed and followed him on board. Without him even saying anything, she ducked down and pushed off her shoes, tossed them into the corner of the boat. "All right then. Show her off."

He gave her an abbreviated tour, his pulse kicking up at the thought of taking the vessel out.

"I'm surprised you didn't move in here," she said when he led her up from the lower deck where the one bedroom had been converted into extra storage.

"I considered it," he told her. "But Sydney can make more money from it as a tour offering. Speaking of which. I'm planning to pitch her a midnight star-gazing tour. You ever see the stars from the water?"

"What do you think?" Marella asked. She didn't stumble around as much as she had her first night on Polunu's catamaran. It seemed as if she'd gotten her sea legs with the way she'd braced her feet apart. "I've barely seen them from my apartment window."

"I can take you to see them now," he offered. "Want to help me find the best spot?"

"You want to go out sailing now? At night? Without any—"

"Plan? Yes." He moved in and drew her to him. "I want you to come out on the ocean with me and look at the most beautiful sight the islands have to offer. Well..." His smile stretched. "Second most beautiful. I'm looking at the first."

She rolled her eyes and playfully pushed at his shoulders. "You are what Pippy would call absolutely incorrigible."

"I don't believe for one second she'd call me that," Keane defended himself. "She's crazy about me. In fact, most of your family is crazy about me."

"Yes," she murmured. "I believe they are." She took a deep breath and let it out in a rush. "If we're going to do this, let's get on with it."

"Yeah?" He almost couldn't believe she'd agreed, but he quickly untied the mooring ropes. "Okay, then up we go. This way." He pivoted and guided her ahead of him to the short ladder into the pilothouse. He pulled the keys out of his pocket and earned a raised brow in response.

"You leave your cell phone at home but always carry boat keys? I've really gotten myself into something with you, haven't I?" She sat in the solitary seat as he turned on the lights and inserted the key into the ignition. When he nudged her away, she planted her feet on the deck. "Nope. If I'm going, I want to learn how to drive this thing." She grabbed hold of the steering wheel and acted as if her knuckles hadn't become completely white. "Heave, ho, Captain Keane."

"Yes, ma'am." He switched the engine on and let the comforting sound of the rumbling ease the last of his worries. He stood behind her, leaned over and brought one of her hands over to the throttle. "Just push forward slightly, yes. There." The metal lever moved and the boat followed. "Keep it slow until we clear the harbor." They eased the boat out of the slip and headed into open water.

It never ceased to amaze him how the world completely dropped away and time all but came to a stop when he was on the water. Normally, he'd have been reticent to allow anyone else to steer the *Kalei*, but as they left Nalani behind and headed south, he felt the tension in Marella's body fade.

He flipped a few more switches, dimmed the light in the pilothouse and turned on the masthead light so they could see where they were going and then the stern light, which made them visible from up to two miles away. The ocean may be large and they might feel as if they were alone, but there was no need to ask for surprises.

He waited for her to speak, to ask questions or start a conversation that may very well serve to keep her distracted from her dislike of the water, but she seemed to be as content as he was to continue in silence.

When the lights and noise from Nalani faded into the distance and only the sky reached out to them, he covered her hand once more and eased back on the throttle until the boat came to a complete stop.

"What's wrong?" She looked at him with concern as he flipped the switch to let the anchor drop from the center of the boat.

"Nothing. We're here." He put on the navigation screen and the sidelights before he drew her out of the chair. "Come on." He stopped long enough to pull out a pair of blankets from under one of the padded benches.

On the lower deck, he sat on the bench and braced himself against the bars, held out his hand and pulled her down beside him. "Here you go." He wrapped them both up and snuggled with her. "Comfy?"

"I'm not entirely sure." She pressed her hand against her chest as her tension returned. "The water's awfully close."

"Yes, it is. There's no weather to worry about. I checked before we left the restaurant. We've got a clear night ahead and a beautiful sunrise to anticipate."

"Sunrise?" She shot straight up and stared at him. "We're staying out here all night?"

"You have someplace to be?"

"No, of course not. I just… We're going to sleep on the ocean?"

"You're the one who said she hadn't been sleeping through the night since she got here. How much worse could this be?"

"Good thing I don't sleepwalk. That could get messy." She allowed him to pull her into his arms. "For the record, not my idea of fun."

Not yet, he thought. But it very well could be. "Stop worrying so much, Marella. Look up. Not at me," he said and laughed. "At the sky. At the stars. At the universe."

It was magical witnessing someone else experience the night's star show. Her gasps of wonder, of awe, how she pointed and questioned and eventually fell silent as she shifted against him and brought his arm around her. She rested her head against his shoulder.

"I've never seen anything like it," she whispered. "It's absolutely breathtaking."

He knew the feeling. And it was a feeling he was going to have to acknowledge sooner than later. A feeling he was going to have to dismiss and push aside before he made the enormous mistake of having her permanently in his world. "Can I ask you something, as your fake boyfriend."

"Sure." He ignored her hesitation.

"Are you really expecting me not to come to your sister's wedding? Or rather, do you expect to be one of the only people there without a date?"

"Maybe I was waiting for you to say you wanted to come." Instead of pulling away from him, she tightened her hold on his arms. "Do you?"

"I was on the fence before. Then I heard Pippy had invited Kahlua the pig and…"

"No one has ever made me laugh like you do, Keane. Yes, I'd like you to be my date at the wedding."

"Great."

"You know, I've been thinking."

"What about?" He rested his hand on her hip, tried not to revel in the sensation of having her in his arms. She was absolutely everything he'd told himself he didn't deserve; couldn't have. Shouldn't want. And yet…

"If you did go back to Cleaver University, Ohio isn't that far away from New York. It's maybe a two-hour plane ride." She shrugged. "On the off chance that might be a determining factor."

"It could very well be one now," he admitted. But the idea of going back when he was currently surrounded by absolutely everything he needed right here in Nalani… "I will take that under advisement."

"Spoken like a true educator," she said. "Now be quiet," she ordered. "I want to watch the stars."

She settled against him. He pressed a kiss to the top of her head, squeezed his eyes shut against the pain he'd no doubt feel when he said goodbye. "Marella, just to remind you." None of this was real. None of it was supposed to be real. Except it was. "Marella?"

"Hmm?"

A new wave of affection rolling over him when he saw her eyes were closed and her breathing had slowed.

"Nothing," he murmured and settled in himself. Moments later, gazing up at the stars, he fell asleep.

CHAPTER TWELVE

"This might be the best beginning to the day that I've had yet." Standing beside Maru's Malasada Hut, a makeshift wood-and-bamboo stand behind which Maru, one of Nalani's most well-known residents sat on her elevated rocking chair, Marella sank her teeth into the softest, warmest filled doughnut she'd ever eaten in her life.

She leaned over awkwardly, attempted to catch the thick coconut filling before it plopped onto her sweatshirt and finally shoved a wholly unladylike bite into her mouth. "Ohmmmgd."

Marella laughed at Keane who was making as much of a mess as she was. Around her mouthful of goodness, she managed to say, "I'm never going to want to leave all this food."

"Don't see any reason you have to go anywhere." Maru handed off the cash for their breakfast that Keane had given her to her teenage granddaughter. "Near as I can tell, you fit here." She eyed Keane. "With him."

"You giving up on me already, Maru?" Keane teased. "I thought you were waiting for me to come to my senses and sweep you off your feet."

Marella enjoyed the banter. There was nothing better than watching Keane charm everyone he met, especially when that person was elderly and female. He just had a way with them that erased years off their faces and probably their souls.

"I need to get back to the resort," she reminded Keane. "Tonight's the rehearsal, then the luau for the wedding guests." Making tomorrow the big day. In a little over forty-eight hours, she'd be heading to the airport to fly back to New York and her life there.

How had the week gone so fast? The better question was, how was she ever going to say goodbye to Keane?

"I'll walk you back," Keane said.

"You don't have to."

"Yes, I do. I don't want your family thinking I absconded with you. See you tomorrow, Maru."

"Challenges ahead," Maru called after them. "Fair warnings for rough winds."

"Um, what did she mean by that?" Marella asked him.

"No idea. She's a little like the island psychic. You listen to her, but you never understand what she means until you're on the other side of things. Have you talked to your brothers lately?"

"Lance and Tag? No. Why?" She finished her *malasada* and with her sticky fingers popped open her cross-body purse to pull out her phone. "I haven't turned it on in days. How about that." She laughed. "Go me."

"I don't think you need to call them," Keane told her. "Here they come."

Phone in hand, Marella glanced up. Sure enough, Tag yelled to his brother across the street before he pointed at Marella and Keane. Next thing she knew they were racing toward her. "What's wrong?" she demanded. "Is it Dad? Pippy?"

"No. It's Crystal," Lance panted. "Where have you been? Everyone's out looking for the two of you."

"Was she hurt? What happened?"

"You aren't going to believe it," Tag said.

"Well, maybe you will. I mean it's not a complete surprise—"

"Tag! Information. Now. Please." Marella snapped him to attention.

"Brita's gone."

"Gone. Gone, how gone? Like she's out exploring Nalani—"

"Gone as in she checked out of her room and is already halfway to the mainland by now," Lance said. "She left a thick envelope at the front desk with your name on it and a note for Crystal saying she'd messed up and that she was sorry."

"Sorry for…"

"Everything," Tag said. "The dresses aren't here. The cake was ordered from the wrong bakery and she forgot to confirm with the florist in Kona and they're all out of flowers because it's graduation season."

"What does that mean?" She turned to Keane. "What does that mean?"

"On the islands, graduates wear leis with their caps and gowns. It's tradition. And it wipes out most of the flowers for weeks at a time. Where's Crystal now?" Keane asked.

"Back at the resort hyperventilating into

a paper bag. She needs help, Marella, and we aren't equipped to give it to her."

"Sure. Yeah, of course." She hurried after them. "In case I forget to say it later. Thank you. For last night. For the stars and…everything you've done this past week."

"You're welcome. I'm going to give Syd and Tehani a call. They can meet us at the resort, help put out some fires."

"Guess I'll find out how many there are in a few minutes." They half walked, half ran down Pulelehua Road to the Hibiscus Bay, darting in around cabs and cars depositing wedding guests at the front door. "Ah, geez. They're getting here already. Mr. and Mrs. Filbert. Aloha!" She gave her parents' longtime friends a quick wave. "We'll have signs posted in the lobby for directions to this evening's event."

"I don't have my cell," Keane said. "I'm going to use the phone—"

"Go, yes, please. Thank you. Crystal's in the bridal suite. Fourth floor. And can you grab that envelope that was left for me?"

"Will do. I'll be up soon."

They parted ways and Marella raced into the elevator that her brothers were holding open. "The guests are arriving," she said as the doors closed.

"We saw," Tag muttered. "What a mess."

Marella tapped her foot, willing the elevator to move faster. "I told her she should have Brita coordinate with the event hostess here at the hotel."

"Not sure how much help she's going to be," Lance said. "It was the first thing Gloria asked Mano about two hours ago. The woman only just started last week when the previous one went on early maternity leave. She's on her way in."

"Okay, we'll manage." Somehow. "I'm seriously going to need your guys' help."

"You've got it." Lance reached around Tag and slugged him in the shoulder. "Told you she'd take care of things."

"So much for ending my vacation on a high note." Or with quality time with Keane. Not that she'd expected too much of that with the wedding kicking into high-gear. Still… "Okay, fourth floor. Lance, until you're told differently, I want you keeping an eye on Crystal. She orders anything from room service make sure it's decaf and sugar free, got it?"

"I can do that."

"What about me?" her other brother asked.

"Tag, you're going to be my assistant. Consider it training for your upcoming job at Benoit & Associates, so buckle up."

"There goes my tour of the hotel kitchen," Tag grumbled.

"Your what?" Marella asked.

"After breakfast yesterday, I asked our server if he could get me into the kitchen, see how things operate. Yesterday they couldn't, but today—"

"Be sure you call down and let them know you have an emergency."

"I already did."

The three of them skidded to a halt outside Crystal's room. Even from out in the hallway they could hear her high-pitched voice of disbelief.

"How could she do this to me, Mom? Where's all my money? I gave her cash for everything. How could I have been so stupid?"

"Here we go." Marella took a deep breath and knocked. The second the door flew open and she saw her father's face, she fell into damage control mode. "I know, I was

AWOL. Keane took me out to look at the stars last night. Don't ask. And don't you comment," she ordered Lance who shrugged and looked a little sheepish. She was used to putting out fires at work. That was the mentality she needed to drop into now. Clean, efficient and clear minded.

"Okay, first things first," Marella announced to her family, who immediately went quiet. "We're Benoits and we handle everything that gets thrown our way. Right, Crystal?" She crouched in front of her sister, who was indeed blowing into a paper bag. Chad, looking completely at a loss, shook his head. "Crystal? Hey." She took in her sister's pale face. "Crystal? Everything is going to be okay. You hear me? Everything that's gone wrong can be fixed. Maybe not perfectly, but enough to get you down the aisle. I promise."

Crystal's voice was muffled by the bag to the point that Marella yanked it out of her hands. "What?"

"No dresses," Crystal panted. "No cake. No flowers. No—"

"Stop." Marella held up a hand. "The panic stops right now. You have your groom, you have a venue and you have your family. Everything else is just extra decoration, yeah? Five, ten years from now, this is going to be a story to laugh about." A knock sounded on the door. "That's probably Keane. Chad, where's your sister and Alexis?"

"I told them to hang out at the pool," Chad replied, his dark hair even more stark against the gray pallor of his skin. "I didn't want them in the way."

"See that? Your soon-to-be husband is already making the right decisions." The last thing Marella wanted to have was Alexis under her feet and poor Shawna was easily overwhelmed. This was definitely not the place for them to be right now. She felt some of the stress melt away when Keane walked in and handed her a stuffed manila envelope. "Hey, we need your island expertise."

"You got it. Tehani's on standby at Ohana. She's ready to make whatever calls you need. Daphne and Syd are on their way here now. I asked Mano to put in a call to Ahuahu at Nalani Floral. She's putting together a list of what's doable by tomorrow and we should have it in a few minutes."

Without thinking, without questioning it,

she went up to Keane and kissed him. "I love you so much right now. Thank you." Ignoring the gasps from her family and the rather shocked expression on Keane's handsome face, she tugged him into the kitchenette that kept her within earshot of her sister and ripped open the sealed envelope.

Marella dumped out the stack of papers and breathed a sigh of relief when two stacks of cash also fell onto the counter. "That answers that at least." She set the money aside and attempted to put the documents into some kind of order. When she started shuffling them around for a third time, Keane covered her hands with his.

"Marella, stop. You're just making a mess. Focus."

She laughed, that panicky disbelieving laugh that came with pressure. But his touch had her taking a breath. "You're right, you're right. Let's take this one document at a time." She held up the first on top of the stack. "Wedding venue contract."

"Nothing wrong with the venue agreement as far as we know," Keane confirmed. "Mano's ready to help however he can."

"Okay, great, then I need him to confirm

not only the space for the ceremony, but also for the reception. It's supposed to be in—" she flipped through the pages to the itemized list "—the Sunset Seas room."

Keane grabbed a small notepad off the counter and began writing as she rattled off the details.

"Here's the printed shipping confirmation for the dresses," she mumbled to herself. "One bridal gown, two bridesmaids." She called out for Lance and held the paper out to him when he rushed up beside her. "Track these. See if you can find them."

"On it." Lance pulled out his cell and went over to the conference-room-sized table.

"What about your dress?" Keane asked. "You're the maid of honor, right?"

"I packed mine in my suitcase." She made a mental reminder to herself to press it with the steamer she'd also packed.

"Of course, you did. Here's the flower order. And…" He plucked up a folded piece of paper and opened it. "This would be for you. It's from Brita."

"She left you a note too?" Crystal dive-bombed over to the kitchenette counter. "What does it say?"

"Let me read it and find out." Marella skimmed the note, her stomach dropping to her toes. It was pretty much what she'd expected; what she'd been subtly or maybe not so subtly warning Crystal about for the past few weeks. Brita had taken on way more than she could handle and the mistakes she'd made were impossible to fix. Apologies aside, she'd seen no other choice but to walk away and leave Marella to hopefully remedy the fallout. "Well." Marella blew out a breath. There wasn't anything else to do but plow ahead. "There's good news and bad news." But it was mostly bad. Like ninety percent bad. "The good news is Brita's retired from her proposed event planning career."

Another knock on the door, followed quickly by, "Hi. Mr. and Mrs. Benoit." Sydney's voice brought a much-needed calm. "Keane sent out a wedding SOS. Ohana Odysseys is at your disposal."

"Come in, Sydney, please," Gloria said. "Thank you for getting here so promptly."

"Anything we can do to help," Daphne said as she also joined the group. "What do you need, Marella?"

Ten minutes alone in a room with Brita to chew her out? But Marella kept that to herself. That urge would pass. Eventually. "Not sure yet." But she was formulating a plan of attack. "Okay, everyone, huddle up." She waited until her parents, brothers, the groom and his mother, as well as Sydney and Daphne moved in to listen. "Other than the venue contract with the resort, it looks as if everything was done, well, for want of a better term, wrong. Delivery times and addresses incorrect. Missed payments. Lack of confirmations."

Tears welled up in her sister's eyes.

"But we're going to make things right," Marella quickly added. "It might not be exactly what you hoped for, Crystal, but we're going to do our best, okay? Crystal? Chad? You both good?"

"Whatever Crystal wants." Chad slid his arm around Crystal's waist. "Whatever you can do," he said.

"So, here's where we have to start. Apparently, there was no confirmation made or contract signed with the caterer for tonight's rehearsal dinner or the wedding. Guests are already arriving, so we need to implement a backup plan now."

"Quick question," Tag said. "Is that the good news or the bad?" he asked and got himself an elbow in the chest from his sister. "Ow. Sorry. Just attempting to insert some levity."

"The cake you wanted was from a bakery in Kona," Marella reminded her sister.

"That's not bad," Sydney said. "I can drive there and back in a couple of hours."

"Yeah, no, that won't work since the cake didn't actually get ordered."

Crystal whimpered but covered her mouth at Marella's look.

"Putting that on a separate to-do list," Keane murmured.

She eyed Keane, who started another page. "The chairs for the ceremony won't be delivered until Sunday." She plucked out the invoice with the order information. "We'll need someone to call the company and see if they can deliver those today for setup or if we need to cancel altogether. Can we ask Mano—"

"Give that to me, please." Gloria took the invoice. "The chairs will be here today."

Marella marked that off her worry list. When her stepmother… No. That was wrong. When her mother wanted something done, she got it done.

"What's next," Keane said.

"The minister from Hilo who is supposed to perform the ceremony canceled on Monday. His wife just had twins so he can't fly in from Maui."

"Father Makani's usually available if the church hasn't been booked," Keane said. "Tehani can probably take care of that for us, yeah?" he asked Sydney, who was already pulling out her phone to text a message.

"Awesome." Already Marella could feel things falling into place. It took her until now to realize something was missing from the papers. And her list.

"What's wrong?" Crystal demanded. "What are you looking for?"

Marella hesitated. "Before we all start running around like wild escapees from the zoo, your wedding license. Please tell me you have it?"

"That one was all me," Chad said and nodded. "It's back in my room with Beck and the rings. My best man is keeping it together."

Another burst of tension popped and she actually smiled. "Best future brother-in-law ever. Lance? How are you doing?"

"Still working on tracking down the dresses!"

"Okay, here's the situation. We have thirty-seven guests arriving for the ceremony that is scheduled for eleven tomorrow morning. According to the RSVP list." Something Brita had apparently been maintaining. "Most of them also plan to attend the rehearsal luau on the beach. We need to divide and conquer. Dad, I think maybe you can be our bridal ambassador and head downstairs to welcome everyone to Nalani. Let them know we'll have details about this evening's event later this afternoon."

"You want me to make sure no one knows anything is wrong," Armand clarified. "Consider that done. Keane? How about I take that list you've made for Mano and save you a few steps."

"Works for me." Keane handed over the sheet and her father offered her an encouraging smile before he left the bridal suite.

"The way I see things," Marella said, "it

looks as if the cake and the food for the reception are our biggest concern."

"I have a few ideas on that." Sydney held out her hand. "Is there a menu plan in there somewhere?"

"There is." Marella shuffled through the papers again, then ripped up the document she found. "But I'm tossing it out. We're starting fresh. New ideas. Practical ideas. Compromises must be made, okay, Crystal?"

Her sister smiled. "I guess. Yeah."

Marella smiled back. "Sydney, whatever you think you can make work—"

"I'm already imagining a mix of island fare and familiar mainland items. Best of both worlds. Don't worry, Crystal," Sydney assured the bride. "Between the kitchen here at the resort and Hula Chicken, we'll get things covered."

"I wasn't planning on a hula-ing chicken at my wedding," Crystal murmured, almost dazedly.

"Well, I'll take a dancing chicken any day of the week if we can make this happen. Daphne. Flowers."

"You're talking my language," Daphne all but snapped to attention.

"Can you liaise with…?" Marella looked to Keane. "What was her name again?"

"Ahuahu."

"At Nalani Floral?" Daphne clarified. "Absolutely. You have any suggestions or preferences on that?"

"Yellow," Crystal, Marella and Chad all said at the same time.

"Mano's already been in touch with the floral shop, so maybe just pick up wherever he's left off?" Marella handed her the appropriate scribbled-on sheet.

"Best done in person," Daphne said. "I've got my cell if you forgot to tell me anything."

"Thanks!" Marella called after her as she too left the suite. "What I wouldn't give for a spreadsheet right about now." She snapped her fingers. "Tag!"

"Here!"

She joined in the nervous laughter. "I need a spreadsheet to keep track of everything we're doing and who's taking care of it. Go get my laptop from Mano."

"Right." The door slammed closed once more and only then did she remember something else.

She got out her cell. "Keane, can you text

Syd and Daphne?" She was already sending a text to her father. "Tell them all receipts should come to the resort at my attention. I'll take care of them after the reception and make sure everyone is paid before we leave," she said to the few people still left in the room, after she'd hit Send. "Now. Let's talk cake."

"I THINK YOU need to do more damage control." Keane's voice sounded gently behind her.

"News flash," Marella said without looking up from their scribbled notes. "Already am."

From her self-isolated spot in the corner of the bridal suite, a luxurious hotel room she had yet to fully appreciate, she glanced up from where she was sitting as he set a mug of coffee in front of her. She scowled. "If that's decaf we're going to have a problem."

"Pity the thought." But Keane's smile told her differently. "Marella, you need to talk to your sister."

He looked out to the balcony where, as far as Marella knew, Crystal had been sulking and pacing for the past half hour.

Marella shook her head. "I don't have time—"

"Yes." Keane touched her shoulder. "You do. And even if you don't, make time. I know you see this as an event-saving scenario, but she's watching her life crumble. Maybe take a few minutes and acknowledge that with her so she doesn't feel quite so useless."

Marella looked across the table at Tag, who had murmured what sounded like agreement. He'd stopped inputting information into the spreadsheet she'd had him set up. "Wouldn't hurt just to touch base with her. Speaking as one of your younger siblings, I can attest to the fact that you're a difficult act to follow. This was supposed to be her week and her wedding."

"It is her wedding," she answered.

"Marella." With one word alone Keane managed to remind her that fixing everything that had gone wrong was more than an expectation of her on her family's part. It was an opportunity to bond with her sister.

"You're right." She frowned at the surprise in Tag's eyes. Surprise that wasn't necessarily aimed at her, but at Keane. "How much have you checked off your list where Mano is concerned, Keane?"

"He's confirmed everything for the ceremony including the wedding arch. Decor is on us, but he'll do what he can to help."

"And the reception?"

"On schedule with setup in the Sunset Seas room," Keane confirmed and then smiled. "On the bright side, it's only going to be slightly more than forty people, which means five tables, plus the head table for the bridal party."

"What's the flip side?"

Keane cringed. "Brita said the centerpieces were being shipped to the hotel and they haven't arrived."

"Probably lost like the lost dresses," Marella muttered. "Okay, centerpieces get added to the list for later."

"The chairs for the ceremony will be here by three this afternoon." Gloria set the chair invoice in front of Marella. "I offered them twenty percent over their normal rental fee for the change of delivery date. Your father and I will cover that expense."

"Works for me," Marella said. "Cake." She poked her fingers against her forehead.

"Keane, what about Little Owl Bakery? Any chance—"

"Always a chance."

"Your father and I stopped in there yesterday for breakfast," Gloria said. "I had a lovely chat with the owner. Let me see what I can do."

"Thanks, Mom." Marella glanced at Tag. "What?"

"You called her Mom." He looked between the two of them. "You never call her that."

"It's what she is, isn't she?" Marella squeezed Gloria's hand. "We make a good team, don't we?"

"The best," Gloria agreed. "I'll text you when I have some ideas."

"Excellent."

"Marella." Keane's warning sounded again. "Take a break. Talk to your sister. Tag? Maybe Chad can help you with what you're doing?"

"Don't really see how," Tag said. "It's really only a one—oh." He had glanced over to where Chad was perched on the sofa by the window, looking more than a bit overwhelmed. "Right. Chad."

"Yes?" The groom stood.

"I could use some help with dictation." Tag

shrugged. "Improv isn't my strong suit," he said under his breath to Marella and Keane. "Don't worry, I've got him. Hey, where's the rest of your gang?"

"Alexis had an all-day thing at the spa, I think? I texted Beck and got him and Shawna in charge of Pippy," Chad told her. "They're spending the rest of the day at the pool keeping her entertained."

"Pippy." Marella touched a finger to her temple. "I can't believe we almost forgot about Pippy."

"Last I checked she was doing fine. All but holding court out there," Chad said as he pulled a chair next to Tag's. "What do you need help with?"

Keane rocked Marella's chair a bit. She glared at him but did as he was suggesting. "Better put this down." She tossed her pen onto the table. "Feeling a bit stabby right now." When she turned and found Keane standing right behind her, she gave in to the impulse to step into his arms. She held on to him tight, rested her cheek against his chest. "I'm so glad you're here." She lifted her face to see him. "I'm also so very glad I kissed you that day on the beach."

He stroked a finger along her cheek. "Me too. Now stop stalling." He kissed her quick and spun her around. "Go talk to Crystal."

As if he didn't trust her to go herself, he walked her over to the patio door and pulled it open, then gave her a little nudge on the base of her spine that had her tripping over the threshold.

Crystal barely acknowledged Marella's arrival since she was ranting into her cell phone like a vengeful Yelp reviewer. "No one should *ever, ever* expect Brita to keep her word or to be remotely competent when it comes to—"

"Tell me you aren't live." Marella snatched the phone out of her sister's hand and stopped the recording button.

"No, I wasn't live," Crystal snapped. "I keep changing my mind about what to say. But you can bet when I've found the right words—"

"Crystal." Marella glanced back at Keane through the glass. He was right again. She'd been so busy trying to fix her sister's wedding she'd forgotten all about the most important part: her sister.

She set Crystal's phone on the tiny glass

table between the chairs and pushed Crystal gently into one of the seats. "Sit for a few minutes. Relax. Decompress. Everything's in hand and we're getting it all together."

"I'm such a screwup." Crystal crossed her legs and then her arms over her chest. The midmorning Nalani breeze kicked up and caught Crystal's hair. "Why can't I ever do anything right? Here you are, riding to my rescue, again. There goes ditzy Crystal, making everything a mess, when all I wanted—"

"All you wanted was the perfect wedding." Marella was taken aback by the bitterness in her sister's voice. "Crystal." She pulled the other chair closer, rested her hands on her sister's knee. "You are not a screwup. And honestly, the only mistake you made was putting your faith in someone who didn't deserve it."

Crystal seemed to be looking anywhere but at Marella.

"Railing online about Brita isn't going to do anything positive for the situation. You've worked really hard these past couple of years to build your reputation as a go-with-the-flow woman who is living her best life. Tearing Brita down, that's not you. That goes against your brand."

"Obviously you haven't seen my night-club reviews."

"No, I haven't," Marella admitted and inwardly cringed. "But you record a message like that and post it to your followers, it might humiliate Brita in the short run, yet it'll damage you eventually in the long run. The internet is forever. You of all people know that. Do you really want to come across as an out-of-control bridezilla who couldn't turn pineapples into a daiquiri?"

Crystal half laughed. "Good one." She gave Marella a long glance. "I'm sorry you're having to clean all this up."

"Me too, but the good news is I was here to do it. And I don't mean physically. I mean emotionally." She nudged her hand against Crystal's leg. "Dad was right. I needed a reset. If he hadn't given me that ultimatum, I don't know if I would have been in the right frame of mind to help make things right."

"Please." Crystal rolled her eyes. "My perfect sister—"

"Okay, stop. Where did this perfect-sister image come from?" she asked. "First Lance and Tag, now you? I have never once claimed to be perfect."

"You didn't have to. You just are. Everything you touch turns to gold. Every decision you make is the right one." Crystal's voice tightened. "You've known exactly what you've wanted to do ever since I met you and you've never once strayed from that path. The rest of us? We're just...blaaaaaaaah!" She waved both hands in the air as if swatting an island full of mosquitoes.

"Okay, but which of the four of us do you think had to ask someone to help her learn how to have fun?"

Crystal eyed her. "You did not."

"I did. Why do you think Keane's always hanging around me? He's my fun coach."

Crystal snorted. "You've got to be kidding me."

"Nope. He really is."

Crystal looked through the glass door to where Keane was looming over Tag and Chad as they filled out the spreadsheet. "You mean the two of you aren't...?" She shook her head. "Nah. I don't buy that for a second. You're crazy about each other. I see it every time he looks at you, not to mention how you look at him when you think no one is around."

"This conversation isn't about—"

"You can't sit there and tell me you don't see it. Heck, you said it yourself when he first walked in the door. You love him."

"I—" Marella sat straight up, her face flushing. "I did not!"

Crystal laughed, the light in her eyes sparking back to life. "Oh, you did so. Everyone heard it. Every. One."

Marella covered her mouth as if she could somehow stop the words. "Uh, obviously I was just keeping the charade going. Him being my rebound boyfriend was simply part of—"

"Marella, it's okay to love him. Actually, I'd think there was something wrong with you if you didn't."

It was one thing, Marella rationalized, to know it herself that she'd fallen hard for Keane. It was another to admit everyone around her knew it too. But that felt too messy to deal with at the moment.

"This conversation is supposed to be about you," Marella told her sister. "About you grabbing this situation and making something positive out of it. You want to take ButtercupDoll to the next level? Rise above the bad. Document everything your family is doing to make your wedding dreams come true, and you *politely*—" she smiled "—thank Brita for everything she tried to do before she understood event planning was simply not for her. Don't throw her under the bus you can drive straight to success."

Crystal stared at her. "That almost sounds as if you have faith in me."

Marella's heart skipped a beat. Up until she'd stepped foot in Nalani, she hadn't realized how completely detached she'd become from her family. A family she loved but had never completely embraced, sort of. "Then I haven't been doing my job as your good big sister." She held out her hands, palms up, and waited for Crystal to grab hold. "Let me tell you what I should have said ages ago. You are the bravest person I know, Crystal. Your leap-first mentality has set you apart in a good way—no, a great way. While it might not be my personal cup of tea, you've built an influencer business that can only get bigger. You've found your niche and you've made it sing for you.

"You've already proved you're capable of amazing things. Everything bad that's happened to the wedding? It's a learning experience. Put what's happened to use. Show your followers what a determined, savvy young woman you are. And forgiving, don't forget forgiving. And how you're willing to take on every challenge that's presented to you. I know you can do it, Crystal. Take that step into what's every opportunity for growth and maybe show other people it's possible for them to grow as well."

Crystal's eyes filled not with sad or panicky tears this time, but with appreciation and love. "One thing I did right was choose you as my maid of honor."

"On that we can agree." Marella laughed and Crystal joined in. "Now." She looked down at Crystal's cell still in her lap. "Are you going to—"

"Marella." Keane motioned for them both to come back inside.

"What's happened now?" Marella asked as she and her sister followed Keane and found Lance sitting at the table, a triumphant look on his face. "You found the dresses?"

"I found where they were delivered to.

Seems Brita got a little confused with all the island resorts." He hesitated. "And all the islands. They're in the admin office at the Hyperion Resort."

Crystal squealed and grabbed Marella's hand. "He found my dress!"

"That's great." Marella had almost leveled up to her sister's excitement. "What's the catch?"

"The Hyperion Resort is on O'ahu," Keane explained.

"O'ahu." Marella did a quick mental search. "But we're on the Big Island."

"That's one problem," Lance said. "The other is that the resort is closing for renovations as of this evening. They can only hold the boxes for a couple of hours."

"Don't!" Marella turned a sharp eye on Crystal who'd started to whimper. "Rise above. There's always a solution. How far away is O'ahu?"

"Well, if you walk there—" Tag stopped himself when everyone glared. "Sorry. I've already looked it up. Next flight from Hilo isn't until five this afternoon."

"Boat?" Marella looked to Keane. "The *Kalei*. Can we take that over?"

"We could." Keane nodded. "Or I have another solution." He began tapping on his cell, then held the phone to his ear. "Hey, Syd."

Marella asked, "What are you doing?"

"Getting us to O'ahu." He dropped a fast kiss on the tip of her nose. "Or did you forget we have a helicopter at our disposal?"

CHAPTER THIRTEEN

"YOU DOING OKAY back there?" Keane yelled over his shoulder from the front passenger seat in Ohana Odysseys's five-passenger helicopter.

"Yep, fine." Marella flipped through the printed-out spreadsheets and blocked out tasks already finished. "Should be done by the time we land." She hadn't looked up once since they'd climbed on board.

"Marella."

"What?" She waved at him as if he were a pesky fly buzzing around her head.

"Get your nose out of those papers and look where we are. Embrace the moment. And mark another thing off your have-fun list."

"I don't have time…" Marella muttered. "I hope Crystal's okay." She was pretty sure her sister would hold it together, but there was still that niggling doubt.

"She said something about turning pineapples into mai tais," Sydney said. "Which makes absolutely no sense. Mai tais don't have—"

"It's pineapples into daiquiris," Marella corrected and glared at Keane. "This is all your fault. Because of you I gave a pep talk to my sister and now she trusts me with everything about her wedding."

"She trusted you with it already." Keane chuckled. "Hey." He stretched a hand back and didn't look away until she took hold. "After this you won't have much left to challenge yourself with on the islands."

"That is the point of completing a have-fun list," she said, smiling.

"I keep telling Sydney she should hire herself out as an island stunt pilot," Keane shouted. "So far this trip is completely boring."

"You know if she wasn't in the back seat I'd take you on a little crater tour around Diamond Head. Maybe drop you off. From fifty feet."

"She's joking." Keane squeezed Marella's hand. "You are joking, right?" Sydney just grinned and managed the controls as easily as he maneuvered a board through the waves. It was natural for her. She belonged in the air.

"Tell me what's going on with the food for the luau and the reception," Marella asked Sydney.

"Both are handled. I put the word out and Akahi called. She's rallying the troops for the luau tonight."

Keane's heart swelled. "Love that woman so much. What about the reception?"

"Tag said he wanted to work on that with Chad." Sydney glanced back at Marella. "Hope that was okay."

"Tag wants to take charge of something, it's fine with me. So where are we going to land this thing?" Marella yelled over the whipping of the blade.

"Friend of ours runs a tour company in O'ahu," Sydney said. "I radioed ahead and asked if we could set down there. It's then a ten-minute drive into downtown." She glanced at the dashboard clock. "We should be there in plenty of time to get the boxes before the office closes. Hang on." She tapped the button on her headset.

"What's wrong?" Marella asked, letting

go of Keane's hand and sliding forward in her seat. "Is something wrong with the—"

"Nothing's wrong," Sydney said. "Your mom can't get through on your cell. She's at the Ohana office with Tehani. I'm going to put her through. Okay go, Tehani."

"Marella?" Gloria's voice came through loud and clear.

"I'm here," Marella said. "What's going on with the cake?"

"The owner has been simply terrific." Gloria cleared her throat, causing a tiny bit of static. Keane adjusted his headphone volume so he could hear better. "Inoa proposed a two-for-one idea. Cupcakes topped with a variety of yellow-and-gold-frosting flowers—"

"Crystal's colors. Fab."

"And then a smaller, two-tier cake for the bride and groom to cut. That'll be decorated with a combination of real hibiscus flowers and buds and frosting that match the color of the cupcakes. The even better news is she can get all of it done by ten in the morning."

"Yes." Marella beamed and gave a fist bump to Keane. He couldn't help but smile back. She really was in her element. "Perfect!"

"I had an idea though," Gloria said. "What if we made the cupcakes the table centerpieces somehow? Maybe there are stands we can use? Then add extra flowers if we can find some that'll suit. Maybe add candles?"

"Daphne said she managed to get one of the stores in Hilo to share their supply. They'll be different colors and varieties, but if the cupcakes and cake have the majority of the yellow, that would work. In the meantime, they're figuring out what to do for the bouquets. I love the centerpiece idea, Mom."

"Okay, then. I'll get back and talk to Inoa and we'll sort the display details. See you when you get back."

Sydney disconnected the call. "Everything's coming up roses then."

"Uh-huh." Marella leaned over to the side, just enough to look out the window. "We're um, pretty high up."

"A little under fifteen hundred feet," Sydney clarified. "We should be landing in about twenty minutes."

"That was fast," Marella said and leaned out a bit more.

"You can switch seats, you know," Keane told her. "If you want a better look."

"I'm good for now, thanks." Right now there was nothing to see but water and a school of dolphins making their way toward the coast of Honolulu. "There's so many of them."

"Good time of year for spotting dolphins," Sydney said. "Nikolao said you could use his car, Keane. I'm going to hang back, refuel and see what new opportunities have popped up out here for tour businesses."

"Always thinking about Ohana," Keane teased. "You've turned into a real businesswoman."

"Maybe. But this businesswoman is starting to feel a little overwhelmed. And that's before Tehani heads off on maternity leave." She cast Keane a side-eyed glance. "Sure would be helpful to know if I'm about to lose any other potential partiers or employees."

"Yes," Keane murmured. "I'm sure it would." He let her comment drift away on the wind, focusing himself on the waves leading them to land. It had been a good long while since he'd surfed these shores. They had a different feel to them than Nalani. Even in the roughest weather, Nalani always seemed to keep control of the water.

But out here? Out here was definitely a challenge.

He heard a click behind him and looked back in time to see Marella slide across the seat and rehook the belt next to the window. He faced forward before she caught him, the smile on his face growing as he thought about how far she'd come. How far she could yet go.

His smile slipped. Futile dreams. Dreams that had been reawakened by Marella's accidental declaration of love in front of her family in the hotel room. A declaration that had brought fear rather than acceptance. For the first time in his life, he wished he could set aside that fear and take a real shot at love.

He knew she hadn't realized she'd said it at the time. But she had uttered the words. And it was the words he'd hold close from here on.

He cared about her too much, loved her too much, to have her take a chance on him.

Sydney reached up, flipped a couple of switches. "You okay?"

"Yeah."

"She can't hear us." Sydney glanced up into the rearview mirror. "She's mesmerized and

I turned off her headset. What's going on in that brain of yours?"

"Just thinking."

"That's what I'm worried about."

He smirked.

"You two make a good team," Sydney said. "This last week you've been different. More settled. Less—"

"Haunted?"

"Good a word as any. She leaves the day after tomorrow. You planning to do something about that?"

"No."

Sydney shook her head. "Men. Some of you never see what's right in front of you. Try as you might, Keane, you couldn't avoid it when it happened. And I saw it happen that day you two met on the beach." She pinned him with one of her know-it-all looks. "You fell for her the second she kissed you."

"Doesn't matter if I did. I'm not dragging her down."

"Is that what you think you'll do? Keane, you've never dragged anyone down in your life."

"And I mean to keep it that way." Just to be safe, he kept his voice low. "I'm not risking becoming something else. Someone else."

Sydney took the aircraft to the left and increased their speed as they approached the shore. "You've always worried about someone bringing out what you consider to be your worst qualities, Keane. Did it ever occur to you that Marella brings out your absolute best? I'll say this, while I'm not read in on a lot about how you grew up, I know one thing Remy always told me. Your father was not a good man."

"No, he was not."

"The fact that you know that is already a step toward breaking the cycle. Also makes me think you don't give much credence to Marella's judgment."

"What's that supposed to mean?"

"It means she's fallen in love with you. The man she met on the beach. The man who has been by her side this entire week. The man who was able to have her waist deep in the ocean she swore she wouldn't step foot in."

"You're proving my point. I have power over her."

Sydney scoffed. "Hardly. She brings out your best, Keane. No one encourages and guides like you do. No one loves like you do. Maybe it's time you realized you are not now nor will you ever be your father and embrace something special that's standing right in front of you. Or sitting right behind you," she added. "Just something else for you to ponder." She flipped the switches again, which must have turned Marella's headset back on because she said, "We're about to start our landing, Marella. You doing okay back there?"

For a long moment there was no response, just Marella staring out the window. "Yeah."

The wonder in her voice warmed Keane's heart.

"Do you think…?" Marella lifted her fingers to her window and pressed them against the glass. "Do you think maybe I can ride in the front for the trip back?"

Keane nodded and looked at the clear blue sky ahead, more than pleased with himself. And Marella. "I think that can be arranged."

BY THE TIME they made it back to Nalani, later than originally anticipated, and after she'd taken the time to check each of the boxes containing the wedding attire to make sure all was intact, Marella handed Crystal her wedding dress causing far less fanfare than she'd predicted.

Crystal set the box down on her bed, opened it and drew out the stunning beaded and rhinestone custom gown with tiny yellow flowers embroidered around the hem, neck and waistline. "I didn't think I'd ever see this again," she said with a surprising laugh. "I should know never to doubt your powers."

"Everything okay?" Marella asked. "You seem, I don't know, kind of subdued."

"That's what happens when your good big sister tells you to get it together. It's a wedding not—"

"A life-changing event?" Marella teased. "Where's your tiara?"

"Back in Chad's room with the rings and license." She pulled the dress out and held it up against her body.

"It's a beautiful gown, Crystal. It's going to be a wonderful day tomorrow."

Crystal nodded, tears filling her eyes. "Because of you, I'm sure it will be. Are these the other dresses?"

"They are. I can take them to Alexis and Shawna if you'd like."

"You've done enough for today," Crystal said. "I'll take care of it. Did Mom tell you she and Inoa found the perfect cupcake stands to use for the centerpieces?"

"Yes, she did. And they're going to be delivered tomorrow morning before the ceremony. I'll make sure they're put in the right places and assembled properly." She backed out of the room, stopping only long enough to grab the laptop Tag had left on the kichenette counter. "I need to check in with Tag and go over where we are with the spreadsheet."

"Okay." Crystal offered her a solemn smile. "I mean it, Marella. I'll never be able to thank you enough for everything."

"Don't worry," Marella teased some more, "I'm sure I'll find a way."

She withdrew from the room and texted Tag to see where he'd disappeared to. When he texted back, she stopped and had to read it at least three times before she hit the elevator button to go down to the front desk. "Hi."

"Ms. Benoit, good afternoon." The young woman who had been on duty at the desk the night of the dinner cruise smiled at her. "How are the wedding plans coming along?"

"Fine as far as I know. Um, can you tell me where I'd find Hema?"

"Yes, of course. She's our head chef in the Southern Seas. It'll be closing in a little while after the lunch service is over."

"So I can just go in?"

"By all means."

"Thanks." Marella didn't take much time to acknowledge the familiar faces she saw milling about the lobby. From what she'd heard, her father had been doing a masterful job entertaining the wedding guests as they arrived and settled into the resort. She spotted Lance pointing and directing people to the elevators or out to the pool.

"Note to self, check on Pippy." She didn't know if it was good news or bad that she hadn't heard anyone mention her grandmother as of late.

"Aloha. Good afternoon," the restaurant hostess welcomed her.

"Aloha. I'm looking for Hema?" Glancing around, she saw only a smattering of customers at a few tables. "I was told she might be in the kitchen."

"Hema is always in the kitchen. Please. This way."

Marella was led to a pair of double swinging doors.

"Hema. There's someone here to see you."

"Yes?" The middle-aged woman who poked her head out from a walk-in freezer and pushed her glasses further up her nose said, "Ah, you must be Marella. Tag! Your sister's here. Come in, come in." She waved Marella away from the swinging doors. Like all the other Hibiscus Bay Resort employees, she was the personification of *welcome*.

"Thanks." Marella pushed the rest of the way through the doors, then stepped to the side.

"I've been going over the final menu your brother's put together for us," Hema told her. "After figuring out what we have extra from our food delivery this week, I think you'll be quite pleased with the plan. Fortunately, for us, forty-one is a manageable number on short notice. Any bigger? Well, we'd have had issues so the winds are blowing fair today."

Marella couldn't help but think she'd stepped through some kind of inter-planetary portal. "The menu my brother—"

"We'll be able to have a lovely plate of

gently roasted salmon with purple potato mash and a selection of seasonal vegetables. No broccoli," she stated and pointed to a loose stack of pages. "Bride's request. Can't forget those."

"No, of course not."

"Second, instead of steak, we're going to do a Kahlua pork roast wrapped in tarot leaves and served with jasmine rice and *lau lau* kale. For the vegetarian option—"

"Hey, sis." Tag rounded the back of the kitchen, narrowly avoiding knocking into one of the kitchen staff. "You got my text."

"I didn't quite understand your text," Marella said. "What's going on? Did we finalize things for tomorrow's reception?"

"Thought you would have checked the spreadsheet. Everything's taken care of. Tehani managed to get ahold of the minister from the church. He'll be here for the rehearsal a little early so he can meet with Crystal and Chad. All set for tomorrow. Let's see, what else." He ticked things off on his fingers. "I know Mom called you about the chairs and the cake. Oh! Daphne sent Crystal some flower pictures and got approval for those. Her bouquet will be a little smaller than expected, but she didn't seem to mind. Instead of the bridesmaids carrying bouquets, they're each going to drop flower petals down the aisle. Since we don't have a flower girl. What else?"

"That might actually be it." She moved back to look at him. "Wh-what are you wearing?"

"An apron." His boyish grin widened. He'd pulled his long hair back into a bun and snapped black latex gloves off his hands. "After I finished the spreadsheet—I see you got the laptop by the way." He pointed to the device in her hands. "I needed something to do. I was talking with Dad in the lobby when Mano walked by, asked if I had some free hands." Tag shrugged. "Here I am."

"You're working in the kitchen? Cooking?"

"Aren't you the one who said I should jump in and see what I was getting myself into?" He shrugged. "I jumped."

"I was just telling Marella about our vegetarian option for the reception tomorrow," Hema said to Tag.

"Crispy garlic tofu served with quinoa and a vegetable medley." Tag's smile told

Marella she should completely understand what he'd just said. "We're going to do the hors d'oeuvres buffet style. It'll keep people moving around."

"Okay." What else was she going to say. "Tag, I'm not sure it's appropriate for you to be in here."

"Appropriate or not, we need his help." Mano came out from around the same corner as Tag. "And speaking of help. Don't worry," Mano told Marella as he pulled his own gloves off and removed the apron from over his head. "He's a natural. And I'll make sure he's done in time for the rehearsal luau. If you'll excuse me." He nodded to Hema. "You know where I am if you need reinforcements."

"Rest of my crew's coming in early in the morning to finish the prep," Hema said, gesturing to Marella. "You all are our guests here and we always treat our guests like *ohana.*"

"Yes," Marella said. "I've definitely learned that this week. Are you sure Tag is—"

"He's green, but he has a good learning curve," Hema assured her. "Never seen anyone have so much fun chopping vegetables. This is all in hand. Go. Relax."

"Ms. Benoit?" The front-of-room hostess poked her head back inside. "Your mother said to tell you the chairs have arrived. She's going to supervise their setup right now."

"Great." How was it possible she'd gone from being in charge of everything to being out of a job in the space of mere hours? It wasn't a bad feeling exactly, but it had her blinking in shock as she joined her father out in the lobby. "Tag's helping in the kitchen," she said, still slightly awestruck. "He's cooking." Before this week she had no idea Tag even knew what a stove was.

"So I've heard." Armand wrapped his arm around her shoulders and squeezed. "I might have mentioned to Mano your brother was considering yet another career change."

"Mano." Marella shook her head. "He's like some kind of island wizard around here. One thing's for sure, Crystal made a brilliant choice with the Hibiscus Bay."

"Agreed. Speaking of brilliant. That was what you were earlier with Crystal. And the chaos."

"I tend to thrive on it. Thanks." She smiled at him. "I learned from the best."

"And you've made Gloria very happy. I'm glad you felt comfortable enough to finally call her Mom."

"Me too. So has everyone gotten here already?" She did a quick count and arrived at least twenty before her father answered. "All the wedding guests who are flying in?" Between her parents' friends and Crystal's semiclose acquaintances, along with a couple or five social media influencers that could qualify as her sister's competition, it appeared as if everyone was going to show up.

"Looks like. I'm going to go retrieve your grandmother from the pool and meet Gloria up in the room to change for the rehearsal."

"Right." She checked her watch. "That's in an hour. Have you by any chance seen Keane? I seem to have lost track of him since we got back from O'ahu."

"I think I saw him heading to the marina. Heard you got an eyeful on that chopper."

Marella nodded. "I swear, if you'd told me this time last week I'd have gone swimming in the ocean and climbed into a helicopter, I'd have laughed."

"I'd have thought the same about you falling in love."

Marella caught her lip in her teeth. "I really said that out loud, didn't I?"

Armand chuckled and drew her into a warm hug. "You really did. And you never disappoint. When you go all in on something, you really go all in."

"It has to be the most irresponsible thing I've ever done. Falling for a guy while on vacation."

"The heart has a mind of its own, so to speak. Especially where love is concerned."

"Could be he's just a rebound guy. After the disappointment that was Craig."

"Not a chance. Keane's the real thing, Marella. You know that."

Yes. She did know that. And standing here so very far away from the life she'd built for herself in New York, she couldn't imagine going back to what—and who—she was. Keane had changed her. Opened her eyes. Cared about her. She stopped short of the *L* word as he hadn't given any indication her feelings were reciprocated. But if she trusted her feelings...

She couldn't imagine he didn't feel the

same way. "I'm going to try to hunt him down before the rehearsal. I'll see you there."

"AKAHI AND POLUNU to the rescue once more." Keane rested one foot on the stern of the *Nani Nalu* and leaned his arms on his knee. "Howzit?" he called out. "Polunu?"

"I'm here!" Polunu's voice rumbled from beyond the sliding doors.

Keane kicked off his shoes and stepped on board, made his way around the hospitality table and into the main cabin area. "Thought maybe you'd be home helping Akahi with the cooking."

Polunu shook his head. "My wife does not need any help in the kitchen. And I'm a smart enough husband to know not to offer." He finished wiping down the bar and tossed the rag into the sink. "That last dinner cruise just about did her in, *keiki*."

The normally lively light in Polonu's eyes dimmed.

"I think we've reached the end of the line. She won't be able to maneuver around the boat much longer. I need to pull the plug on our business before she gets hurt."

Despite not being surprised, Keane couldn't

help but feel he'd been punched in the gut. He wandered to the window, looked out to the other vessels that, while they were stunning in their display, didn't possess the heart of the *Nani*.

He loved this boat. Had spent some of the best moments of his life here, not only with Polunu and Akahi, but Remy and his grandparents as well. "I won't be the only one who says... Hey, what's that?" He stopped, pointed to the large square sign Polunu pulled out from behind the bar.

"It's a For Sale sign." Polunu spun it around to examine it. "Finished it up last night."

"You aren't keeping her? You're selling the *Nani*?" He knew it was ridiculous, but he'd lowered his voice so the boat wouldn't hear him. "Polunu, this is your home."

"My home is with Akahi," Polunu said. "If I don't sell, she'll talk me into keeping the cruises going and I can't let her do that." He walked over to Keane and set the sign in the window. "There. Done." He stood back and clapped his hands together. "Wasn't as painful as I thought."

It was for Keane.

You'll know it when you see it—the right thing to do.

Marella's words floated back into his mind as if on the wind. She was right. He did know.

"Sold." He turned to the window and grabbed the sign. "I'll buy her."

Polunu shook his head. "That's impulse talking, Keane. Not logic."

"Since when have you known me to be logical? I won't have her being bought by a possible stranger. I want her. Ohana Odysseys wants her. We'll take over the cruises." Somehow. "We'll keep her afloat. How much?"

Polunu narrowed his eyes. "Five bucks."

Keane rolled his eyes and tossed out a significantly higher counteroffer. It was a fraction of what he'd get for his house back in Ohio. A house that had never once felt like a home. But the *Nani Nalu*? Nalani itself? There was no question. Besides, he could use the rest of the money to buy a share of the partnership in Ohana Odysseys. Sydney would finally be able to quit asking him to.

"Oh, and there's something else. I'd like to keep Edena on if she's willing. And—" he tried to find the right words "—I could use a bartender. And a head chef. If she'd be willing to do the cooking at home and we'd transport it to the boat before the cruises…" He was going out on a limb, essentially offering Polunu and Akahi jobs with Ohana Odysseys, but Ohana already rented the vessel a few times a month. This was just simplifying the procedure for the future. Hopefully, for everyone's benefit. "The buying price should keep the medical bills at bay and you can both continue to work as long as you want." He held out his hand. "What do you say?"

Polunu looked torn between laughing and crying. But he slapped his hand into Keane's before pulling him into a tight bear hug. "Don't know a better man than you, Keane Harper. Not a better man." Polunu released him and he stumbled backward. "I'm going to take your deal before you come to your senses and change your mind."

"He won't change his mind," Marella's voice drifted in through the open door. Keane's gaze held Marella's and he grinned. "Keane knows a great deal when he sees it."

Polunu looked between them, slowly made his way toward Marella. "He's—"

"A good man." She nodded, but her smile didn't quite reach her eyes. "Yes. I know."

"I'm going to go home and tell Akahi. She'll probably be so happy she won't get mad at me for setting foot in the kitchen." He touched a hand to Marella's shoulder. "Mahalo. Both of you." He left.

"So." Marella clasped her hands behind her back and rocked forward on her heels. "You bought the *Nani*."

"I guess I did." For the first time, he couldn't identify what he saw on her face.

"I guess that means you made up your mind about not going back to the college. That two-hour plane ride didn't tempt you at all, did it?"

"The plane ride didn't, no." It was on the tip of his tongue to tell her she was the only incentive to return to his old life. "I probably should have talked to you about this before—"

"Keane." She walked over to him, took the sign out of his hand and tossed it on top of the bar. "You made the right decision. And as much as I'd like to have been a consideration, there's no reason for me to be. Nalani is your home." She lifted a hand to touch his face. "The *Nani* is your home. You're where you belong."

"And New York is where you belong."

He didn't know what he expected. A nod of agreement, a sad smile. A realization shining in those beautiful, hypnotizing eyes of hers that argued with him. Instead, she rose up on her toes and kissed him. "You were a wonderful fun coach. I'm never going to forget Nalani. Or you." She stepped back, trailed her hand down his face, his neck, his chest. "I've got the wedding rehearsal in a few minutes. I hope I'll see you at the luau?"

He nodded. "You will. I'm helping Sydney and Daphne set up the picnic tables and torches. We'll be minus the pig in the ground but—"

"Have to say I'm not disappointed to miss that." She smiled again. "I'll see you there."

CHAPTER FOURTEEN

"I THINK TOMORROW'S going to be even better than originally planned," Gloria told Marella as they stepped onto the beach after the wedding rehearsal. "The minister is absolutely lovely and the chairs are perfect, if I do say so myself."

Marella forced a laugh. "I will completely agree with that assessment."

"With as much as went wrong," her mother continued, "everything seemed to fall easily into place when it came to fixing it. You are a wonder, Marella. Calm in the eye of the storm."

"I'm only as good as my team and when my team is my family, how can we not succeed?" She rubbed a hand against the odd pit in her stomach. The pit that had formed upon hearing Keane offer to buy the *Nani Nalu*.

"I think that family's gotten exponentially

larger this past week." Gloria tucked an arm through Marella's and looked back to where Armand was leading Pippy down the slope. "Crystal even laughed at the idea of Pippy's date bringing his pig."

"She may have laughed, but she still said no." Marella paused to clear her throat. "I hear Kahlua will be making a guest appearance tonight, however. Benji doesn't usually attend luaus if there's an emu around."

Gloria bent down and pushed off her sandals. "Today's chaos aside, I can't recall a more enjoyable family vacation. You know, your father mentioned looking at some property Sunday morning before we fly home. What would you think about us getting a house here?"

"I think that would be a great idea for the two of you. And Pippy."

"And you? It would give you a reason to come back." Gloria cast her gaze across the sand to where Keane and Ohana's jack-of-all-trades Wyatt Jenkins were moving picnic tables around so Sydney and Daphne could tack on the bright yellow flowered fabric covers. "If you didn't already have one."

"It's best for everyone if I cut ties completely once the plane takes off." She swallowed hard, tried to dislodge the tears that tightened her throat. She'd met some wonderful people during her stay; some she now considered friends. Sydney and Tehani. Daphne and Mano. The staff at the resort, who always had a smile to share or a hand to offer. "He knows how I feel and he knows I'm leaving." She shrugged as if it wasn't the most painful gesture she'd ever made in her life. "He's convinced he's not good enough for anyone and he doesn't believe it when someone tells him he's wrong." Besides, she had a nice, steady life back in New York. A career she loved. Even if all of that felt a million miles away from her now.

"Sometimes it's difficult to make a life-changing choice when there's a past to cling to."

"He's terrified of becoming his father." Now it was Marella's turn to kick off her flip-flops. "Which doesn't make sense because I've only ever witnessed him being kind and caring and lov—"

"Loving. Yes. I've seen it. We all have." Gloria tightened her hold on Marella's arm. "He has to come to the belief on his own. Or maybe he has to realize that being without someone is far more painful than taking a chance on loving them."

"He's such a good man." Marella couldn't stop the rush of tears any longer. "I'd give anything if he could just see it for himself." She turned away and Gloria squeezed her hand.

"Marella!" Sydney waved with both arms just as Marella turned back, her emotions under control. For now. "We're just about ready!" Sydney pointed to the lineup of plastic banquet tables that had been set up and decorated near the trio of firepits that Keane headed over to light.

"The guests should be on their way over anytime." Marella extricated herself from Gloria's hold. "We put up a sign in the lobby." Sure enough a flood of guests emerged from the doors of the Hibiscus Bay.

"So, we have coolers filled with all kinds of drinks, water, beer, sodas. Supposedly Akahi shared her rum punch recipe—"

"Uh-oh." Daphne joined them and frowned. "Keep me away from it."

"We had her kick down the amount of rum, don't worry," Sydney explained. "All the plates, utensils are biodegradable and we have receptacles set up at multiple stations. We planned for a hundred—"

"A hundred?" Marella gasped. "But that's—"

"Welcome to a luau in Nalani," Sydney said. "Even without the catering, it always turns into a larger event. Aloha, everyone! Marella, can you greet folks, tell them they can get comfortable with some drinks while we wait for the food? I see our ukulele players are here. Just need to get them positioned around the fires."

"No problem, that I can do." It was probably just as well, postponing another conversation with Keane. She didn't know what they had left to say to one another. It was maybe better to leave with a self-inflicted broken heart rather than step into a circle of rejection.

"Over here, everyone." She imitated Sydney and waved the wedding guests to where she was standing. "Feel free to kick off your shoes, grab yourself a drink. We're going to start lighting the torches pretty soon. The food will be here shortly." She hoped. Until she saw that first hint of aluminum foil or plastic-covered dishware, she wasn't entirely convinced this was going to happen. "Aloha... Hello."

Marella and Gloria played hostesses as the guests filed around the tables. Lance and the rest of the bridal party, along with Tag, who was only now pulling off his apron, found themselves in the middle of the happy fray and joined in the greetings and welcomes.

Pippy made a beeline for Benji and Kahlua, who made their entrance to the party via the beach. When Pippy bent over and planted a kiss on Kahlua's nose, the pig's squealing response had everyone laughing. The music started, that festive plucking acting as a melodious escort as the bride and groom, along with their recently booked minister, made their appearance.

Crystal's gorgeous sunshine-yellow dress was accented by a beautiful white hibiscus lei around her neck while Chad wore a *kukui*-nut lei necklace. Everyone cheered at the first sighting of the beaming couple.

"Am I the only one worried about the food arriving?" Marella twisted her hands together.

"Yes," Sydney told her as she joined her, Daphne and Gloria. "Vivi texted. They're packaging up the *huli-huli* chicken now. Believe me, they're bringing enough for an army."

"Good thing we have one then," Gloria teased Marella.

"There they are!" Daphne nearly fell over in the sand when she jumped and pointed. "I can see them. Akahi's leading a parade."

Marella couldn't think of another way to describe what she was looking at.

Sure enough, Akahi, wearing a pretty yellow muumuu, her hair knotted on top of her head, walked at the head of a long, winding line, her cane almost setting a rhythm for the many behind her.

Marella and the others stepped back as Akahi and Polunu reached them.

"I…" Those darn tears again. She lost count of the number of residents who trailed behind. Dozens of them carrying all different trays and bowls and containers. "Mahalo, Akahi." Marella bowed her head. "Mahalo."

"She looks shocked," Akahi teased to the group. "You all do. Well, except for you, Sydney. Nothing surprises you anymore, does it?"

"No." Sydney motioned to the tables. "The tables are yours to fill."

Akahi nodded and stepped back, waved her arm for her entourage to display their home-cooked offerings.

"I still don't believe this," Marella whispered to Sydney. "You've all been so kind. So generous. I feel like—"

"You're home?" Sydney dropped an arm around Marella's shoulders and squeezed. "That's because you are. All this? It's the Nalani way. The Ohana way."

Emotion flooded through her. Strong enough to push away any doubts she had about Keane. About her feelings for him. About his doubts about himself. She had the words now and the spirit and courage to speak them. Except...

"He's gone." She pulled out of Sydney's hold, walked toward one of the firepits and scanned the crowd all the way down to the ocean. He hadn't stayed.

She shouldn't have been surprised, but Keane's absence popped that balloon of hope that had been building in her chest. She knew where he'd gone. To his cottage.

To his waves. To his ocean. And he'd done so knowing where she would be.

She wouldn't follow and intrude. She certainly didn't expect him to attend the wedding and especially not as her date. Until he accepted himself as the man she knew him to be, no words she uttered could change things. Best to just leave them as they were now.

With an unspoken goodbye that had broken her heart.

KEANE HAD EVERY intention of staying for the luau. Not only because he was starving— he hadn't had much to eat since that *malasada* this morning before chaos had broken out. But after seeing Marella arrive with her mother, after feeling that pain in his heart that reminded him she was leaving in forty-eight hours, he couldn't bring himself to join the crowd.

He bided his time, finished with the firepits, before he'd told Wyatt he was shoving off. Wyatt looked confused for a moment before he'd nodded.

Keane had planned to head home, straight down to the beach and allow the ocean to soothe the hurricane of emotions currently spinning through him. Instead, he circled around and made his way up to Pulelehua Road. Walking through town as the party started meant most of the storefronts were already closing up for the evening. He heard the door chime as Seas & Breeze retrieved their specials sign. He noticed Shani closing up The Hawaiian Snuggler before she hurried down the street toward the celebration.

He hadn't planned to make any stops until he found himself pausing to look in the window of Earth & Sea Jewelry.

"Keane. Aloha." Malie Koa, whose father owned the shop that featured locally hand-made jewelry, opened the door and popped her head out. "I thought you'd be down at the beach for the luau."

"Not my scene tonight," he said. "That necklace." He pointed to the one Marella had been admiring the other day. "Is it for sale?"

"The olivine pendant? Absolutely. Would you like me to gift wrap it?"

"Just a box will do." Marella wasn't ostentatious or concerned with pretty wrapping. She'd appreciate the box for the simplicity the necklace offered. "Thanks, Malie."

A few minutes later, box in hand, he continued on his way to the cottage. The timing of his delivery had to be just right. He'd wait until he knew the wedding was under way and leave it for her at the front desk. A going-away gift. A thank-you gift.

An I-hope-you'll-remember-me gift.

Theo Fairfax waved and called out to Keane from the front porch. "Sydney owes me fifty bucks. I told her you wouldn't stay for the luau. She insisted you weren't that foolish."

Keane was too emotionally drained to laugh and walked up the porch stairs. "Sounds like it might be a kind of draw to me. You get that out of the fridge?" He pointed to Theo's soda.

"Yup. Grab one. Pull up a chair."

"Uh, Dad. Are you going to lecture me about my women issues?"

"Your sense of humor is growing on me," Theo told him. "And I hadn't planned a lecture. Noodles might have though. Right, Nood?"

The gecko perked up and lifted his head as if he were going to respond.

"I appreciate you checking up on me, but honestly? I'd really just like to be alone."

"Totally get that." Theo nodded, drank and gave no indication of leaving. "I didn't realize you were into self-pity and punishment."

Keane's temper caught. "That's how this is going to go?"

Theo glanced at his watch. "I'm running out of time. I have a luau to get to. For the record, and I admit this really isn't any of my business—"

"Au contraire," Keane muttered.

"But I think Sydney's right. You aren't foolish. What you are is scared."

"I'm scared." Keane leaned against the railing. "Do tell."

"You're scared of being happy. Scared you somehow don't deserve her or that you'll mess the relationship up and hurt her. Ask me how I know."

"Gee, Theo, how do you know?" But Keane already knew the answer.

"Because not so long ago I was right where you are now."

Noodles zigged and zagged, and Keane wondered if that was the gecko signaling his agreement. "I was faced with the very real fact that meeting Sydney meant my life had been changed forever. And for the best. Everything that had mattered before then, ceased to exist. Sydney was it for me. My future. After I realized and accepted that, my life choices got a whole lot easier."

Keane didn't know how to respond. "I'm not who any of you think I am. Especially Marella."

"Nope." Theo shook his head. "You're exactly who we know you to be and it didn't take you buying Polunu and Ahati's catamaran to prove it."

Keane winced. "Word's out already? Does Sydney know?"

"Your punishment for not giving her a heads-up is a one-on-one employee meeting Monday morning at 6:00 a.m. But I digress. Pressure defines a person. How he reacts to things going wrong defines a person. How you respond to a ticked-off stranger trying to get revenge on her cheating boyfriend defines a person. Defines you.

"If you can honestly tell me you'll be happier without her. That you won't think of her anytime you step on the *Nani* or the *Kalei*, if you can stand there and tell me Marella Benoit won't haunt you until your last breath, then you can ignore me."

Keane's doubt cracked. "Maybe I'm okay with being haunted."

"Then maybe you are foolish, not to mention making the worst mistake." Theo toasted him with his almost-empty soda can. "Seems a pretty ridiculous choice to live with the memory of her rather than the woman herself." Theo shoved himself up, gave Noodles a one-fingered pat on his head and stepped off the porch.

"Say you're right." Keane couldn't ignore the long-dismissed pull inside him. "What do you think I should do about it?"

"You know what you should do about it." Theo walked backward down the beach. "Call me if you need help."

"SO STAY TUNED, all you super-delicious ButtercupDolls." Crystal spoke brightly and beamed into the phone Alexis held up in front of her face. Marella noticed her sister used her bare ring finger to touch one of the sparkly yellow earrings, then the other. "This week has been filled with awesome

events and between you and me, the celebration is just getting started!" She blew her
followers a kiss. "Ta for now." She waggled
her fingers as Alexis stopped the recording.

"Got it." Alexis turned the phone around,
handed it back to Crystal.

"It's uploading now," Crystal said. "Stop
giving me that look, Marella. You told me
to make the best of this weekend and that's
what I'm doing. They've gotten a play-by-
play of the past two days, including you
hula-ing your backside off at the luau last
night."

Marella almost checked to see if her backside was still in place. "It's just my face,
Crystal, it's not a look." She admired what
Crystal had made of herself, but Marella
knew she wasn't ever going to fully understand it. "You ready for this?"

"I am. Are you?" Crystal pulled Marella
in front of her, held her by the shoulders
and made her look in the full-length mirror. "That dress is perfect on you. Elegant.
Poised. Simple."

Marella touched a hand to her still-jumpy
stomach. She had to admit, when it came to
fashion choices for each of her attendants,

Crystal had gone above and beyond. While Alexis's sexier one-shoulder knee-length gown was in a brilliant, blinding yellow, and Shawna's princess-neckline short sleeve was a soft butter shade, Marella's dress was a subdued gold tone in an off-the-shoulder style that didn't dip too deeply into her figure. She did feel pretty. Prettier than she had in a very long time.

The narrow band around her waist sparkled with the Crystal's trademark rhinestones and accentuated her curves.

Alexis, who was performing double duty as bridal party hairstylist, had swept Marella's hair into a combination of curls and whisps that complemented her subtle neutral makeup.

"Anyone need touch-ups for the pictures?" The photographer—a friend of Tehani's from high school—had been snapping away all morning and had just returned from getting pictures of the groomsmen with the groom.

"I think we're good," Crystal whispered. Her sister's misty eyes met Marella's as they stared at their reflections in the mirror. "Are you nervous?"

"Isn't that supposed to be my question?"

Marella stepped back to appreciate her sister's gown. A fairy-tale princess creation for sure, and the tiara on the top of her head made the perfect finishing touch. "You're more calm than I expected you to be."

"Am I?" Crystal gave Marella's hand a squeeze. "If you say so. Okay. Now, flowers. Got my bouquet right here. Marella, here's yours. Roses front, please."

"I thought I had a basket of flower petals…"

"I made an executive decision," Crystal said.

"Shouldn't Mom be here?" Marella asked.

"She and Dad had something to take care of before the ceremony. Ladies, let's get this wedding started."

Feeling a bit more like a racehorse leaving the gate, Marella followed Crystal out of the bridal suite. Shawna and Alexis trailed behind them.

"So." Crystal waited until they were in the elevator and heading down to the lobby, before saying, "Chad and I had a long talk last night at the luau and we agreed I've taken ButtercupDoll as far as I can. At least in this incarnation. We're going to start a new destination vlog together. ButtercupAdventures. When we get home, we're going to make a list of every place in the world we want to visit and we'll document our travels."

Marella nodded. "That's actually not a horrible idea."

"It's a rave." Shawna laughed.

"I figure as long as Chad and I are partners in life, we should be partners in everything else. We're really excited about it."

"I can tell." Marella noted that Crystal almost seemed more excited about her new career prospects than the idea of getting married. "Congratulations."

"I'm glad to hear you say that because we're going to need a branding expert to help us make the changeover. I want to hire you as our consultant."

Marella gaped. "You...do?"

"If you have the time. We can talk details later, but we'd make a fabulous team. Especially since you really don't have any problem telling me off."

"This is true," Marella confessed. "Okay. We'll talk. But can we please get you married first?" The longer this day went on, the more time she had to think about whether she'd made the right decision not to track down Keane last night.

"Sure, yes. Of course." The elevator dinged and the grouped stepped out to find her father, with Tag and Beck, waiting for them. The men's tuxedos were absolutely pristine.

"Shawna." Tag stepped forward and offered his arm.

The younger woman smiled and blushed in such a Benoit family way that Marella and Crystal exchanged wide-eyed glances.

"Alexis." Beck repeated Tag's gesture and they all disappeared toward the door leading to the side sanctuary where the ceremony was taking place.

"Crystal." Armand stepped forward, took Crystal's hands and kissed her cheek. "I don't know how you managed it, but you're more beautiful than ever."

"Thanks, Dad."

"Okay then." In the distance Marella could hear the strumming by the same trio of ukelele players who had entertained at the luau last night. "Let's do this, yeah?"

She took the lead, wanted to focus on doing her best for her sister, but in the back of her mind she was counting down the seconds until she left Nalani behind. The town had slipped into Marella's heart, just like Keane had. The idea of likely never seeing it again was almost as painful as the image of one day coming back and finding Keane had moved on.

Marella paused at the doorway, scanning the attendees briefly before stepping out onto the satin carpet draping the stone walkway. She multi-tasked, praying her ankle-breaker heels wouldn't fail her.

She spotted Sydney, Daphne and Tehani in the last row of seats, beaming at her as if she were family.

The music was a lovely tune, gentle and easy to move in time to. She kept her eyes pinned to the minister standing beneath the flower-draped archway, but gave in to the impulse to look at Chad and best man Lance as they watched and waited for Crystal's arrival.

Marella smiled at her mother, but then her gaze was drawn to someone else in that front row.

She very nearly tripped for real.

Keane was seated, right there, between Gloria and Pippy. He was holding on to

Pippy's hand while her grandmother beamed like a lighthouse.

Marella did her best not to give in to the shock even as her face went luau-firepit red. Her mother gave her a knowing wink, and Marella heard the silent warning to be careful.

She couldn't look directly at him. Glancing sideways, her hands began to tremble. She couldn't believe the sight of him in a tuxedo as smart as the one her father wore.

As she reached the minister, she stepped to the side. The processional music started.

The crowd rose as one, but she couldn't take her eyes away from the man standing in the midst of her family. He was the only one not looking at the bride. The only one looking at her. He touched a hand to his heart, inclined his head. And smiled.

She felt the tears pool as her heart reawakened.

Crystal's approach to her groom was done in typical Crystal style, with a little bit of a shimmy and more than her share of sass. Armand kissed his stepdaughter's cheek and Crystal handed off her bouquet to Marella.

"Surprise," Crystal whispered so only

Marella could hear. "You didn't honestly expect he wouldn't come, did you?"

Marella tried to look stern and disapproving, but it wasn't possible. Not with the hope filling her soul.

The ceremony was short and sweet, with the couple's vows as quirky and thought out as Crystal was wont to do given that every second was being recorded by Alexis.

The audience clapped and cheered when they were pronounced husband and wife and kissed beneath a spray of hibiscus and roses.

Marella prepared herself for walking back down the aisle, for passing by him once more. What should she say? What should she...

Crystal held up hers and Chad's linked hands.

Applause and congratulations rang out. Marella dabbed at her eyes, wondering how her heart could be both full and broken at the same time. Until this moment she didn't understand that Crystal had managed to grab hold of the best of both worlds. Rather than thinking she had to sacrifice one dream for another, she'd simply found a way to make them both work. Together. With the man she loved.

"Weddings make me all sappy." Pippy's voice overtook the quieting cheers. "What do you say, handsome?" She elbowed Keane and beamed at him. "Minister's just gotten warmed up. Want to exchange I do's with an older woman?"

Laughter roared from the crowd, and Marella's cheeks warmed in embarrassment for him, but Keane lifted an arm over Pippy's shoulders and drew her close.

"Tempting, Pippy." He hugged her tight. "Very tempting indeed." He shifted his gaze to Marella. "But I'm afraid I'm spoken for."

Her breath caught in her chest. Only a short time ago, where she'd seen doubt and fear, now she saw hope. Amusement. Temptation.

Resolution.

Marella opened her mouth, but there was no thought coherent enough to utter. She blinked, wondering if it was possible...

She'd kissed a stranger on the beach, Marella reminded herself, as her mind began to clear. All the things keeping them apart—his fears, his lack of belief in himself, her clinging to a life that while fulfilling in a lot of ways, didn't make her feel anything close to the man currently looking at her as if he never wanted to let her go.

Marella had only taken one impulsive leap of faith in her life. That time had landed her right in Keane's arms. If that had been possible, who knew what else was?

She inclined her head and smiled at him, just for him, and the corners of his mouth curved up, his entire face lit with love.

He nodded. Just once.

But once was enough.

"He's right." Marella stepped forward and cleared her throat. "I'll share him at family functions, Pippy, but otherwise he's all mine." She handed her bouquet off to an almost-squealing Crystal as Keane joined her at the altar. "If he wants to be?"

The confused murmurs of the guests faded into the background. There was nothing she saw other than Keane.

"You sure about this?" he asked.

"Shouldn't that be my line?" she teased, her heart fluttering to life at the same frenetic speed as the wings of a butterfly circling overhead. "Keane..."

"I forgot to say something to you yesterday in the bridal suite," he said. "When you told me you loved me. I convinced myself I was too late, that I'd lost my chance." He cupped her face in his palm. "I'm not going to miss it again. I love you, Marella."

Tears flooded her eyes and she held on to his arm. But only for a moment before he bent down on one knee and reached into his pocket.

She gasped at the sight of the pendant he clasped between his fingers. The beautiful olivine pendant she'd told herself to remember to go back and buy.

"You did what no one else has ever done for me, Marella. You made me believe in myself. In us. I love you. Will you marry me?"

She let out a sobbing laugh, covered her mouth as she nodded. "I— We don't have a license."

"We can get one after the fact."

She looked to her father, saw only pride and joy on his face as Gloria threw both arms around him and hugged him. "Dad? What about—"

"Listen to your heart, Marella," Armand said quietly. "The rest will all fall into place."

"Marella?" Keane asked again. "You going to leave me hanging here?"

"Never." Laughter burst from her lips and she cried, "Yes, of course! I will absolutely marry you!"

She didn't wait for the vows. She didn't wait for her father to give her away. She didn't even give Keane the chance to latch the chain around her neck after he stood.

Instead, she raised her arms, grabbed him around the neck and pulled him in for a kiss that put their first one to shame.

"Last chance to make a break for it," she whispered against his mouth.

"Don't need anything other than you."

"Wait." She held up her hand when he started to turn away. "Just one second, if you don't mind?" she asked. "I love the necklace. It's perfect. But…"

"But?" Keane suddenly looked uncertain. "I didn't have time to get a—"

"Rings can wait. There's something else I want you to get me." She leaned forward and whispered in his ear, "I want my own surfboard."

Keane slipped his arms around her waist and, laughing, spun her in circles until she was dizzy. "You are most definitely the perfect woman, Marella Benoit." He set her back on her feet, straightened his jacket, and slipped his hand into hers.

"Well, what are you waiting for, Padre?" Pippy yelled out. "Hit it!"

"Take two it is." The minister smiled as the audience chuckled.

Marella joined in, gripping Keane's hand, knowing she was never ever going to let go. Not of him.

And not of her family. Her *ohana*.

* * * * *

More island romances are on the way from acclaimed author Anna J. Stewart and Harlequin Heartwarming!